WILD GOOSE CHASE

A QUILTING MYSTERY

WILD GOOSE CHASE

TERRI THAYER

WHEELER
CHIVERS

This Large Print edition is published by Wheeler Publishing, Waterville, Maine, USA and by BBC Audiobooks Ltd, Bath, England.
Wheeler Publishing, a part of Gale, Cengage Learning.
Copyright © 2008 by Terri Thayer.
The moral right of the author has been asserted.

The text of this Large Print edition is unabridged.
Other aspects of the book may vary from the original edition.
Set in 16 pt. Plantin.
Printed on permanent paper.

LIBRARY OF CONGRESS CATALOGING-IN-PUBLICATION DATA

Thayer, Terri.
  Wild goose chase : a quilting mystery / by Terri Thayer.
    p. cm. — (Wheeler Publishing large print cozy mystery)
  ISBN-13: 978-1-59722-779-7 (pbk. : alk. paper)
  ISBN-10: 1-59722-779-X (pbk. : alk. paper)
  1. Quilting — Fiction. 2. Specialty stores — Fiction. 3. Retail trade — Ownership — Fiction. 4. Murder — Investigation — Fiction. 5. Santa Clara Valley (Santa Clara County, Calif.) — Fiction. 6. Large type books. I. Title
  PS3620.H393W55 2008b
  813'.6—dc22   2008013154

BRITISH LIBRARY CATALOGUING-IN-PUBLICATION DATA AVAILABLE

Published in 2008 in the U.S. by arrangement with Midnight Ink, an imprint of Llewellyn Publications, Woodbury, MN 55125 USA.
Published in 2008 in the U.K. by arrangement with Midnight Ink.

U.K. Hardcover: 978 1 408 41217 6 (Chivers Large Print)
U.K. Softcover: 978 1 408 41218 3 (Camden Large Print)

Printed in the United States of America
1 2 3 4 5 6 7 12 11 10 09 08

ACKNOWLEDGMENTS

Thanks are many. Becky Levine and Beth Proudfoot, both great writers and the best critique group ever, were instrumental in seeing Wild Goose Chase finished. Writers Susan Lee and Deb Lacy lent me their homes and their expertise. I would not have become a writer without the example of the California Writers Club, South Bay Branch. The Book Passage Mystery Writers Conference spurred me on. Lee Lofland, and DP Lyle lent me their expertise, which I alternatively embraced and ignored, and most likely, mangled, in the final product.

My brother, David Thayer, who kept me going with his exploits, and set the bar really high. To Mom, who is the best cheerleader a girl could ask for. To Matt, who inspires me to do better. To all my family and to GSI, who will be seeing me on their guest room bed for the book tour. Thanks to Will for keeping the bank account stoked.

My quilting buddies, especially Maureen, Robin, and Virginia, who challenge me and make me laugh and dare me to buy more fabric. Lillian, Carol, Ruth, and all the Fabrics 'n' Fun gang that gave me plenty to write about. Thanks to the QTC and the Quilt Book Club for their early readings and encouragement. To all of them, I owe so much.

Having a great agent like Jessica Faust of Bookends, LLC makes the whole process easier.

Thanks to Barbara and her wonderful team at Midnight Ink. They made my dream come true — a rotary cutter dripping blood with my name on it!

Finally to Dan Niemi whose End of Watch came too soon, on July 25, 2005. His smile and love of police work imbues my fictional characters in a way that I hope honors his memory.

WILD GOOSE CHASE PATTERN

The Wild Goose Chase block has been a popular mainstay of quilters for nearly two hundred years. The early piecers found that by combining two half-square triangles, they could create the arrow shape, reminiscent of birds in flight. Variations followed as the block was used in quilt squares and borders. The modern quilter still relies on the Wild Goose Chase block, sending the geese curving through space or in circles.

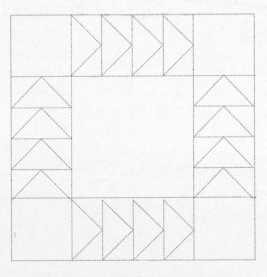

ONE

"Dewey Pellicano, you nearly killed me! You left the blade open. Again!"

I looked at the blood dripping from my sister-in-law's elbow. Sure enough, I'd forgotten to close the safety cover on the rotary blade. If Kym found out that I'd used it to cut through the plastic on an impossible-to-open ink cartridge instead of using it to cut fabric, she'd really flip out.

I tried a diversion. "Where's the packaging? I just opened that cutter. I left it right there."

Kym pushed the safety cover back on the blade with a forceful click and gave me a pout that probably worked on my brother, but did nothing for me. "How many times do I have to tell you that a rotary cutter is dangerous? I barely brushed against the blade, and look how I'm bleeding. I could have opened a vein."

A girl could dream. I pressed on. "I need

the barcode so I can take that cutter out of inventory. Otherwise, the computer says we have more than we do. And it's bad when the inventory numbers don't jibe."

My tactic was working. Like a time-lapse photograph, I could see Kym tuning out. Any mention of inventory or computers and she went slack-mouthed and glassy-eyed.

She daubed at her elbow with a tissue. With a giant sigh, she tossed the packaging to me and began folding fabric. Obviously, her injury was not life-threatening.

I needed this weekend to go well. I'd done an end run around Kym, bringing the computer to power the cash register despite her threats. I needed to use the new program at the quilt show so I could bring the store online and make my job tolerable.

Next to Kym was a wire crate. The honey-comb partitions designed to hold milk bottles were the perfect size for the half-yard cuts of fabric she was arranging. I went back to hooking up the computer. It was Thursday morning, and we were almost finished setting up the Quilter Paradiso booth at the Seventeenth Annual Northern California Quilt Extravaganza.

Kym stopped shoving fabric into the partitions, dove under the table next to me, and came out with a purplish thing in each hand.

"Here, put on your apron," Kym said. "I just heard Eve and Justine in the next aisle making their rounds. We need to look good when they get here. I *am* going to win Best-Decorated Booth this year."

There was no way I would wear that thing. The lavender gingham apron with purple rickrack on the pockets complemented her attire and the old-fashioned general store booth theme, but would look really stupid over my khakis and Quilter Paradiso T-shirt.

Kym yanked on her apron, flipping the strings around her waist and pulling them tight, crafting an expert bow centered on her flat belly. The ruffled shoulders fell perfectly into place. I winced at her efficiency. That kind of knot-tying ability explained the short leash she had my brother on.

I balled up the apron and stuffed it back under the table. "If I stop what I'm doing," I explained, straining to keep my voice even, "the computer won't be up and running when the customers arrive."

"So what?" she said. "I don't understand why you picked this weekend to start using the new system."

Kym was ignoring the fact that she'd refused to work on the test version I'd installed at the store last week. Forcing her

11

to use the system here was my only option.

"Do you realize how many customers will be coming through our booth for the next four days?" Kym whined.

"And we will accommodate them faster than ever."

"Ha."

I tried to stare her down, but she had the advantage. Her eyes were the same blue color as the inexorable summer sky here in Silicon Valley. Each July, when the sun had been shining without interruption for months, I'd search desperately for a cloud or two to break up the monotony. Kym had the same lovely, relentless streak. Hard to rail against something so pretty, but if you didn't, you might lose your soul.

Kym broke off eye contact to straighten a picture of my great-great-great grandmother behind the counter of the Dewey Mercantile, her slouched shoulders unconsciously mimicking the sack of dried beans in front of it. Guarding the penny-candy barrel had given Great-Great-Great Granny a permanent scowl.

Kym hijacked my heritage to win a hundred-dollar prize. Under her watchful eye, last night's taped-off 16' × 24' bit of floor in the cavernous convention center had become a charming replica of the

Dewey Mercantile. She hated the fact that the silver laptop didn't fit in with the tall, wooden bobbins, the pickle barrel full of buttons and the shelving that smelled slightly like prunes because it was made of floorboards Kevin had salvaged from a fruit-drying shed in Campbell.

I had to admit Kym had made the booth look pretty. But pretty wasn't everything. Even before my mother had died in a car accident six months ago, and I'd been thrust into the role of shop owner, I'd been computerizing Quilter Paradiso. My mother had pressed me into installing the free trial version of a very expensive point-of-sale system she'd received from a friend six weeks before she'd died. Laid off from my high-tech job, I'd agreed.

This weekend's show would be the first time we would use the POS system to record actual sales. I wanted to prove to my skeptical sister-in-law how valuable it could be to keep track of the customers and their sales electronically.

"We need to account for the inventory," I continued.

"Never did before."

"Exactly, and because of that, I have missing inventory."

Kym rummaged in her pockets and came

up with a lipstick. She pursed and applied the color without taking her eyes off me. I gave her credit for that; I had trouble putting the stuff on with a magnifying mirror. She ground her lips together and flicked her Disney-heroine blond hair off her shoulder. I liked to keep my brown hair short but it was no good for expressing disgust.

I flinched as she reached to pick a stray thread off my T-shirt. "Face it," she said. "We both know if the economy in this valley hadn't tanked, you'd be back in high tech by now."

And Kym would be running Quilter Paradiso. Kym was the daughter my mother never had. Unlike me, she loved anything to do with — her words — the home arts. Even as a kid, I'd chosen a Commodore 64 over needle and thread.

She might be right, but that didn't change anything. My mother had died, and I was the new owner of Quilter Paradiso. Kym moved on to fuss with a length of calico laid over the front table, gathering up a handful and tying a graceful knot. The cloth draped artfully, much better at taking direction from her than I was.

I punched the plug to the cash register into the back of the laptop and positioned the computer closer to the edge of the table.

I adjusted the free-standing monitor, making sure the transaction screen was clearly visible to the person taking cash. I pushed the buttons that opened and closed the register drawer and tucked the separate keyboard on a lower shelf for easy access. The merchandise scanner sat next to the drawer.

Kym bent down, parting the curtains she'd velcroed to the fake wood table and pulled out what looked like a quilted casserole cover.

"What's that?" I asked, my blood pressure rising. "I will not wear whatever . . ."

"A computer cozy." She came toward me, holding the elasticized ends apart like a shower cap. "Get out of the way. Justine and Eve will be here any minute."

"You can't cover the laptop with that."

"That ugly thing is ruining my booth theme. First impressions are important."

I lunged for Kym's cozy and stubbed my toe against an old-fashioned soda-bottle cooler. I swallowed a curse as I hopped on one foot, rubbing the throbbing toe.

"You can't cover up a laptop while it's being used," I said, when the pain had passed enough that I could speak again. "The computer needs ventilation. It'll overheat." I grabbed, but missed the cozy.

My cell phone rang. Before I could stop her, she closed the lid and swathed the laptop in calico.

"Dewey?"

I recognized my brother's voice. "Kevin? Why are you calling my phone?"

"Kym's not answering hers."

"Of course not. It clashed with her outfit."

Kym stuck her tongue out at me. I handed my phone to her and turned away, to get clear of the baby talk I knew was coming.

"You people got everything you need?" an unfamiliar voice asked.

Two women, probably in their forties, approached the booth. They wore matching black bowling shirts with red lettering embroidered over the pocket that identified them as Justine and Eve, of JustEve Productions. I recognized the name as the company responsible for putting on this quilt show, the people who'd cashed our six thousand dollar check for the booth fee.

Although dressed alike, these two couldn't have looked more different. Justine was tall, slender, and ash blond, with a heart-shaped face and pleasant smile. The lipstick she wore was bright red and shiny, the color of rain boots I'd coveted as a kid. I'd bet she didn't need a mirror to apply hers either. Eve was shorter than Justine by several

16

inches, with dark hair cut short, losing the battle to gray. No lipstick that I could see, not even the eaten-off kind.

Justine appraised our setup. "Nice. Love the old-fashioned general-store idea."

Kym hung up on Kevin in mid-coo. She dropped my phone into her apron pocket and smiled, the kind that didn't reach her eyes. She had to be nice to Justine if she wanted to win the prize, but I could see it was difficult for her. She hadn't forgiven JustEve for awarding last year's prize to a vendor who decorated her booth like the solar system, complete with imploding black holes.

"It's the family business." Kym said.

My family. Not yours. I bit my lip to keep from saying the words out loud.

She spoke in a monotone, pointing out the features of the booth. "We celebrate the entrepreneurial spirit with our booth. The Dewey family has been in business in the same building for over a hundred consecutive years."

I opened my eyes wide to stop them from rolling involuntarily at her air hostess delivery.

Justine moved into the short aisle between our tables, clucking over the American flag with the historically accurate forty-six stars

17

that Kym had sewn. I couldn't stomach another tour of the authentic décor, so I turned my attention to Eve, who was scanning the booth, her heavy eyebrows nearly meeting in the middle as she creased her forehead in what looked like a permanent furrow. She cocked her head and barked into the phone she held in front of her. I had the sense that Eve thought if she relaxed for one moment, the whole show would fall apart. For all I knew, she was right.

When she'd clicked off her phone, I stepped out of the booth and approached Eve with my hand extended. "We haven't met," I said. "I'm Dewey Pellicano."

Her eyes scanned my chest. "You're not wearing your badge. You must wear your vendor ID at all times."

So much for small talk. "Big problem of folks sneaking in without paying, huh?"

I thought I was being funny, but she nodded gravely. "People will try to avoid the admittance charge."

"Quilters? Really — those little old ladies?"

"Most quilters aren't arthritic blue-hairs, as you well know," Kym put in from several feet away, always ready to correct me.

Little old ladies and women like Kym who lived in the past. I shrugged. "I'm surprised.

My mother always said quilters were honest people."

"Do you need another ID badge?" Eve asked.

"No, no, mine's around here somewhere."

"Put it on," Eve said. "And leave it on."

Kym grinned at my chastisement. She'd nagged me earlier about wearing it, but I'd ignored her. Her badge was in a calico holder with scalloped edges that she'd sewn to match her outfit.

Justine broke the tension, touching my upper arm gently and smiling at me. I saw a weariness in her eyes. Smoothing over Eve's rough edges must be a full-time job. I felt her pain and knew she and I would get along.

"Ten minutes until show time," Justine said. "All ready?"

Kym snapped, "Of course we are."

"Great," Justine continued, pushing past Kym's snarkiness. "From now until Sunday, we'll bring in the shoppers. All you have to do is sell 'em stuff and make 'em happy."

I smiled. "We'll do what we can."

Justine and Eve said their goodbyes and moved away, hailing the woman selling quilt jewelry at the booth next door.

Kym turned to me, her face suddenly twisted. "Why'd you have to set up that ugly

19

computer this year? You've spoiled any chance I had of winning."

I bit back nastier words. "So I should forego accuracy so you can win a hundred-dollar prize?"

I stripped the cover off and started the computer again. The familiar whirrs of the hard drive booting up soothed my frayed nerves. I clicked on the icon, a smiling woman in a patchwork vest, to open the sales software. I entered the password and was rewarded with the bells that meant the system was open. To be sure, I started a sale under my name and scanned the packaging from the cutter Kym had opened. A satisfactory ping chimed and the SKU number popped into place on the screen. I canceled the test sale, put the packaging in my backpack to take to the store for the tax board report, and pushed the backpack under the table with my toe.

"Okay, Kym, the computer is ready to go. Do you remember what I showed you?"

"Never mind that contraption, Dewey, come here. Someone wants to meet you."

I turned to see a man standing next to Kym. His hooded green eyes were locked on her ample breasts, which were emphasized by her prissy long-sleeved blouse and apron.

He was dressed in a Nehru-type jacket, made of red, shiny fabric, a style that had never been in and so couldn't be considered retro-chic now. The brown hair on top of his head was thinning, strained by the straggly ponytail he'd pulled the strands into. He was no taller than me, probably about 5'9".

Was this her idea of the right man for me? Kym thought being single was only one step away from being dead. She never believed me when I said I was happy on my own.

She identified him as Freddy Roman of Freddy's Fine Fabrics in Los Angeles. He finally tore his eyes from Kym's bust and turned to look at me, first taking a quick detour at my chest. When he found it lacking and looked up at my face, I saw his eyes flash.

"Oh, my god, you scared me. You look so much like your mother, I thought I was seeing a younger, prettier ghost."

I didn't notice the hot tears spilling from my eyes until one hit my hand. By that time, I was well away from the booth and Freddy's spirit sighting, heading blindly for the nearest exit. My heart was pounding wildly in my chest.

I'd prepared myself for the possibility that people here would compare me to my

21

mother. She had been a vendor at the first Extravaganza and made friends with many of the people who returned year after year. I'd thought I was ready to handle her grief-stricken colleagues.

Then, faced with the very first person to mention Mom, all I could do was bolt. I felt like a fool. My stomach tightened, and the tears dripped freely.

I needed air. My nose began to run, and I wiped my face on my sleeve. I kept my eyes straight ahead, ignoring the looks I was garnering from other vendors making last-minute adjustments to their displays.

I moved over one aisle and into a row of hanging quilts, maybe thirty total. Ignoring the colorful display, I spotted light through the glass transom over a row of exit doors and headed that direction.

I pushed open the door and found myself in a glass-walled two-story atrium. I was nearly bowled over by the crush of women on the other side. Their bleating voices echoed off the steel rafters. I covered my ears to protect myself from the din.

I was stunned by the size of the crowd. Were all these people here to see quilts? A mass of middle-aged women filled the space and disappeared down the hall. I couldn't see the end of the queue.

I took a step forward and the door closed behind me. People looked at me expectantly as I came out of the place they wanted to be.

This mob was between me and fresh air. There was no way I was going to get to the outdoors.

Static crackled, and I heard Eve's voice come over a loudspeaker. The crowd quieted and tensed like swimmers at a diving block.

"Okay, quilters, the Seventeenth Annual Northern California Quilt Extravaganza is officially open. Step this way to pay the entrance fee and get your hand stamped. Fifteen dollars, exact change very welcome."

A security guard moved the crowd back so he could open the door. The women began to move toward him.

I took a deep breath. I was feeling better. Freddy had probably gone to his own booth by now, and I felt ready to face the shoppers and Mom's friends. I started through the door, but was stopped by a skinny arm.

"Your ID badge?" the security guard, dressed in faux police blues with shiny buttons, asked. He was blocking the door I'd come through.

I realized I'd never put on my vendor badge. Kym's gloating face hovered in front of me. "I don't have it with me."

He gave me a pained look. "No entrance without a hand stamp or vendor ID."

"You just watched me come out that door," I said.

The security guard waved through a woman in a tie-dyed mini-dress holding up her badge. "Next." He made a come-forward motion, cupping his hand and closing his fist like a Caltrans flag guy in a cone zone.

The line of people began to move slowly through the door as the pimply security guard checked hands. I looked around for help. Halfway across the atrium, Eve and Justine were collecting fees and stamping hands. I couldn't get their attention.

A gray-haired woman in a pink and purple patchwork vest decorated with three-dimensional Easter eggs shook her arm at me triumphantly as she entered the show. I fought down panic as the crush of people closed around me.

Moving backward, I found an open piece of floor near the restroom door. How was I going to get in? Kym had my phone in her damned apron pocket, I had no money on me to buy a ticket, and it was impossible to get Justine or Eve's attention. I was screwed.

We'd picked up four badges yesterday. Kym and I had two, and I'd left the others at the store for the staff working in the booth. My employees, Jenn and Ina, were due to start work soon. They could be in this line. I'd have to intercept one of them and have them bring me my badge. I leaned heavily against a pillar and searched the crowd, hoping to see one of them. Looking for two women, one silver-haired, one blond pony-tailed, in this crowd? Talk about a needle in a haystack.

"Problem?"

I turned to see Claire Armstrong, the grande dame of the quilt world, addressing me. Even I recognized her grandmotherly face from the covers of countless quilting magazines. We carried a dozen of her how-to books at the shop. She'd developed patterns to be used with the rotary cutter before anyone else realized the tool's potential. Like all superstars, she was known by her first name. Bono. Sting. Oprah.

Claire.

The crowd stilled. Friends nudged each other and pointed. A low buzz began as the quilters realized they were in the presence of a true celebrity.

"The guard won't let me in," I whispered. "I don't have my ID badge. I'm a vendor, Quilter Paradiso. I came out to get some air, and he won't let me back in."

"Follow me," she said.

A thin woman in a blue suit at Claire's elbow spoke up. "We can't go in there. We need to prepare for our class."

Claire answered in a tone that brooked no discussion. "You won't be coming with us. Go up to the room, Myra. Make sure we have enough handouts. I don't want a repeat of last year. I have some business with Miss Pellicano."

Claire knew my name. Another friend of Mom's, no doubt. I straightened up. I could handle this. The tears had dried on my cheeks.

"Stay with me. I'll get you into the show," she said.

I coasted in Claire's wake as she glided through the crowd imperiously, head held high, leading with her pillowy bosom like the figurehead of a ship. The crowd parted and murmured, but Claire didn't acknowlededge anyone. Her head bobbed slightly, so I knew she heard the sighs and greetings, but she kept her eyes averted.

From behind, her white hair barely concealed a pinkish scalp. She was dressed in a rose-colored polyester pantsuit with sensible shoes. An overly large purse dangled from her elbow. She smelled like violet dusting powder.

Claire bestowed a nod on the security guard. The guard glared at me but let me pass. Once inside, I thanked Claire and started for the QP booth. I could see my mother's calico banner with Quilter Paradiso on it one aisle over. Claire stopped me with a hand on my elbow and led me to an unoccupied space beneath a row of wall hangings.

"Dewey, isn't it?" She tapped me; her nails were short with pink polish, matching her pearl earrings and necklace. She had a puppet's face; her jaw was hinged with deep lines, and her cheeks were apple dumplings.

I nodded.

"I want to talk to you," Claire said. "Before she died, your mother had agreed to sell Quilter Paradiso to me."

Two

I took a step backward, nearly colliding with an impatient shopper in jeans and a poncho. Claire put a hand out to steady me. I shook her off. I didn't need her help.

"That's the most ridiculous thing I ever heard," I said. "QP was my mother's life. She would never sell."

Claire was looking at me closely. "You didn't know?"

"Know?"

"Your mother and I had reached a verbal agreement about the shop last October, right around Quilt Market in Houston."

Just before my mother had been killed. Could this be true? I'd been busy getting the inventory and store accounts online. Did I miss hints my mother left? Had she discussed selling with Dad? Oh, God, with Kym?

People eddied around us. The line in the atrium must be diminishing, as the aisles were getting more crowded. I could barely see the booth now. The idea that Mom would sell the shop, her connection to her quilting and her friends, was crazy.

I looked at Claire, who was waiting for a reply. "She never told me, and then . . ." I couldn't finish the sentence.

"I heard she was hit by a drunk," Claire said.

"The driver's never been caught." I let the subject drop, not wanting to talk about my mother's accident.

We stepped aside to let a woman using a motorized cart pass. The back of her plus-size T-shirt said, "Old quilters don't die; they just go to pieces."

"I wonder why she wanted to sell," I said, my voice squeaking. I suddenly felt like a child, trying to grasp the unknowable grown-up world.

Claire's voice turned gentle. "Do you want me to tell you what I think? The shop had grown larger than your mother was comfortable with."

"But that was her heritage . . ." I stopped when I heard myself using Kym's word. But it was true.

Dewey Mercantile had morphed into Dan's Hardware, my grandfather's store, before I was born. When I was eleven, Mom had begun Quilter Paradiso in a corner of the hardware store with a couple hundred bolts of fabric, the first quilting magazine, and a few dozen books. Hardware was phased out, Grandpa Dewey retired to Ireland, and the quilt shop took over the whole 10,000-square-foot building.

Today we had two classrooms and six thousand bolts of fabric. We sold twenty-five different quilting magazines, plus quilt books and patterns numbering in the hundreds. With annual sales of nearly a million dollars, maybe the shop had been too much for Mom to handle. It was certainly overwhelming me.

Claire's hand on my arm brought me back to the present. "Running a shop like Quilter Paradiso is a big job."

Was she talking about me or my mother? A long-legged woman wearing pink cowboy boots stopped next to us. She was talking loudly into a cell phone, describing the chaotic scene like a racetrack announcer. Claire glared at her.

"The cell phone is ruining polite society," Claire said. "I'd like to speak to you in private. Would you be interested in coming up to my hotel room to continue our talk?"

I shook my head. "I've got to get to the booth. We're using a new software system, and I need to be there to answer any questions."

"Yes, your mother mentioned that," Claire said, her voice drifting off as she saw something over my shoulder. She frowned, clearly not happy. I glanced behind me. An African-American woman dressed in an expensive suit was heading relentlessly toward us. Her business attire contrasted sharply with the colorful handmade patchwork jackets, jeans, and T-shirts that most of the show-goers were wearing.

She was focused on Claire, never slowing or noticing as people got out of her way. Trailing her were a bearded man with a shoulder TV camera and a young woman with a boom microphone.

I tried to bring Claire's attention back to me. "I'm not interested in selling the shop."

"Don't make up your mind just yet." Claire started moving away from me without taking her eyes off the approaching trio. She talked quickly. "I'm staying at the hotel for the duration of the show, room 605. Come and talk to me."

Without waiting for an answer, Claire sped off, leaving me standing in the aisle by myself. The TV crew passed me, following in Claire's footsteps. A logo pasted on the side of the camera read, "Lark Gordon and

31

Her Wonderful World of Quilts."

That was the name of an extremely popular quilting show on the cable home channel, with tie-in books that we carried. This woman must be the hostess, Lark Gordon.

Claire ignored Lark as she caught up to her. Lark grabbed her arm and pointed at the camera, obviously trying to talk Claire into being on the air. Claire kept moving, putting distance between them. Lark followed but Claire lost her in a crowd of quilters by the entrance. Finally Lark stopped and watched Claire disappear. She said something to her entourage and stalked off. The two trotted after her to keep up. As she passed me, the fierce look on her face made me wonder if the TV show was all Claire and Lark had been talking about. Seemed a bit more personal.

I dodged a stroller as big as a first-class airline seat and went to our booth. Ina and Jenn had arrived and were already waiting on customers. Ina, a long-time employee of Quilter Paradiso, was a small, wiry woman with hair the color of a chrome grill and a matching grin. She made her own clothes, favoring natural fibers in asymmetrical jackets and elastic-waist pants with wide legs. Today she was dressed in a turquoise raw-silk. Her practical sneakers were bedazzled with jewel-tone crystals.

Jenn had been at the store for several years, working part-time while her kids were in school. She was a thirty-eight-year-old soccer mom who wore her hair in a sleek ponytail. Most of her pay went toward what she called "supporting her habit." She cashed her paycheck at the store, spending it on fabric that she made into quilts. Her usual uniform was a white blouse with khakis. Today she was dressed exactly like Kym, right down to the cameo pinned on her chest.

Kym, perched on the stool next to the checkout stand, was ringing up sales. I allowed myself a frisson of pride as she pushed a button on the keyboard and the drawer flew open, completing the sale. My hard work was paying off.

As I watched, things began to fall apart. Kym muttered under her breath and tapped a half-dozen keys. I moved up behind her.

"Trouble?"

"Dewey, don't hover, you're making me nervous."

"I was ten feet away — you looked like you were having a problem."

"I'm fine. This computer is stupid, that's all," Kym said.

"Can I take a look?"

The program was hanging up, most likely from Kym banging on too many keys. With two swift strokes, I closed it down and brought the program back up.

"Don't keep pounding on the keyboard, Kym," I said. "You'll confuse things. Do you want me to do this for a while? You can watch me."

"No, I can do it." Her teeth were gritted. She was going to break a cap if she wasn't careful. That would be my fault, too.

"Okay," I said, as the system came back up. I smiled at the waiting customer and entered the password. "Try not to hit two keys at once. Call me when you get frustrated. I'm right here."

Kym turned back to the computer with a scowl. I knew she was not trying very hard to learn the system. My job today would be to stay close and make sure she learned. A customer thrust her credit card at Jenn, who was helping Kym finish the sale.

"Think they can do it?" Ina whispered, as I joined her. "Kym is so resistant. And Jenn will follow her lead."

"It's pretty foolproof. The system is designed so you don't have to be computer-literate to use it. They'd have to try hard to screw it up."

"Don't underestimate Kym's determination to stay out of the modern age. Look at our booth, for crying out loud. Did you know she wanted me to wear a snood?" Ina said.

Whatever a snood was, the idea of wearing one was pissing Ina off. I didn't want that. I made some soothing noises.

"I saw you talking with Claire Armstrong earlier," she said. "What did she want?"

Ina's question sounded casual, but her lips were tight. I looked at her face, trying to read her emotions behind the question. Did she dislike Claire? Did she know about Mom selling?

Before I could ask Ina what she knew about Mom and Claire, we were interrupted by a customer looking for an Indonesian batik. Ina went off with her and two women in matching lime-green Delta Quilters Guild T-shirts requested Lark Gordon's latest book from me.

Customers steadily entered the booth. I cut fabric, recommended patterns, and demonstrated notions with Ina and Jenn. I kept a watchful eye on Kym.

Two hours later, when the first rush of customers ebbed, Kym came down off her stool. She stretched her hands over her head and bent from the waist several times.

"Been a good morning for sales," she said.

"I've taken in probably a thousand dollars."

I didn't dare ask if the computer was making the sales go smoother; she'd never admit if it was. "I can run a report right now if you want to know the exact amount," I said, heading for the computer.

Kym shrugged as though she didn't care. "I'm going to take a break," she said, her body humming with tension.

"Okay," I said. "Jenn, want to go with her? Ina and I can handle things."

Kym was already in the aisle. "That's okay," she shot back. "I need to be alone for a while."

Working at the computer must have stressed her more than I realized. I shrugged at Jenn who glared at me and stalked over to man the cash register.

"I thought those two went everywhere together," I whispered to Ina.

"Usually they do. Maybe Kym has an assignation," she said with a phony French accent. She clamped her hand over her mouth. "Sorry, I forgot for a moment that she's married to your brother. I didn't mean . . ."

"No problem. Sometimes I wish she would find another man and let my brother go."

I slapped my cheek as Ina giggled. "Did I

say that out loud?"

"Don't worry, I'll never tell," Ina said.

I straightened the fat quarters that had gotten messy from the morning's groping. A hoot of laughter came from my left. In the convention center, the atmosphere was like a street fair. Booths of colorful merchandise lined the aisle. A man walking and juggling what looked like pin cushions cut off a trio of women in colorful saris. A neon sign over a booth across the aisle read, "Quilt Naked — Free Your Mind."

I had never understood my mother's need to make quilts, but I was here, in the middle of the West Coast's biggest quilt show, with entries from the most famous names in the business. Whatever drew my mother to quilting was here at this show. Maybe all I had to do was free my mind.

As a kid, I'd steered clear of Quilter Paradiso. To my three brothers, sewing was for sissies. They were always poised to catch me doing anything girly and exploit it as a sign of perceived weakness, taunting me mercilessly. One pot holder crocheted on a spool when I was six earned me the nickname of "Knitting Nincompoop" that stuck until I was eleven. Consequently, I'd spent much of my childhood proving I could kick the ball, take a punch, and give a wedgie like a boy. I left my mother to her feminine pastimes and mastered the soccer field instead of a sewing machine. My chosen career was in a man's world, computer programming. Lately, I had begun to wonder if I had cheated myself.

Kym tapped Ina on the shoulder when she returned and took over the computer duties. I watched from a safe distance. The computer beeped irritably as Kym tried to push items through the scanner too quickly. I heard another beep as Kym tried a function that wasn't open. In the hour she'd been gone, she seemed to have forgotten how the system worked.

I moved closer. The drawer was not opening. Kym tapped on the keyboard. A white-haired lady with dangling purple earrings and two circles of rouge approximately on her cheeks was waiting to pay.

"I think you forgot to hit the total button." I tried to insert myself in a non-threatening manner, but Kym turned on me, eyes flashing.

"I've got it," she snarled. She pressed the correct key, and the drawer flew open.

I backed off.

Finding a lighted seam ripper for a smiling Japanese woman with minimal English grabbed my attention for the next few minutes. Her friend wanted the latest ruler. That led to a stilted, half-spoken, half-signed discussion about which ruler was easier to read, the clear or the yellow. I was rubbing my fingernail along the rough surface on the back of the clear ruler to illustrate its usefulness when I noticed a line forming near the register.

Five customers were waiting to pay. The same white-haired woman was still standing next to Kym, her sale not finalized. Ina was entertaining the waiting customers with knock-knock jokes, talking fast like she did when she was nervous. I heard someone muttering that this used to be her favorite booth, as she put down the hundred-dollar quilt kit she'd been planning to buy and walked away.

I struggled to see what Kym was doing from where I was positioned. A large woman stepped aside. Suddenly, I had a clear view of Kym pulling the plug out of the laptop.

I felt heat rush to my face. What did she think she was doing? She knew that wasn't the right way to shut down. I tried to make my way over, but the line of waiting customers clogged the small inside aisle, and I could make no headway. I had to watch from ten feet away as she tugged on the power cord, dislodging it from the strip underneath the table, and took out a pad of sales slips from her apron.

Only the presence of customers stopped me from screaming. The sales slips in her apron meant one thing. She'd never intended to use the computer this weekend.

I leaned over a table toward Ina, who was already in the main aisle and closer to Kym and the cash register. "Go take her place. You and Jenn get these customers moved along quickly."

Ina looked startled at my tone of voice. I modulated. "Please. Tell Kym I need to see her."

I walked away, wanting to pace but finding no room to take more than two steps without running into a disgruntled customer. I plastered a smile on my face, and murmured assurances that things would be fixed soon.

"Dewey?"

My sister-in-law tried to arrange a sincere look of remorse on her face, but I could see she was barely suppressing a smile.

"What happened?" My throat was so tight, I barely got the words out. I felt the customers staring at us. I took several steps away with Kym in tow. Ina and Jenn hurried through each sale, bagging items and getting signatures on the old-fashioned credit slips.

"The computer started acting funny." She tried the little-girl voice. I narrowed my eyes at her. She looked down at her folded hands.

"So you unplugged it? I was right here, Kym. Why didn't you call me over?"

"Did I do something wrong?" Her guile was amazing.

"I'm sure I could've solved the problem. I would have walked you through. We need to use the computer here this weekend." I leaned in close, not caring that I was spitting on her apron. I saw my cell in her pocket and snatched it, jamming it into the carrier on my belt.

"I don't see the big deal." She fanned a pad of sales slips at me. "We'll be fine working the way we used to."

Could she really mean that? I saw that she did. She was happy with the old-fashioned methods my mother had always used. My sister-in-law was not going to allow me to computerize the store.

It was clear to me now that Kym had wanted me to bring the computer to the show to prove we didn't need to get our systems online.

My face burned with the realization that Kym would never be on my side, and yet she would always be a part of the store. I couldn't fire my brother's wife.

Claire's offer to buy the shop came back to me. That was a way to get out from under Kym and her schemes. Sell the shop. Now. I would be free to return to my real life. Claire Armstrong had delivered me the solution. All I had to do was take it.

THREE

I made my way through the crowd, turning my back on Kym and the line of customers, and shoved the laptop into the padded section of my backpack. I would have to find someplace quiet and turn the computer on to know for sure if data had been lost. But first, I would go talk to Claire.

Ina, Jenn, and the customers stared at me as I left the booth without saying goodbye. Let Kym explain.

I would sell the shop and go back to my old job in high tech. Before I'd turned thirty, I'd been able to construct and furnish an entire fantasy house in the first ten minutes of a date with an eligible guy. I used that skill now, except instead of envisioning life with bamboo floors and a fireplace in the bedroom, I imagined life without Quilter Paradiso. I saw myself returning to a programming job. Going to a corporate office park instead of the dingy office under the shop stairs. Working in a clean, organized cubicle rather than the old, wooden partner's desk with its stuck drawers. Dealing with silent, male co-workers instead of chatty, conniving females.

As I walked across the now-empty atrium, my loafers echoed loudly on the marble floor. With each step, my stomach clenched. I rubbed my gut, without relieving any of the pain.

Down a glass-fronted corridor past the hotel bar, I found the elevator that led to the hotel rooms. Soon I was on Claire's floor. I looked left and right to see where number 605 would fall. At the far end, I caught sight of a blonde disappearing through the stairwell door. The entwined J&E of the JustEve logo was visible on the back of her shirt. Justine was on her way back to the show.

Better her than me. I was never going back.

My phone rang, but when I saw it was Kevin, I turned the phone off completely. I would pay for that later. He would not be happy with me, but I didn't need to hear his pleas for mercy for Kym.

I didn't want to discuss what I was about to do.

I found Claire's room. A Do Not Disturb

44

sign hung from the door knob, but that was no deterrent. She probably just wanted to work in peace. I knocked. There was no answer. I listened, but couldn't hear anyone moving inside. I knocked again, louder. Still nothing. Damn, she had said she'd be here.

What a letdown. Once I made up my mind, I wanted action. If Bo hadn't answered my knock the night I went for my tattoo, my ankle would still be unadorned. I liked it so much better with the poppy.

Would I be able to go through with the sale if I had more time to think? I didn't want to find out. I wanted an agreement from Claire to buy the shop. Now.

I knocked again. My knuckles hurt, and I blew on them. I had to see Claire. I didn't have an alternative plan.

The hall was empty. Most of the hotel occupants were gone for the day, in quilt classes or at the show. I heard a door open behind me. A man carrying golf clubs headed for the elevator. Some quilter's husband on his own for the day.

The man with the golf bag reminded me of my father. What was he going to think about me selling the store? He hadn't had much to say about my running the shop to this point. I didn't know if he'd approve or not.

I tried again. "Claire. You in there?"

The elevator pinged, and a thin woman in a business suit disembarked as the golfer got in. I recognized her as Claire's assistant, Myra. She would be able to help me. I took a step toward her.

"Oh, good, you're here," I said.

She was carrying a lunch tray with an apple, a container of cottage cheese, and a Diet Coke. A napkin was wrapped around a plastic fork. Between the fingers on her left hand, she held a key card.

She looked at me expectantly. "Need something?"

"We met earlier, remember? Dewey Pellicano," I said. "I'm looking for Claire."

The woman eyed me. Her clothes were drab, a uniform more suited to a bank than a quilt show. The only bright color she wore was a beaded bracelet on her right arm.

"How did you know she was here? She never gives out her room number."

"We had an appointment." That was an exaggeration, but I hoped this guard dog of a woman would believe that.

"I calendar Claire's appointments," she said. "We had none this morning."

"Look, Claire and I have business to discuss. Obviously, if you're bringing her lunch, she's in there. Let me in."

"I can't do that. Claire specifically asked not to be bothered. She's busy with last-minute preparations for our class."

I'd had my fill today of passive-aggressive women whose only power came through their connections with others — Kym via my mother, Myra through Claire. I felt the need to exercise a little power myself. I threw my shoulders back and faced Myra down.

"I've got to see her," I said.

She remained unmoved, feet planted in front of the door, blocking me. She wasn't going to let herself in until I was long gone.

My resolve deepened. Downstairs, Kym was running the QP booth the way she wanted. I was not going back to that.

I reached for the key and got two fingers on it before Myra tightened her grip and I lost my grasp of the plastic. I grabbed the soda can. As I'd hoped, the sudden weight shift caused the plastic tray to teeter. Myra scrambled to keep it balanced. The apple slid, and the cottage cheese began its descent to the floor. I grabbed the room key from Myra's loosened fingers, reached over her arm, and swiped the door before she could react. I heard the apple hit the floor with a dull thud.

The green light came on, and I pushed

47

the door open without waiting to see if Myra followed. Immediately on the left was a bathroom. I set the soda can on the counter, eager to let go of the cold sliminess.

I shifted my gaze toward the bedroom that opened up off the short hall. The room was very large, dwarfing the king-size bed and round table beyond. The table had been pulled up close to the bed. On the table was a green rotary-cutting mat. A clear acrylic ruler lay across the mat with a piece of fabric underneath, as though Claire had been cutting. Looking up, I saw a quilt pinned to the curtains. It looked off-kilter until I realized the quilt had borders on only three sides. A work in progress.

"Claire?" I called out. I looked back at Myra. She had picked up the tray and the lunch. I was glad to see the lid was intact on the cottage cheese. I hadn't meant to ruin Claire's lunch. "Where is she?"

"She's not here. As you can see."

"I'm going to wait for her to come back."

I took another step into the room, heading for a chair. A strange smell lingered in the air, metallic and earthy. It caught in my throat and swirled around, making me catch my breath and hold it. The smell was familiar; I remembered the butcher shop next to

Grandpa's hardware store. It had been closed for years, why was I thinking of it now?

Suddenly Myra was right behind me. I felt her breath in my hair and I turned around and glared, trying to get her to back off. She was looking past me, over my head; her nostrils flared. I took several steps forward to see what she was looking at.

Past the far side of the bed, Claire lay on the floor, almost under the table. She was on her back, her eyes open but unseeing. From the waist up, she looked untouched. But she was in a puddle of blood. Her pink polyester slacks were red. The upper part of her right thigh was visible through a gash in the fabric. I could see the muscle showing on either side of a deep cut.

Next to her hand was a bright yellow-handled rotary cutter.

I was surprised how obvious it was that she was dead. The blood was fresh, still bright red in spots, but Claire looked so icy cold, I was sure no life remained.

I heard Myra gasp behind me and felt the air rush out of my body in response. We stood at the foot of the bed, unable to move or stop staring. My backpack slipped off my shoulder and clunked to the floor, landing on the rucked-up bedspread. I worried for a second about damage to the laptop, then, without warning, I felt the gorge rise in my throat and pushed past Myra to the bathroom.

I retched and retched, my body shaking with the effort of throwing up food that wasn't there. When I was finally finished, I felt bruised and battered. I lay my head down on the closed toilet lid, welcoming the cool porcelain on my cheek. The smell of bleach irritated my nose.

A small noise came from the doorway of the bathroom. Myra leaned against the jamb, a feline keening sound emanating from her. I pushed myself up and pulled her into the bathroom. Myra was docile. I steered her toward the edge of the bathtub and sat her down. Her shoes tracked blood onto the clean white floor. She must have tried to revive Claire.

"Myra, sit down. I'm going to call the police."

She didn't answer, dropping her head into her bloody hands.

I reached for the phone on my belt and dialed 911. Myra had slipped onto the floor and was leaning up against the tub, her skin the color of the porcelain, her black hair in sharp contrast against the rim. I was reminded of Snow White lying, poisoned, waiting for her prince. Too bad no prince was on his way today.

"I think she's dead," I said to the woman who answered the phone. Saying the words out loud, I felt the enormity of the situation. The 911 operator coaxed the details from me and promised help was on the way.

"Myra, let's get out of here. We can wait in the hallway."

"I told her to be more careful," Myra said. "She insisted she could sit on the bed and cut from there. I told her." Myra's eyes were fixed as though she could see through the tile wall into the bedroom where Claire lay dead. She reminded me of my neighbor's dog that sat at the gate for weeks after he died, sure that its master would come up the walk any minute.

I took a deep breath, regretting it immediately as the smell of blood caught in my throat again. Shuddering, I choked it down. I perched reluctantly on the edge of the toilet and patted Myra's shoulders. She didn't move, her body stiff under my touch.

I knew nothing about shock. Perhaps that's what was going on with her. I pulled the towels off the rack and covered Myra's hunched shoulders. She looked ridiculous, like she was at the beauty parlor about to get her color done, but I felt like I had contributed something. I hoped help would be here soon.

Claire — what had happened to her since I last saw her? She'd left me a few hours ago. Then what? She came back here to do some work and cut herself with her rotary cutter while Myra was out getting her lunch. She must have hit an artery. By herself, she had no way to staunch the blood.

Dying alone was the worst thing I could imagine.

Finally, I heard loud voices in the hall, and firemen in black and yellow suits swarmed into the room. Two paramedics broke off from the others and came into the bathroom.

I assured them I was okay, and, after they turned their attention to Myra, I moved into the hall. The air felt cool against my super-heated skin. My stomach was still roiling and sore from the heaving I'd done earlier. I leaned against the wall across from Claire's room. I slid down and sat on the floor, the industrial carpet scratchy and rough. A draft from an air-conditioning vent overhead sent cold air down my neck, but I was unable to move away. I closed my eyes, but I could see only Claire.

"Miss?"

I opened my eyes to see a man hunched

down in front of me, his graceful hands resting on his knees. His head hung low as he peered into my face. His pants broke on his shiny, tasseled loafers at the perfect length. He was a small man, and I thought about the expense he must incur to have his pants hemmed.

I pushed my back against the wall to get some leverage to stand up, but he stopped me, laying his hand on my shoulder. I sat back down, grateful I didn't have to move.

"Stay put," he said.

I nodded.

"You the one who found her? How did you get in?" he said.

"Myra had a key."

"Myra?"

I indicated the room inside.

"That her in the bathroom? Who's the woman in the other room?"

"Claire Armstrong. She's pretty famous. Just Claire."

I felt myself babbling, trying to spill out everything I knew.

"Come with me." He pulled me to my feet. My legs didn't hold up, and he frowned as I collapsed. He let go of me, and I hit the floor hard.

"Who are you?" I said, angrily.

"Sergeant Roy Sanchez, San Jose Police

Department. Homicide." He flipped his badge open for me to see. "I need you to follow me into the conference room down the hall." He offered his hand a second time but I waved him off. I didn't want to risk getting dumped again.

My cell banged against my hip bone as I stood. I heard Myra crying, her bleating voice echoing off the tiles. I was glad to move into the quiet of the conference room.

It smelled like bagels and coffee, although the sideboard along the wall to my left was empty. A small refrigerator was tucked underneath. Straight ahead, in front of the windows, was a large mahogany conference table with a dozen chairs around it. I sank into the nearest seat.

"We're going to need your clothes," he said.

"Excuse me?"

"All evidence must be preserved."

"Evidence?" What was he talking about? "Why are you treating me like a criminal? I found a woman dead."

"Yes, and until we find out what happened . . ."

"She cut herself."

"Were you a witness to that?" he asked, making notes on his pad.

"No, that's not what I meant. Look, I've

never found a dead body before. I don't know the procedure."

"Exactly. So please listen to me." His tone hardened. "Do you have a change of clothes?"

"I have a gym bag in my car," I allowed. I always carry workout clothes, in the never-ending battle to find enough time to exercise. I tried to remember what was in the bag. I didn't want to spend the rest of the day in a holey tank top and bike shorts.

"Give me your car keys. I'll send someone to get your things and you can clean up."

For the first time, I looked down at my clothes and saw I had blood on my khakis.

"I didn't realize. I helped Myra stand up . . ." My voice faded.

Detective Sanchez waited as I took my car keys off a hook on my belt. I described my car. I couldn't get out of these clothes fast enough. A policewoman came in the room and handed me my bag, escorting me to a restroom and waiting as I undressed hurriedly in a cubicle with the door open. I didn't look at the policewoman as I gave her my clothes.

The T-shirt in my bag was a wrinkled ball, but an unworn jogging suit, along with clean socks and sneakers, lay alongside.

Once changed into my running clothes, I

was left alone in the conference room. I walked the length of the room, trying to assess what was happening. What were the police doing?

Where was Myra? Surely if the police had wanted my clothes, hers would be taken. What would she change into? They would have questions for her, too. She must be going through hell, finding her boss dead. I couldn't imagine how horrible that would be.

My jumbled thoughts returned to what Sergeant Sanchez had said — that he was from Homicide. Why Homicide? Claire had obviously hurt herself and bled to death.

I glanced at the clock on the wall. It was nearly three o'clock. I'd been alone in this room for nearly an hour. Enough. I would find that policeman, answer his questions, and get out of here.

I strode to the door, pulling it open. Sergeant Sanchez was about to enter, followed by a younger man, also dressed in a suit and tie. The new guy was tall, and bulky without being fat. His shoulders were wide and I knew he'd played soccer in high school. I stared at him. The cognitive dissonance of seeing a familiar face in this room was muddling my brain.

Sanchez moved past me across the room,

straightening the wooden chairs, positioning them closer to the conference table.

"Dewey?" the young detective said quietly. "What are you doing here?"

That voice. The voice that was my lullaby. "Buster."

It was Buster, Benjamin Healy, Kevin's best friend since second grade. I'd talked him into eating a tadpole when he was seven and I was nine. He'd beaten me at ping-pong one hundred and sixty-eight times one long summer. I'd towered over him until he hit a growth spurt when he was fourteen. My fifth child, my mother had called him, like the mythical fifth Beatle.

This was Kevin's best man.

This was the fourth pallbearer who had helped my brothers carry Mom's casket.

This was the guy who had been leaving messages on my answering machine since November, looking for a date.

FOUR

"Buster." I saw by his sharp look that no one called him that anymore. He glanced over at Sanchez, but the thin sergeant was distracted, talking into his cell. Buster put his hands in his pants pocket, spreading apart his suit jacket, exposing the gold badge clipped on to his narrow brown leather belt. Detective Benjamin Healy, he seemed to be saying, that's who I am now.

"Sit down, Dewey."

Buster moved further into the room, steering me with a gentle touch toward the conference table chairs. Gone was the baby-faced kid. I could see the beginnings of wrinkles around his mouth and eyes. I wondered if they were squint lines or frown lines — wrinkles from the sun or the work he did.

"Homicide, Buster?"

"Just assigned, Dewey. Six weeks ago."

"Congratulations, but that's not what I

meant. Why are homicide detectives here? Claire had an accident."

"Routine," Buster assured me. "Unattended death in a hotel room. Dispatch sends a team out."

Even though I'd seen Buster off and on over the years at family functions, right now I could conjure up only two images of him as an adult. One was from Kevin and Kym's wedding, two years ago. Dodging the affections of an usher feeling entitled to a post-reception grope, I'd bumped into Buster, his arm slung around my brother's neck, his grin mirroring Kevin's, flush with drink and the excitement of the day. The usher had slunk away when faced with the protective duo who gathered me into their boozy embrace. Last November, I saw Buster with his arm around Kevin again, but this time his face echoed the pain surrounding us in the anteroom of the funeral home.

I'd been grateful that day for his quiet strength. The men in my life had not handled Mom's death well, alternating between sudden tears and explosive rage, with little warning. Although I'd never acknowledged his role, Buster had alleviated my burden, taking one brother or the other for long walks; sitting with my father as he recounted worn-out tales of long-ago barbecues.

Now he was here in an official role. I looked to him for a clue on how to proceed. His face was shuttered. This was not the bocce ball champion of the Pellicano backyard.

"I just have a few questions," Buster said.

Sanchez clicked his phone closed and joined us at the conference table. I sat in the chair Buster had pulled out. Sanchez stood across from me, his feet spread wide apart. I had to turn slightly in the seat so I could see Buster at my elbow. I looked from one detective to the other.

"Can't you see what happened?" I spoke quickly. "She was working on her quilt, cutting the final border, from the looks of it. Her rotary cutter slipped, and she cut herself. Badly." I remembered the ugly cut on her leg and stopped to breathe in a painful gulp of air.

"Rotary cutter?" Buster had his pad out now, ready to take notes.

"Didn't you see it? The big blade? With a yellow handle?" I asked.

Neither detective changed expression. They must have seen it, so it was obvious to me they didn't know what a rotary cutter was and were not going to reveal their ignorance.

"A rotary cutter?" I continued, proscribing the shape with my hands. "Looks kind of like a pizza cutter? Quilters use them. Very sharp blade. Really lethal."

I winced at my frivolous choice of words, but their potential danger had been drilled into me from the time my mother brought home the first rotary cutter twenty years ago.

"Do you use the rotary cutter, Miss Pelligrino?" Detective Sanchez asked. He over-pronounced the t's in cutter, as though he'd never heard the word before.

"Sure. We use them every day at Quilter Paradiso, my shop." Something about Sanchez demanded complete answers, so I corrected myself. "Mostly, my employees do. To cut fabric. I do the computer work. And it's Ms., Ms. Pelli*cano.*"

Sanchez didn't seem to register the correction, gesturing for me to continue. My temper flared at his dismissive attitude.

"The tool is very common," I said sharply.

"Where does one buy this tool?" Sanchez asked, drawing out the word enough to let me know that real tools have power cords at one end and a man at the other.

"Any quilt shop or fabric store." I laid on the *any,* informing him he was the one out of the loop.

I felt Buster's eyes on me, pleading for me to play along. He knew my tendency to smart-mouth. I swallowed the sarcastic tone and spoke civilly. "We sell them in our shop and, this week, in our booth. Many of the booths carry them, I'd guess. You do know there's a convention of quilters this weekend, don't you? I'd bet there are hundreds of these rotary cutters around here." The sarcasm had crept back into my voice. Had they missed the hordes of fabric-toting women downstairs?

"So these cutters are used extensively?" Sanchez said.

"Yes," I shouted. Years of dealing with brothers who never seemed to hear me unless I yelled, had turned me quick-tempered when confronted with deliberate obtuseness. "And how about this — not only are they used all the time, most people use the same brand, so they all look alike. They come in different sizes, but still have the same yellow handle. To tell them apart, people put their names on them. Did you find a name on the one on the floor, Detective?"

Buster clasped a large hand on my shoulder, sending tiny waves of energy through my body. The warmth from his hand soothed my jangled nerves.

I settled against the back of the chair and modulated my tone. "Quilters use these cutters all the time, that's all I'm saying."

"But you don't use one?"

"I'm not much of a quilter."

Sanchez dismissed me, turning his attention to Buster. "What's your plan for interviewing witnesses?"

"We can question people on-site," Buster said. "According to hotel staff, most of the guests are associated with the quilt show and knew Mrs. Armstrong."

"She *was* famous," I put in. I suddenly felt too confined and jumped up, knocking over my chair. Buster caught the back of the chair before it hit the ground.

"A famous quilter," Sanchez qualified with a sneer. "Take your seat, Miss Pelican."

I did not want to sit down. "It's Ms. Pellicano," I corrected, biting off each syllable. "Why can't you get it straight?"

Sanchez gave Buster a look as though to say I was his problem now. "I'm going back to the scene," he said.

As he left, I sat heavily back in the chair. I felt the kinetic energy drain out of me.

"You okay? Sanchez can be a little rough."

"I'd hate to see him around someone who was guilty of something." I rubbed my eyes. I hadn't seen much of Buster since going away to college, just a few times a year at family events. That's why I'd been taken aback when Buster's voice floated out of my answering machine several days after the funeral.

At first he'd offered a shoulder to cry on. I'd been tempted, but had been unable to summon the energy to dial. When I didn't return his initial call, he left several more messages. It became clear he wanted to see me on a more personal level. I hadn't been sure how to deal with the idea of dating Buster, so I'd ignored his phone calls. I thought not responding had been a pretty good tactic — until now. Now, it just seemed rude.

Buster said, "I'm going to tape your statement, all right? Don't be nervous, it's standard procedure."

He was wearing glasses. I didn't remember ever seeing him in glasses before. They made him look smart, and the look contrasted with his wide shoulders and small waist, imbuing him with an intellectual sex appeal. This didn't seem like the right place to be noticing that Buster was hot, so I looked away.

His ministrations with his handheld tape player were taking longer than I thought necessary. I fidgeted in my seat. My legs twitched uncomfortably.

Finally, he spoke into the recorder, establishing the time and place of the meeting, inserting my name and his. The official tone of his voice made my stomach clench in fear. I was finally getting the idea that, despite the size of his tiny recorder, this was a real police investigation.

Buster indicated I should begin. I started haltingly to tell what happened.

"I came up here to meet with Claire Armstrong. She was going to buy Quilter Paradiso."

Buster's eyebrows shot up in question. I reached across the table and put my hand on his, restraining him.

"You can't tell anyone, Buster. Especially not Kevin or Kym. I just decided today to sell the shop," I said.

He nodded. "I won't say anything. Start with what happened this afternoon," he said.

"Kym . . ." I didn't want to finish that sentence. What happened at the booth would stay at the booth. The police didn't need to know every detail of my miserable morning. Only the worst part.

I started over. "I needed to speak to Claire. When I came up to her room, she didn't answer. After I knocked on the door a few times, her assistant showed up with her lunch. She didn't want to let me in, but I convinced her." I glanced at Buster to see if he could tell I'd omitted grabbing the key from Myra. I didn't want to admit I'd bullied my way in.

I lied a little more. "We went in together, thinking Claire was coming right back. Then we saw the body, and I couldn't understand how so much blood could be on the floor. It was pooled, thick and sticky." I stopped as I remembered Claire's inert form, and the huge gash in her thigh. My eyes filled with tears.

"I felt sick and ran to the bathroom to throw up. Myra came in and we called 911. That was it." It was impossible to describe how helpless I felt at that moment, so I didn't try.

"Was there blood anywhere else in the room?"

I pictured the scene and shook my head. "I don't think so."

Buster made me describe the color of the blood and Claire's position. He asked a lot of the same questions over and over, changing the words, never explaining, but I was sure he was trying to trip me up or see if I changed my story. I just told him again and again what I'd seen.

Finally, he turned off the recorder. He sat

near me, taking my hand in his and patting it awkwardly.

"You've had a rough day."

The sympathy in his voice was genuine and hit me like a wave, knocking the adrenaline out of my body in a rush, leaving me feeling wrung out. I crumpled against the back of the chair, pulling my legs in around me. I leaned my chin on my knee, trying to gather myself together.

Buster got a can of soda out of the small refrigerator and handed it to me. I drank thirstily, the caffeine and fake sugar doing its magic, reaching my limbs and revitalizing them. I stretched in the chair, twisting my neck back and forth.

"Better?" Buster asked.

I nodded.

"Diet Coke still a favorite, I see."

I knew where he was going with this. "Hey, I was ten."

He looked around and whispered dramatically. "You made me steal a liter of Coke from Baxter's store."

"Paula and I were thirsty."

"I was almost caught. Only old Mrs. Wright knocking over that Pringles display with her walker saved me."

"How did I know you were going to grow up to be the police?"

We laughed at the memories of simpler, innocent crimes.

"You always could get me to do anything you wanted," he said quietly.

I squirmed. This conversation was going to a dangerous place. I did not want to talk about the power I had over Buster when we were kids. I was two years older, that was all. In the neighborhood pecking order, age ranked highest.

"Buster, I'm sorry I didn't return your calls . . ."

My apology was interrupted as the door banged open, and Sanchez took the room in several long strides. He was carrying my backpack in a plastic bag.

"Hey, you've got my backpack. Great." Coming out of my chair, I reached for the bag.

Sanchez pulled it out of my reach. "Sit back down, please."

My arms were still outstretched. What was with this guy? "I'm not a golden retriever . . . you can't just tell me to sit."

"Sit now."

I heard in his voice a certain undeniable authority. I tried a quick look at Buster, but he was studying Sanchez. I sat, harder than I intended, jarring my butt and clinking my teeth.

"We found your satchel at the scene." He waited for me to answer.

Satchel? How old was this guy? "Yes, that's mine," I said.

"Can you identify this?" He held up the cardboard I'd put in it earlier.

"Of course, that's the packaging from a new rotary cutter." I looked at Buster, who remained stone-faced. "I opened one this morning to use in the booth."

"You put it in your bag."

"Not the cutter, just the packaging. The State Board of Equalization requires us to pay sales tax on everything we take out of our own inventory even if it's for our own use. I needed to take that to the store so I can include the barcode in our monthly report."

I looked from Sanchez to Buster and back. Neither one said anything. Buster was watching Sanchez's face. He was taking his cues from the older detective.

"I don't understand," I said.

Sanchez stood in front of me, his voice stentorian as though he was projecting across a crowded theater. I saw the frustrated actor — or maybe lawyer — in him.

"Ms. Pellicano, did you use the cutter in this packaging to kill Claire Armstrong?"

My first thought was that he finally got

my name right. My second was that he was accusing me of murder.

FIVE

"Of course not," I said, my voice wavering. I struggled to get under control. I stood, hoping being upright would stave off how vulnerable I felt. "Can I go now? I've been here for hours. You've got my clothes, my shoes, and my backpack. Just let me go back to work. I'm needed there." I stopped talking as I heard my voice veer off into a pathetic whine.

It dawned on me that, without the computer, my last statement wasn't really true. I didn't have any business in the booth. Still, I needed to get out of here.

"No," Sanchez said.

"Okay," Buster said.

Their voices blending as they spoke at the same time, Buster and Sanchez looked at each other. Buster frowned.

Sanchez shook his head. "We need to hold her until we've finished questioning everyone."

"We have more witnesses to interview. She's got a business to run," Buster said. "I have her statement."

"She had access to the murder weapon," Sanchez said.

"We're not sure we have a murder here."

His partner lowered his voice; Buster bent to hear him. He was at least eight inches taller than Sanchez, but it was clear Sanchez was used to being in charge.

"Healy, put your dick back in your pants." Sanchez spoke softly, but I heard him.

Buster's head snapped back, and a red blotch started creeping up his throat as he saw I'd overheard. He glanced at me, an apology in his eyes. He pointed his chin at Sanchez.

"She's told us all she knows." Buster's voice was steely. "We have no reason to hold her."

Here was a glimpse of the man Buster had grown up to be. Tough when he had to be. I was grateful. Sanchez backed down with a tiny shrug.

"Leave your cell phone," Buster said. "We'll keep your backpack. Don't disappear."

"I'll either be at the store, home, or here."

"More importantly, don't talk to anyone about what you've seen," Buster said.

He dismissed me, inclining his head slightly toward the door. I flew out into the hall, wondering what price Buster would have to pay for my freedom. I looked at my watch; it was nearly five, almost closing time. I'd spent the whole afternoon with the police. With Buster.

As I pushed the button for the elevator, I noticed a faint smear of blood on my hand. I'd washed my hands when I changed out of my clothes, but I missed this. The blood was caught in the cuticle like the blood you see after getting a paper cut you didn't know you had. I scrubbed at my fingers, rubbing the redness out of the nail, feeling very, very alone.

Claire's was the first dead body I'd ever seen outside of a funeral home. I'd always felt cheated not seeing my mother before she was fixed up and put in the pink silk-lined box. That hadn't been my mother in there, not really. At the viewing, I'd snapped at anyone who said she looked good.

Now I felt grateful to the mortician who'd made her look as normal as possible. I hadn't understood what a great distance that was, from alive to dead. A vision of Claire's pale eyes danced in my memory, the arch of her eyebrow, now extinguished forever. Sadness washed over me.

Downstairs in the atrium, the show was closing and quilters were streaming out, returning to their cars and their everyday lives. Several remained behind at tables scattered around the space, basking in their purchases. I heard cries of "Where did you get that?" and whines of "I would have bought some of that if I'd seen it," as purchases were passed around.

Their frivolous fun grated on my exposed nerves.

I hesitated outside the door to the show. They'd be expecting me back at the booth, wondering where I'd been all day. Ina, Jenn, and Kym had no idea I'd nearly sold the shop this afternoon. They had no clue I'd found a dead body and spent my day with the police. I couldn't tell them about finding Claire, and I wasn't going to tell them about selling the shop. But I needed to collect the day's receipts and bring them back to the store.

No one checked my ID as I bucked the tide of exiting quilters and went in to the show. At the booth, Ina and Jenn were saying goodbye to the final customers of the day. Did they know about Claire? It had been hours since I found her, but I had no idea if word of her death had spread.

If the news had gotten around, death

didn't deter Kym. Her problems, as usual, took precedence.

She blocked my way at the entrance to the booth, hands on her hips. "Dewey, where have you been? I've been calling you and calling you. Don't you have your cell on? We need to cash out."

"What do you need me for? You know how to do that." I couldn't keep the annoyance out of my voice.

"I don't know what to do," she whined. "Some stuff was on the computer, the rest of the day wasn't."

"Do whatever you used to do before the computer," I said. Leave it to Kym. She'd caused this trouble, yet expected me to fix it. Well, I wasn't taking the bait.

Kym stomped a foot in frustration, but I turned my back on her. Ina and Jenn were draping lengths of fabric over the displays, shrouding the tables, closing down the booth for the night.

"We had a good sales day," Ina offered.

I nodded, like I cared.

"Did you hear about Claire Armstrong?" Jenn said. "She had an accident and died in her hotel room."

"I heard," I said curtly.

A garbled announcement came over the

loudspeaker. I looked at Ina. "I didn't get that."

"The show is closed," she translated. "The vendors have fifteen minutes to shut down their booths and get out."

"Or what?" I snickered. "You're locked in?"

"JustEve productions takes security very seriously, Dewey," Kym said.

Jenn was nodding her head gravely. "The guards make sure everyone is out and then lock the doors so our things are safe. No one can steal a quilt, or our merchandise, for that matter."

"It's true, Dewey," Ina said. "They only give us a few minutes to get out each night."

"So what should I do about reconciling the cash?" Kym said. "We've got to get out of here."

Kym touched my arm, to start pleading with me anew. I pulled myself away angrily, my voice squeaking from exhaustion. I reached under the table for one of our QP personalized totes, stuffing my ugly gym bag and wallet inside.

"Just handle the drawer please, Kym."

She let out a huge sigh. I lost my temper and whipped around. Getting right in her face, I found the strength to raise my voice.

"This is your fault, remember? I had a

procedure for closing using the computer, but you decided to quit using it halfway through the day, so that's useless. I don't care what you do. This is your mess, now deal with it." I ran out of steam pretty quickly, and with nothing left to say, I walked away from the booth. I wanted to be finished with Quilter Paradiso and Kym more than ever.

I heard Kym call after me, but I threw back my shoulders and kept walking. In my haste to get out of the booth, I'd turned left instead of right, sending me deeper into the quilt show, instead of to the outside. I didn't want Kym to know this wasn't a deliberate choice, so I walked as though I had a destination in mind.

The aisles were deserted; it wouldn't be difficult to find my way out. I still had a few minutes before being locked in. I would cut over as soon as I could and go down a neighboring aisle to the exit.

The only sounds were the murmurs of vendors closing up, their voices soft and subdued with the weight of the day's work behind them. Tired from ministering to customers all day, they were caching energy to do the same thing all over again tomorrow.

A voice came over the loudspeaker. This

time in the relative quiet, I heard Eve clearly. She called out the attendance like the announcer at PacBell Park — paid attendees: 2,423 people. A cheer went up from the sales floor. I waited to hear if Eve would mention Claire's death directly. Instead, she thanked the vendors for their hard work on a difficult day. She reassured everyone that there would be no changes to the schedule. I heard a murmur of approval.

Were these people nuts? I saw a man give his wife the thumbs up. It was ridiculous that the show would go on tomorrow as usual.

At the end of the row, instead of being able to make a U-turn down another aisle to the front door, I found myself at a dead end. Without realizing it, I'd entered an alcove off the main room. A sign overhead read "Award Winners." Straight ahead was a quilt with Claire's name on the artist's card. I stopped, saddened that this was the first time I was seeing any of Claire's work when she was already gone.

The quilt was a large rectangle, made up of pieced arcs and circles. The colors were blues and browns. I noticed plaids, stripes, and print fabrics. The effect was calming and exciting at the same time.

A tap on my shoulder made me jump. It

was the diminutive security guard I'd met earlier this morning.

"Time to go, miss."

I'd been staring at the quilt without seeing it, my mind lost, Claire's death replaying in my mind. I swallowed my resentment at being startled. I felt unjustly accused of something.

"I was just leaving," I said.

"This way."

He stepped away from me, allowing me room to pass, but staying close. The hall was deserted. I must have been looking at that quilt for longer than I'd thought.

Once we were out the door and into the atrium, he made a big show of locking up. He was pretty pleased with himself. After dealing with the real cops all afternoon, I was in no mood for a Target reject, pushing his weight around.

"That's a lot of keys on your belt," I started but checked myself. Let him be. He was just doing his job.

He was oblivious to how close he'd come to getting bitched out. "Just make sure you have your ID card with you tomorrow," he said.

I held it up, showing him I'd been wearing it around my neck since I put it on this morning. He didn't acknowledge me.

Eve was sitting in her information booth in the atrium. I wanted to know if she'd considered Myra's feelings in going on with the show as usual. I crossed over and knocked on the wooden frame to get her attention. She looked up, scowling.

"Eve, hi. I heard you say there would be no changes to the activity schedule. You did hear about Claire, right?"

She nodded. "Of course," she said, looking at me quizzically. Her cell phone began playing a Sousa march. She glanced at the readout, her face screwed up into a moue of frustration.

She snarled into the phone, holding it six inches from her mouth, "Just handle it, okay? I'm sure she'll be along any minute."

Out of the corner of my eye, I saw Freddy approach.

"How about a drink?" he said.

Eve waved him off gruffly.

"Come on, you two," Freddy persisted. "We all deserve a libation after a day like this. I'll buy." To me he said, "I need to make up to you for what I did this morning."

"What did you do?" Eve asked Freddy.

"I mistook her for her mother."

He answered without taking his eyes off an attractive young woman in a crisp white fitted blouse and tight jeans who cut between us. Eve came out of her booth, locking the flimsy wooden door behind her.

Eve looked me up and down. "I don't see it."

"I could use a drink," I said, the truth of the statement only hitting me after the words were out of my mouth. A tall glass of syrah would go a long way toward smoothing my ragged edges tonight.

"He won't, you know," Eve said to me.

"Won't what?" I asked.

"Buy drinks. Freddy never does. We go through this every year. Every show, for that matter. He talks a good game, but he never ponies up."

Eve's phone rang again; she frowned and answered it. She shook her head vehemently and hissed into the phone. I felt a wave of pity for the person on the other end. She clicked it closed.

"Have you seen Justine?" She punched Freddy on the arm to get his attention, as he followed another pretty girl with his eyes. He turned reluctantly, rubbing his bicep.

"Justine? She's around here somewhere."

"No, she's not. I haven't seen her since she took the deposit to the bank this morning. I'm getting calls about the fashion show." Eve's voice rose, her frustration with her partner evident. "She's supposed to be in charge. The lighting people want to focus, and she's got the keys to the stage. It was the only thing she had to do this whole weekend, damn it."

"Chill, Eve. The fashion show isn't until Saturday night," Freddy said.

"Easy for you to say. Rehearsal is tomorrow," Eve said.

"You're not going to stop any of the events?" I asked.

Eve turned to me. "Why would I?"

"Claire's death." I left off the "duh?" but it seemed obvious enough to me.

"Listen, Dewey, I know you're new to all this, but a show this size is like a small town. Heck, it's bigger than lots of towns up north. Every day in Smalltown, USA, people die and life goes on. It's just the way it is."

My eyebrows arched in surprise at her condescension. I started to protest, but she interrupted with a wave of her hand.

"I'm not insensitive, but people come from around the world to this show, Dewey," Eve said. "Take the fashion show. We've got outfits from sixteen different countries. I couldn't stop these festivities if I wanted to."

"Plus, she doesn't want to. Business might even be better," Freddy put in.

She shot Freddy a look.

He pulled away, laughing, out of Eve's reach. "You know it's true. Same as grief sex. Consolation shopping. Spending money proves you're alive, unlike the dead sucker . . ."

Eve put up a hand to silence him, and he obliged, his poor taste under wraps for now.

"And the lecture on Saturday? I saw on the schedule that Claire was supposed to give a talk Saturday afternoon." I asked, still stuck on the idea that the show could not go on as planned, determined to show her things were not normal, no matter what she thought.

"Sold out," Eve said.

This time I didn't bother to hide my double take. "Who's going to speak?"

"Myra said she would fill in."

"When did you talk to her?" I asked. Did she get out of police questioning sooner than I did?

"About an hour ago."

Right about the time Sanchez was pawing through my backpack. He must have questioned Myra, found the packaging in my bag, and let her go. He didn't find any reason to hold *her*. I was singled out.

"She said she would put together a grouping of quilts. Do an Armstrong retrospective," Eve said.

"Claire Armstrong — the Wonder Years," Freddy put in.

"How could she do that, so soon after her boss' death?" I could barely talk about my mother, nearly six months later.

Eve shrugged. "We'll see. If anyone can pull it off, it'll be Myra. She's really good at focusing on the task at hand. Besides, it'll be good for her. Like a wake, a memorial service."

Wow, Myra wasn't the only one who could focus. Eve was pretty good at putting unpleasantness behind her, too.

"It'll be good for everyone involved. The customers loved Claire, too," Eve said.

"Justine will really miss Claire," Freddy said, his voice lilting up in a way that meant he was teasing.

"You really are a bastard, Freddy." Eve lunged for him, and he danced away. He ran in front of us, laughing. Eve was visibly upset, but I was just puzzled. Why would Justine miss Claire more than anyone else?

"Come on, lighten up," Freddy said, holding his arms out to Eve, offering her a hug that she ignored. "I was just kidding."

When he couldn't get more of a rise out of Eve, Freddy inserted himself between me and Eve. "Look at the thorn among the roses," he said.

"More like the prick," Eve scowled.

Suddenly, I wanted to go home. The fake bonhomie and inside jokes were making me sick to my stomach. Claire had only been dead a few hours. "Look, you guys, you don't need me to tag along. I'm going to go . . ."

"Suit yourself," Eve said. "Your mother always came for one drink the first night of the show." She moved ahead of us, striding toward the bar as though the drink awaiting her was the only thing that mattered.

"Besides," Freddy continued. "Now that Claire's dead, aren't you going to look for a new buyer for Quilter Paradiso?"

Six

Freddy was facing me, walking backward.

"How did you know?" I said, grabbing him by the arm and forcing him to stop. Eve never hesitated, just kept moving toward the bar.

"Claire has been interested in your mother's shop for a while now."

"Why?" I asked.

"I think she was tired of being on the road and liked the idea of having her adoring fans come to her for a change. When I heard you were talking to her this morning . . ." He shrugged.

"But I wasn't selling to her then. I mean, when she and I met this morning, that was the first time I knew anything about a sale."

"So I put two and two together and got six. Sue me. But judging from the look on your face, you're thinking about selling now."

"I am," I admitted. "Know anyone who

might be interested?"

"Not me, I've got my hands full," Freddy said. "Let's go in the bar. I'll introduce you around. Lots of vendors from the show will be here. Pretty soon this place will be crawling with potential buyers."

We entered the darkened space. Straight ahead was a long wooden bar with red upholstered stools and a mirror reflecting rows of neat liquor bottles. To my right, round tables with matching tub chairs were scattered around the floor. We headed for the table in the back where Eve was already seated. I sank into the chair next to her.

There were about twenty people in the bar, most sporting vendor IDs from the Extravaganza. Freddy produced a hundred-dollar bill from his wallet and announced that he was paying for drinks for everyone.

Eve looked up in surprise. "Now I've seen everything. He's actually going to buy drinks."

"What that man won't do to impress a pretty girl," she continued, after Freddy left to go fill our orders. "He likes you."

I shrugged. "I doubt it. He just feels bad about this morning."

I helped myself to a handful of pretzels. "I do wish Justine were here though. I'd like a chance to talk to her," I said.

Eve's eyes narrowed as she checked out the room. "I wonder where she is. We always go to the bar the first night of a show. Our little tradition. I'm surprised she's not here already."

"I'm sure she's fine, Eve."

"I know *that,*" she said sharply. "Justine and I are a team. We're so connected, I'd know if something bad happened."

Oh boy, I knew how untrue that was. When my mother lay dying in her Volvo, I was at happy hour with a bunch of engineers. We were comparing worthless stock portfolios, cursing the Alternate Minimum Tax and doing Jell-O shots. Before that day, I'd thought I would know, too. Now I knew better. The moment my mother died, I was laughing at a joke about the size of Larry Ellison's plane.

I hadn't been in a bar since that night, I realized. I would only stay long enough to meet potential buyers.

Eve's phone rang, playing "Let It Be," and her eyes lit up. It was the first time I'd seen her smile. Her face brightened, her features softened, and she looked years younger. "Hey, babe," she shouted, holding the phone with one hand and clamping the other over her free ear. "Where are you?" She moved to a quieter corner toward the front of the room.

Returning with our drinks, Freddy rolled his eyes. "Must be Justine."

Freddy had linked Claire and Justine. I'd seen Justine outside in the hall before I knocked on the door. What was their connection?

"Why did you say that about Claire and Justine?" I asked him.

Freddy's answer was drowned out as cries of "Bonnie" and "Rick" rang out. A middle-aged couple dressed in matching plaid shirts came in. The room was filling up quickly.

"I know, it's not really funny that Justine borrows money from Claire," Freddy said.

"What are you talking about? Why would Claire lend money to Justine?" I asked.

A large bang jump-started my heart. Freddy and I looked in the direction of the noise. Across the room, a large man with a sweater vest almost covering his belly was standing. His table was still rocking from his fist pounding. His beer glass was raised high, slopping the liquid over the side. He licked his hand and lifted his glass even higher.

"To Claire!" he shouted. "Claire, who had the biggest balls in the business. May she rest in peace."

A cheer went up from the crowd.

"News travels fast in this place," I said to Freddy, over the din.

"What else would people talk about?" he said. "It was too good to ignore — the woman who taught the world to rotary cut, the queen of strip-piecing, falling on her rotary cutter? How much more Siegfried and Roy can you get?"

I cringed at Freddy's characterization.

"Which one was it that got eaten by the tiger?" he continued, hand on his chin. "Roy? No, Siegfried. Or is that the same person? I can never remember."

A rash of toasts broke out from all corners of the room. I swiveled, trying to follow the cheers from my chair.

"To Claire, who taught quilting to the klutzy, math-challenged, uncreative masses," a brassy blond chimed in from her bar stool.

"To Claire, whose sense of decency never got in her way."

"To Claire, who never met a dollar bill she didn't like."

From behind me, a stout woman in black jeans and a red denim jacket said, "Remember that time Claire arrived at the Extravaganza by helicopter?"

"Scaring every living creature within a square mile," another woman put in.

"How about that time she decided to

decorate the fountain out front to match her latest quilt? The dye killed every plant within a hundred yards. She didn't know the water was recycled into the sprinkler system."

A roar of laughter filled the space.

Eve came back to the table. She picked up her drink and took a deep sip. "To Claire! That rotten bitch. May she rot in hell!" she said, low enough that only Freddy and I heard her.

We exchanged a glance. Freddy watched Eve over his glass, his reptilian eyes following her as she tossed back the rest of her drink. Eve turned, her face creased with a false smile. "At least Justine's up a thousand dollars."

"Up a thousand dollars?" I said, not understanding her meaning.

"Gambling," Freddy put in, sotto voce.

Eve shot him a look and explained to me, "She's playing poker at the local card club. That's how she blows off steam."

I tried to hide my surprise that a woman like Justine had spent the day gambling. It seemed kind of tacky.

"You okay with that?" I asked Eve, trying to keep the judgment out of my voice.

"Why not? She always comes home when she's finished," she said defensively.

"Granted, it would have been nice if she'd told me where she was going. She thought she was on track with the fashion show, figured she wouldn't have to deal with anything until tomorrow. She'll be back later. It's fine."

"Whatever gets you through the night," Freddy said.

Eve took a sip of her second martini and glared at him. I felt like a kid in the crossfire of an adult argument. I didn't understand exactly what was going on, but it was uncomfortable. I tried to move the conversation to less incendiary topics.

"This seems like a very different crowd than the quilters I see at the store," I said, pointing at a representative table. "Younger for one thing, more my age."

Eve agreed. "With business savvy. When quilting became a billion-dollar industry, the corporate world started to take notice."

That meant Mom had been on the right track with the software. I needed to finish computerizing the store to attract a good buyer.

Freddy sighed and sipped his scotch. "I'm old school, like your mother was. We were interested in quilts and spreading the word. We started vending at these shows for the same reason we started our shops — because we loved quilts. We made the mistake of making our avocation our vocation."

"Why was that a mistake?" I asked. "Seems like you should be happy doing what you love to do."

"Things changed," Freddy said and lowered his voice. Eve looked bored as though she'd heard this diatribe before. "This new generation of vendors are business people first. They could be selling sewer pipe, for all they care."

Eve's face twisted with impatience. "Just because owners have starting running their shops like businesses meant to turn a real profit," she said, "doesn't mean they don't care about the industry."

Freddy pouted. "They don't give a hoot about quilting. These people are direct descendents of the snake-oil salesmen. They're vagabonds, setting up at quilt shows like itinerant traveling salesmen. Claire, for all her faults, was one of us."

Eve sniffed and took a drink. "Selling is selling, Freddy."

"Quilting is big business now, run by people ignorant of the art," he continued.

Was he including Eve in that characterization? I glanced at her to see how she was taking this. Her eyebrows were gathering like thunderclouds.

"That's the type of owner I am," I said, trying again to lighten the mood. "I know nothing about quilting."

"Yeah, but you're different because you know nothing about business either," Freddy quipped.

I punched him in the same spot Eve had hit earlier. He grunted and rubbed his bicep. I had more experience inflicting pain than she did.

"What was Claire, artist or businesswoman?" I asked.

Freddy brightened. "Claire was the exception. She managed to do both."

I thought about Claire's assistant. What would she do for a career now that Claire was dead? "And Myra?" I asked.

Eve and Freddy exchanged a look and laughed. "She's all business, that one," Freddy said.

Eve picked up her drink. "I'm going to make the rounds," she said.

"Watch her work the room," Freddy said as Eve put on a smile and stopped at a nearby table. "She's like a bride at her wedding, greeting her guests. All she's missing is the money bag to collect her gifts."

To sell the store, I had to talk to some of these people. Swallowing a sudden shyness, I tapped Freddy on the arm. "So what about it, Freddy?" I said, with far more enthusiasm than I felt. "Are you going to introduce me around or what?"

Freddy and I followed in Eve's wake as she circumvented the room. For the next hour, Freddy made good on his promise. I met at least thirty new people. Conversation centered around two things: the amount of business done today and Claire's death. I was surprised to hear several men comparing the sizes of their daily totals, and I felt stupid when I didn't know exactly how much business the booth had done today. I ducked any conversation about Claire. No one knew I was the one who found her and I wanted to keep it that way.

The muscles in my face were beginning to ache from constantly smiling so I decided to have one more glass of wine and leave. I gave Freddy a twenty and sent him to the bar and found a seat at a table just vacated by a group from Fresno. It felt good to be alone.

Freddy returned with a fresh drink for me and one for himself. A commotion went up at the front door. He stood up to see what was going on.

"Sweet. Lark Gordon in the house," he reported. "Have you met her yet?"

I looked where he was indicating. Over

95

the heads of a barrier of people, I could see the elaborate pattern Lark's tiny braids created on the back of her head.

I shook my head. "I saw her earlier, talking to Claire. She's got a show on cable, right?"

"Yes, *Wonderful World of Quilts.*"

"I hear customers quoting her all the time," I said. "Too bad she doesn't have a way of letting the shops know what's coming up on her show. My life is hell if she mentions a tool on the air that I don't have in stock."

"I'll introduce you and you can suggest it."

"Oh yeah, right. I'm sure she's interested in what I have to say."

Freddy stood up and snagged Lark as she went past. I got out of my chair, and he introduced us. When Lark turned, I could see why she was a successful television personality. With her eyes on me, I felt like I was the only person in the room.

"So sad about Claire. I saw you talking to her earlier," she said. "She was a frequent guest on my show. We were good friends."

Good friends? It hadn't looked like that to me. If that was true, then something had happened between them, because it was obvious that Claire hadn't wanted to talk to

Lark this morning.

Lark peered into my eyes. "You might have been the last person to see her alive. Do you want to go on camera?"

"TV?" I took a step back to break the intensity of her gaze. "No."

Freddy interceded. "Come on, Lark. Give the girl a break. She's here trying to forget the events of the day."

Lark interrupted him. "How about getting me a drink, Freddy?"

He looked at me. I waved him off. I could handle Lark. He headed for the bar.

Lark said, "Your shop is Quilter Paradiso, right? That's a great place. I don't sew much, but since I started this job, I've become quite the fabriholic, buying tons of fabric I'll never use."

"You're not a quilter?" I asked.

Lark reared back and laughed. Her laugh was a very girly giggle, at odds with her sophisticated exterior. "Can you keep a secret? I can't sew, let alone quilt. I'm a journalist, although I've been working as a television personality lately."

"So how long have you been in this job?"

"Five years."

"Is that how you met Claire?"

A frown crossed Lark's pretty features quickly, and then she composed herself.

97

"Yes, she had a great interest in television."

How many pies did Claire have her fingers in? Was that what they had been arguing about? I could see Claire as a hostess of a quilting show. If she had lived, that might have been something she would have done.

Lark looked around the room, playing idly with her earrings. They were large gold hoops, the size of a salad plate. She wore a gold necklace with a diamond at the neck and several charm bracelets. Rings, but no wedding ring. Her jewelry and her clothes looked expensive. A cable TV hostessing job must pay better than I thought.

She sat down and leaned toward me. "How about the local news? I've got contacts in the local market. I'm sure I could get air time. We could probably get on the local early morning show, talking about Claire."

I shook my head vigorously. Lark settled back in the chair, with a pretty pout on her face. She turned away from me. Her eyes lit on Freddy's back. He was leaning against the bar.

"What's he doing up there? Schmoozing the cute bartender?"

When I didn't answer, she asked, "Is your shop doing well?"

I hesitated, then shook my head. "Not

great. In fact, I'm looking for a buyer."

The noise in the bar suddenly abated as though the air had been sucked from the room. I felt eyes staring in my direction and looked up to see Myra standing at my elbow.

Lark stood abruptly. "My condolences," she said to Myra. "Tell Freddy never mind the drink." She took a step back and was immediately swallowed up by the crowd.

Lark's fascination with Claire didn't extend to Myra, for some reason.

Myra had changed into navy pants with a pale-blue silk blouse. The last time I'd seen her, she'd been covered in blood. The only sign of upset was the slight tremor in her hand. I pulled out a chair for her to sit down next to me.

"Hello," she said quietly, twisting the colorful bracelet on her arm.

"How are you?" I asked.

She shrugged.

"If you need to talk," I said, "I'd be willing. After all, I was there with you. They say talking helps. We could get a more private table . . ."

"Ha!" The syllable burst out of her; her eyes were flashing with anger. "That's the most ridiculous thing I have ever heard. Why would I want to *talk* about what happened today?" Her voice dripped with sarcasm. I felt singed by her tone of voice. I didn't dare look around, but figured every eye must be on us again. I shrunk against the seat back.

She continued her rant. I fought off the urge to jump up and leave. "Do you want me to sear every detail in my brain, guarantee myself a lifetime of nightmares? Ensure that I never forget a single detail? So I can always remember what Claire looked like, lying in her own blood? No thanks. Give me good old-fashioned repression. People talk way too much."

Her words stung. I sipped my drink, watching her over the top of the glass. I would cut her some slack. She was grieving; I knew people grieved differently. Dad went fishing; Kevin sought solace in his marriage, sublimating his own personality so much as to disappear; my brother Sean threw himself into his work, building stage sets at twice his normal speed; and Tony, the oldest, sought solitude in the desert, coming home every couple of months to do laundry before going back to categorizing succulents.

Where was Freddy? I could use his silliness right about now.

"Great jewelry," I said, trying to shift focus.

Myra looked down, and stopped twisting.

Her shoulders relaxed. "I made it from the buttons we've used in our projects over the years."

"Buttons? They look like beads."

I took her wrist in my hand and examined the bangle. It caught the light, and the buttons glittered.

Myra took her hand back. "Nope, I glued them on a Bakelite bracelet I found at a flea market. All of them came from Claire's button collection." Her eyes misted.

My throat closed up. "Detective Sanchez thinks I killed Claire," I blurted, to avoid telling her that every little thing would be fraught with meaning now that Claire was gone. I faced that feeling every day when I went into the shop.

Myra looked shocked. "That's crazy. Why would he think that?"

I looked around the bar. The jukebox was playing loudly but I wanted to make sure no one heard me. I moved my chair closer.

"He found an empty rotary cutter package in my backpack," I whispered.

Myra sneered. "So what? Does he seriously think you would open a new cutter, kill someone, then put the cardboard in your backpack and go back up to her room and find her body?"

"Guess so." Out loud, that scenario

sounded ridiculous. I relaxed against the back of the chair, feeling the plush sink beneath my shoulders.

Myra leaned in and said, "Dewey, it was obviously an accident. She was sitting on the edge of the bed and cutting fabric. I told her that was not the way to use that blade. Did she listen? Of course not."

Myra's conviction that Claire had just had an accident was beginning to calm my nerves. I hadn't realized how much Sanchez's accusations had unsettled me.

"I'm glad you don't think I killed Claire."

Myra laid her hand on my shoulder. "I know you didn't, Dewey."

A geeky guy with wire rims and a small goatee appeared next to Myra's chair and insisted she come to his table and meet his wife. I told Myra to go ahead. I needed time to think.

"I can see Claire," Freddy slurred, bumping into the table as he finally returned, slopping his drink on the table. I looked up sharply before realizing he was talking metaphorically. He must have had several shots at the bar. He pointed across the room.

"She always held court at that corner table over there. People came to her with their questions. She was like . . . a godfather, no godmother. The Godmother of Quilting."

I got an image of Claire behind a big desk, dispensing favors. "She made offers people couldn't refuse?"

He grimaced at my awful Brando. "No more," Freddy continued morosely. "The balance has shifted."

I'd had enough drama for one day. "I'm out of here," I said, pushing up from the table and grabbing my QP tote. I looked around to see who I needed to say goodbye to. I couldn't see Eve. Myra was deep in conversation far across the room. Lark tried to catch my eye, but I looked away quickly. I told Freddy I'd see him tomorrow and left.

Outside, it wasn't dark yet. I still needed to go to the shop; I felt a pang of guilt that I'd been out of touch so long. There was the question of missing inventory that I still needed to figure out. A new owner, especially a corporate one, would insist that all the store accounts were reconciled.

Was the next owner of Quilter Paradiso in that bar? I hadn't come right out and asked anyone to buy my shop but I might have met the potential buyer tonight. It was going to take more investigation, but I felt like I'd made some headway. At least I knew more vendors by name than I had this morning.

I started down the sidewalk toward the garage where I'd parked my car.

Suddenly, Eve cut across the path in front of me. She was talking angrily into her cell. I had to stop short to avoid running into her.

"That was money we needed," I heard her say as she held the phone out in front of her, walkie-talkie style.

Like so many people, she seemed to forget that her cell conversation was audible. She passed in front of me again, nearly tripping me. I tried to gauge where she was going next.

"I want you to come home now. You need to get help, J."

This conversation was obviously a private one, despite the fact that it was being held in a very public place. I held back, resigned to waiting her out, hoping she would get off the phone soon.

"Claire's gone now, honey, so you don't need to worry about the money," Eve said.

What were they talking about? Freddy'd said Claire lent money to Justine. I'd seen her outside the room. She could have been paying Claire back. Had Justine been the last person to see her alive?

"When will you be home?" Eve shouted, as she wheeled around heading right for me.

Behind her the sun was setting, the few clouds streaking the sky pink and red.

Eve walked quickly past without registering that I was in front of her. My path to the parking garage was suddenly clear and I took advantage, dodging past Eve and heading up the concrete walk toward the structure. The last thing I heard was Eve's exhortation to Justine.

"Do not miss the fashion show, whatever you do."

Seven

The small gravel parking lot behind Quilter Paradiso was full; I backed out and parked on the street in front. The shop was still busy, despite the fact that we were scheduled to close in a few minutes, at eight.

I stepped outside my car, breathing in the cool air, trying to get the echoes of Eve's phone conversation and the sad events at the quilt show out of my head. The sun had finished setting, leaving the sky the color and texture of navy blue velour.

Lights from inside the shop glowed invitingly. The neon "Open" sign sent colorful contrails streaking down the glass. The front window was dominated by one of Ina's signature Lone Star quilts. Neighborhood people often dropped in on their way home from errands to tell us how much they enjoyed our ever-changing window displays. I felt a swell of pride, not for me, but for my mother. This was the shop she had created. I was just trying to keep up and falling short constantly.

Inside, I could see customers milling about, some already carrying their bags, others waiting at the cutting table, still others fondling the fabric. Vangie, Tess, and the rest of the staff had everything under control.

I'd used my quota of social energy at the bar, so I stuck to the sidewalk and went around to the back of the store, running my fingers over the old masonry siding as I walked. My great-great-great grandfather, determined to recreate his Boston childhood, had shipped these bricks overland. The shop stood out from the Spanish-style stucco architecture of the rest of the block. It was perfect for a quilt shop, although the traditional feel ended when the customer walked in the door and got a glimpse of the brightly colored fabrics. California twisted tradition, Mom had called it.

Of course a new owner would change all that. I felt a twinge of doubt. Was I doing the right thing in looking for a buyer? Kym was leaving me no choice.

I entered through the back door, nodding to a customer as she opened the door to my left that led to the bathroom; the door to the right opened into the classroom. A second classroom was in the loft space. My office was on the other side of the bathroom, and a kitchen was beyond that. From there, it was a short distance to the store's main space.

I could hear Vangie singing "My Boyfriend's Back." That meant a customer had bought six yards or more of fabric to use for the backing of a quilt. Vangie, despite having just turned twenty-one, was an aficionado of sixties music. She liked to refer to herself as a hippie.

Shrieks of giggling filtered back to me as Vangie hit the chorus. "Hey now, hey now, you've bought a back." I crossed over to my desk, listening to the joviality, but not being part of it. This was a familiar feeling, being an outsider in what was supposed to be my shop. I felt a flare of anger at my mother for leaving me in this position. I quickly stuffed it down. It wasn't her fault she had died too early.

Entering my office, I felt my focus shift. The talk at the bar had brought home the fact that Mom had been right about computerizing the sales and accounting systems. I'd spent the last six months entering every item we had for sale, every bill we owed, every invoice we sent out into the laptop. It had been a huge job, and I had finished last week — except for one outstanding invoice.

When I'd put the store accounts into our new software, I'd found checks being paid out to a company named WGC, without a corresponding bill of sale. I knew this much from my basic college accounting class — expenses and outlays had to be the same. There was no documentation of what we'd purchased from this company. I'd asked Vangie to get copies of all of the checks made out to WGC, thinking they might reveal information about the company. On my desk was a folder with her handwriting on the outside.

Attempts I'd made to contact the company had not panned out. There was no phone number to call or any explanation of the charges on the monthly statement. Just a new bill each month, coming from a post office box in San Jose.

I fanned out the seven checks. More than $3,750 worth of payments to WGC. Under the old system, there was no reconciliation between receiving and accounts payable, so this kind of discrepancy would never have come to light.

The first check was signed by my mother, the rest by Kym. I turned the checks over and squinted at the blurry endorsements. No signature, just a stamp that read WGC, followed by the imprint of a local bank, one with branches all over the country.

The checks told me nothing new.

I threw the folder into the top drawer, disappointed. I'd let myself hope that the answer was here in the checks. Now I would have to double check my inventory input and I couldn't do that without the laptop.

A bulging envelope with Kym's distinctive curlicue writing was on my desk. I pulled it open and swore. She'd had the last word after all. In the bag was a copy of every receipt from today's business at the booth, along with the cash, checks, and credit card receipts. From the size of the pile, they'd been very busy all day. That was great news for Quilter Paradiso, but rotten news for me. Under the old system, I had to enter all these transactions in the ledger by hand before I could balance the money and get the bank deposit ready.

Worse yet, I'd have to sort out which sales went through the computer and which had not. I'd have to match every check and each credit card transaction with its receipt. A tedious, time-consuming, mind-numbing chore. Brought to me by Kym.

I was not going home anytime soon. Laughter again erupted from the front of the store. I felt very sorry for myself as I closed the door and returned to my desk.

I was deep in the process when the phone rang.

"Dewey," my brother said, recriminations already evident in his voice. His timing was impeccable. "Kym's a mess."

The top of my desk was a sea of receipts. "Kevin, don't start with me. Your wife . . ."

"She's really upset about the computer, sis."

I put him on speaker phone and lit into him. "She's upset? I'm furious. She refused to learn the program, she pulled the plug on the laptop and left me with a huge mess to clean up. She's doing everything she can to make me look bad."

"Come on, Dewey. Cut her some slack. You knew she wasn't happy about the store going online."

I sighed and rubbed my fingers against my temples. Kevin owed his loyalty to his wife, but I wasn't used to this alliance. As kids, it had always been me and Kevin against our two older brothers. His relationship with Kym had snuck up on me. Busy with the pressures of working at a startup, I didn't know how hard he was falling for her until it was too late and they were engaged.

When I didn't answer, Kevin changed to a more sensitive subject. "I just spoke to Dad.

He's stuck at Donner Pass. He won't be home until Sunday."

"That figures." I couldn't hide my disappointment. My father was unable to deal with the first Quilt Extravaganza since his wife's death. His job had always been to help my mother with setup and teardown. This year, he'd had a sudden urge to go fishing. Late spring snows in the Sierras were conspiring to keep him away. I needed him here.

Kevin sighed. "He's avoiding me because I'm trying to get a line of credit at the bank. I can't take these big jobs without one, but he refuses to listen."

Kevin and Dad were always at odds over money. Dad thought Kevin took too much liberty with his credit cards, and Kevin thought Dad's stand on remaining debt-free was ludicrous. It was an old argument, one that would probably never be resolved until Dad retired and Kevin took over Pellicano Construction completely. I made a neutral noise, unwilling to get bogged down in his fights.

Kevin realized he'd hit a conversational dead end. "Kym told me about Claire Armstrong. Weird, huh?" Kevin said.

"You have no idea," I said, suddenly feeling exhausted. I wanted to tell him about finding Claire. I wondered if he knew about Mom selling the store to her. I couldn't believe that if Kevin or Dad had known, they wouldn't have told me.

"I've got to go," he said suddenly. "Kym wants me to watch *Survivor* with her."

I wanted to keep him talking to me. "Kevin, you know QP hasn't been doing very well, don't you?"

"The valley's economy is not that great. Things'll turn around."

"I don't think it will." I took a deep breath. "Kevin, Mom —"

"Dewey, not now. Kym's waiting for me."

Not now. It had been like this ever since Mom died. No one in my family would talk about her. Mentioning her favorite dish at a family dinner put everyone off their feed. If I started an anecdote about her poor sense of direction, Sean got out his portable GPS unit and started talking about geocaching. Pulling out the family albums, I could clear the room in six seconds.

"She was going to sell the shop to Claire," I said, but the phone was dead. "I found her body," I finished although I knew no one was there.

The door to my office opened as I was hanging up. Vangie was framed in the door-way.

113

"Whoa, Dewey. I was shocked to hear your voice. We were so busy out front, I didn't know you were here," she said.

Evangeline Estrada, Vangie, had started working at the store several years earlier as a high school kid, part of a work/study program. After graduation, she'd left QP and drifted, getting in with a bad crowd, doing drugs and getting caught. She'd spent time in custody, but when she got out, Mom had hired her back, convinced her innate goodness would win over her addictive personality. So far, so good. She knew as little as I did about quilting, but she knew computers.

She was relentlessly honest — it was what kept her to her straight path. I relied on her to tell me the truth.

I leaned back in my chair. "Everyone gone?"

"Yup, we had a great day."

Her chocolate eyes flashed with pride as she held up the bulging deposit bag she had readied from the cash register up front. She had thick brown eyebrows that matched her long curls.

I held up the mesh bag Kym had left. "Looks like the booth did okay, too. Trouble is I don't have the laptop, so I'm trying to balance the old-fashioned way."

"Where's the laptop?"

"In police custody."

"Get out! Did you have Kym arrested for something?"

I laughed but sobered up quickly when I realized she didn't know I'd found Claire's body and spent the afternoon with the police. Vangie harbored a deep-seated resentment of authority figures.

"You heard about Claire, right?" I asked.

"Yeah, I couldn't believe it. First Kym called and then of course the customers were yammering on about it all afternoon. Her death was the number one topic of conversation."

"Well, I found her, and I left my backpack in her hotel room. The cops took it as evidence. The laptop was in the backpack."

Vangie's gaze unfocused. "What were you doing in Claire's room?"

My turn to tell the hard truth. "I went to talk to her about buying the shop. Vangie, my mother was planning on selling QP to her."

She looked away. "I knew that."

"You knew?" It was my turn to be shocked.

"Yes, but I thought it was a moot point once your mother died. Until today, I figured Claire had given up."

"Vangie, we've got to keep this between us. No one else knows."

Vangie glanced up at me quickly, her expression giving her away. I grabbed her hand. "Come on, Vangie. Spill."

"Kym knows. She saw you talking to Claire this morning," she said quickly, trying to soften her words with speed. "She called here and caught me off guard. She asked what Claire would want with you and I told her about the shop sale."

I said, "Well, if she was trying to change my mind about selling, trashing the laptop was not the way to do it."

Vangie turned pale. "Did you decide to sell?"

I nodded.

She put on a brave face. "No worries. I'll find a new job."

I curled back into my chair, a knot forming in my stomach. In my haste to get out from under Kym and her machinations, I hadn't considered what would happen to my employees. Selling the store would mean putting people out of work. I'd have to make sure that didn't happen. I felt the weight of my responsibilities pressing on my shoulders, and I shrugged to release the tension.

"You found the copies of the checks?" Vangie asked.

I nodded. "Yes, thanks. I looked at them but I still don't know why we're paying WGC that money each month."

"What does WGC stand for anyhow?" she asked.

"I don't know. Warm Gouda Cheese?"

"Wacky Girl Consortium," Vangie added. "Wild Grannies Corporation."

I laughed. I could always count on her to lighten my load.

"We'll figure it out," she said. "In the meantime, let me balance the receipts from the booth."

"That'll take hours," I protested.

"No, it would take *you* hours." She tugged on my chair. "Come on, take off. I can straighten this out in no time."

I got up from my desk, grateful to go home and get into bed.

"Want to hear the worst part?" I said, as she began expertly sorting the credit card slips.

"Worse than Claire dying?" she said, without looking up. Her forehead was creased with concentration on the task.

"The homicide detective, Sergeant Sanchez, thinks I did it."

She looked up. Her expression was concerned. "Thinks you killed Claire Armstrong? Is he crazy?"

"I mean, it's ridiculous. She had an accident with her rotary cutter. But he's not convinced and thinks I had something to do with it."

"I bet she was murdered."

"Vangie, how can you say that? She was a quilter, for crying out loud."

Vangie put more slips into a pile, sorting by a method I could only imagine.

"What?" she said. "Quilters can't kill each other? Come on, all that slicing and dicing — what's that about? I bet Claire had a lot of enemies."

"I don't think so." I remembered the toasts in the bar. Except maybe Eve. And Lark.

"What's more important is what the cops think."

"What do you mean?"

Vangie looked up. She pointed her chin at me, eyes narrowed.

"You need to be proactive. You can't just lay down and let the cops walk all over you. Go out there and find someone else who might have done it."

"Vangie, you're not serious."

"Dude," Vangie continued. "You've never been in trouble; you don't know how the system works. Once the police know your name, everything changes."

EIGHT

I loved my neighborhood, and after the day
I'd had, the familiar streets lined with
mature olive trees, cracked sidewalks, and
yellow roses were like a balm on my frazzled
nerves. The houses were a brew of Spanish
and craftsman architecture with the odd
Cape mixed in. Most of the houses were
small; the large Victorians on the Alameda
had long ago been turned into law offices
and real estate firms. I'd only moved back
to the old neighborhood two years earlier
when my company stock split and left me
with a windfall that made a sizable down
payment. Even with that money, my house
was tiny and on the wrong side of Park
Avenue. And the monthly nut was large
enough to make my mortgage-free parents
gag.

I parked in the driveway and went in
through the back door.

My bungalow was a work in progress,

what Ina would call a UFO, Unfinished Object, but I loved the graceful proportions of the built-ins, the warmth of the wood floors and the arched doorways. When I'd first moved in, all I had to do was enter my back door and I felt renewed and safe. That sense of security had been spoiled by my mother's death.

It was only lately that the sheltering feeling in my house had returned. And it was because of Buster. For weeks after my mother's death, I'd found it impossible to sleep through the night. I'd wake up about three in the morning, too keyed up to read, too unfocused to watch television. I tried to knit, but ended up with a twisted mess of yarn in my lap that looked like a psychotic kitten had been playing with it.

One night, after Buster had left a particularly disarming message, I pushed play again to hear his joke at the end. Alone in the dark, I found the sound of his words comforting.

All of his messages had been stored on the voicemail system, filed neatly under Buster's return number. I'd played another and discovered if I rewound clear to the beginning, the messages would replay one after another. In the pre-dawn emptiness of my small house, Buster's deep timbre filled the space up.

He was shy in the first few messages, growing bolder as he called more often. His monologues were funny, endearing, and sometimes pathetic, but they always drew me in. After that first night, I used his voice as a lullaby many times. I knew every modulation, knew where the self-deprecating chuckle would come, where his voice broke with pride, where it fell off in thought.

There was something very intimate about his disembodied voice coming out of the answering machine. Each evening, I'd looked eagerly for the blinking red light that meant I had new messages.

I hovered by the phone now. No new messages. I nearly pushed the button to hear the old ones, but after spending the afternoon being questioned by him, Buster's voice held new meaning. I wasn't sure I'd be able to separate Homicide Detective Ben Healy from Buster.

I started the water in the tub instead. A long, deep soak would have to serve as comfort tonight.

I stripped off my running suit, wondering where Sanchez had taken my clothes. When would I get them back? Did I want them back?

In the tiny mirror over the sink, I was surprised to see the same face that I'd seen this morning looking back at me. So much had happened since then. I felt like I'd changed so much, but the trauma of finding Claire didn't show. I couldn't even see a new wrinkle.

The combination of the emotional day and the hot water lulled me to sleep almost as soon as I lowered myself into the tub. I awoke to pounding on the front door. My heart echoed the rhythm. The water in the tub had gone cold. I dried myself quickly and pulled on a pair of boxers and a tank top. The rooster clock on the kitchen wall read just after eleven, too late for visitors. It had to be family. Maybe Dad, back early, or Sean, down from the city and needing a place to crash. I shuffled to the front door and looked through the peephole.

Buster stood on the front porch, dwarfing the pillars, filling up the small space. My craftsman-style bungalow had the proportions of a dollhouse, built when people were shorter. At six foot four, Buster was definitely no doll.

The oak door creaked loudly as I opened it. Why was he here? I looked past him. He was alone. He had changed into a scuffed leather jacket and jeans.

"Can I come in?" he said, one foot over the threshold. The shy smile on his face told me I wasn't going to be taken into custody.

"Are you going to arrest me? I don't see any handcuffs."

"Oh, I'm sorry," he mocked. "Did you want me to bring handcuffs? I've got some in my truck."

"Very funny. Come in."

The front door opened directly into the living room. I knocked a pile of books off the faux Stickley armchair and took a seat on the couch. Buster sat down in the chair. Feeling underdressed, I pulled a fleece throw off the back of the couch and wrapped myself up. I stroked the soft nap, stopping when I saw Buster's eyes following my hand.

He reached into his jacket pocket and pulled out my cell phone. "I brought you this."

I lunged for it, dropping the throw to the floor. "Oh, thank you. You have no idea what this means to me. I felt so . . ."

"Disconnected?" he supplied, sporting a goofy grin.

"Well, no phone does make it hard to reach out and touch someone."

Buster groaned. "Bad joke begets worse one. Nice." He sat back. "We're done with the cell, so there was no reason you should be without it."

"Hallelujah." I hugged the phone, which beeped complainingly. It had been nearly nine hours since I found Claire. I couldn't remember ever going this long without retrieving messages. I wanted to get started. I looked expectantly at him, but he had moved to the fireplace, rubbing the wood grain on the surround appreciatively.

"Great mantel. This is the old Colombo place, isn't it? Bobby and I were in grammar school together."

"I bought it from a young couple," I said. "I didn't know the people that owned this house before that."

"I spent many an afternoon in that bedroom right there." He pointed over my shoulder at the wall the living room shared with the spare room.

"Really?"

"Bobby and I, playing with our joy sticks."

I gave him a sidelong glance. "You called them joy sticks?"

"Bobby had a Sega," he said innocently. "What did you think we were doing?"

"Gee, I don't know, two teen boys, maybe a *Sports Illustrated* swimsuit edition."

"Wow, you have an evil mind."

"No, just three brothers, remember?"

"Good point. Bobby and I were pre-pre-puberty, far more interested in our Star Wars figures than bikinis."

"That's a relief," I laughed. "I'd have to strip the floors again."

He laughed, too. His face was open and expressive. "You remodeling?"

I nodded. "Just about every room in the house is in an uproar. The only room that's done is my bedroom. I made sure that I had one place to retreat to."

"Can I see it?"

"My bedroom?" I yelped.

His eyes twinkled at my discomfort. "The whole house. I'm a big fan of bungalow architecture. I'd like to see what you've done with it."

I stood and crossed my arms across my stomach, conscious of the thinness of the boxers I'd changed into and the fact that I wasn't wearing a bra under my tank top. He followed me into the dining room. My running commentary about home improvements would end at the back door, and me showing him out.

"We redid the floors before I moved in, and now we're stripping and staining the built-ins."

"We?"

"Me, mostly. Kevin and Dad help out

when they can."

"I thought maybe you had a boyfriend," he said, rubbing his hand over the door jamb appreciatively.

"Not right now." I reddened, glad he wasn't looking at me.

Stick to talk about hardwoods, I cautioned myself. The house was only 950 square feet, so the tour didn't take long. Living room across the front, dining room, and kitchen along the back of the house. Two bedrooms and a bath off a short hall, unfinished attic space upstairs.

We stopped in the kitchen near the back hall that led to the bedrooms and bathroom.

"You've done a great job," he said.

"Thanks, I still have a long way to go."

Buster rested his hand on a kitchen chair. I leaned my butt on the counter. The proximity of his body to the speaker where his voice had come out so many nights was too much for me. I blushed, remembering how often I'd played the messages.

Now he was here and I wanted to hear more of his voice. Without the answering machine between us.

My guitar lay across the kitchen table, along with a teach-yourself chord book, open to Lesson Four. I hadn't gotten very far. He picked it up, put a sneakered foot up on the chair and plucked the strings, humming softly. I liked the look of his hands, nearly too big for the neck, his thick fingers moving nimbly as he tuned the guitar. He wasn't wearing his glasses, and he squinted as he worked the strings. His head curving over the guitar made one lock of black hair fall over his forehead.

"You learning guitar?" he asked, without looking up. He played the first few notes of "Here Comes the Sun," then turned the top key.

"Trying." Many of our family parties ended with the guitars coming out. Buster was a good player with a raspy, sexy voice. "I'm always jealous when you guys jam. I feel left out."

"Yeah, but you're the only one that remembers the words to 'Losing My Religion.' "

"A vital skill, I know, but I'm looking to expand my repertoire."

He looked up from the guitar, smiling. "I'd love to come over and play with you. I might be able to teach you a few things."

I bet. Just behind him was the doorway to my bedroom. My mind went to places it didn't belong, picturing his fingers on me instead of the fret. I was a sucker for a boy with an acoustic guitar. MTV Unplugged all the way.

I shifted farther into the kitchen, away from the danger zone.

He lowered his head back to the strings, fingers moving quickly, squeaking now and again. A leather thong on his wrist dropped down. I hadn't noticed it under his suit earlier. He had showered and changed into a SJPD black T-shirt and jeans, but he hadn't shaved, so his chin was blue-black. The five o'clock shadow, the man bracelet, and the guitar was a dangerous combination. I smelled a spicy aftershave and felt a low burn in my belly. I swallowed hard.

He brushed the hair back off his forehead and caught me looking at him. He stopped playing, leaned over the guitar and smiled.

"I was surprised when you said you were selling. Kevin told me you liked working at the store."

"He did?" I couldn't keep the surprise out of my voice.

"I wondered about that. The quilt shop was the last place I thought you'd end up. I can't really picture you working with a bunch of women."

"It's tough. I don't always feel like I speak the language," I said.

"Didn't you get into computers or something? Is that easier?"

"Much. At least I feel competent. At the store, most of the time I just feel stupid. I knew nothing about quilting when I started. And I still don't know much."

"Did your mother leave you the shop in her will?" he asked.

I nodded, chewing the side of my finger. I didn't want to say any more about the shop.

After a moment of silence, he spoke again, pointing his chin at the answering machine.

"You never returned any of my calls."

I couldn't keep up with the change of topic. "Why did you keep on calling me?"

"I wanted to talk to you about your mother," he said bluntly.

"Oh." I didn't know what to say to that.

Buster strummed a familiar tune that I couldn't name. "Her death hit me hard," he said into the belly of the guitar. "It was the first time someone I knew died while I was on the job. I couldn't talk to Kevin; he didn't need me, he had Kym. I thought maybe you'd want someone to talk with. Someone who remembered her."

He was right. I had needed someone to talk to about her. I just hadn't known if he was the right person.

"Did you know she sent me packages when I was away at school?" he asked. "Candy, and beef jerky, and toys."

I nodded; I got those packages too. "Once I got a set of jacks."

He stopped playing and pointed at himself. "Nerf basketball. I was the envy of my floor."

We were quiet, remembering my mother and her knack for keeping connections alive. I heard the clock tick and the compressor on the refrigerator kick in. The only light was coming from the nightlight on the stove and the lamp I'd left on in my bedroom, and from the huge full moon shining in through the back door. The world didn't seem to extend beyond this space. We could be the only two people awake in the neighborhood.

"You know how sometimes just saying something aloud can help you come up with an answer?" he said softly into the stillness. "That's what it was like leaving those messages on your machine."

He brushed the hair out of his eyes, the guitar leaning across his knee. The thin leather strap on his strong wrist made me breathless. The whole picture was making me swoon. It had been a long time since anyone had made me feel this way.

I fought the urge to move closer. I leaned farther into the countertop, trying to play it cool.

"You stopped calling for a while," I said. The calls had ended about two months after my mother's death. Lately, they'd started again.

"Well, it's pretty weird, you've got to admit. Leaving messages on a machine to a person who never returns your calls. I tried to stop. Went cold turkey."

He'd left the last one a week earlier. "But then you started again."

Buster pulled back and looked away, slightly embarrassed. "When I was assigned to the detective squad, I wanted to tell you. I would drive home from work, trying out the story of my day. I'm sorry if I disturbed you," he said formally.

I shook my head. It was my turn to confess. "I enjoyed your messages. I tried calling you back once or twice in the beginning but then I'd let it go so long, I didn't know what to say. I did like hearing from you, though."

Buster chuckled, and pushed up from the table. "We're a couple of sick puppies. Trying to communicate without ever speaking to one another." He leaned the guitar against the wall and started toward the screen door.

I didn't want him to leave now.

"I like this face-to-face stuff much better," I said, so quietly I wasn't sure he heard me.

He turned back, his eyes following mine as I looked into my bedroom, just a few feet away, and widening as he got the idea.

I took the steps that separated us and slipped my arms around his neck. His shoulders were broad, and I felt his potential strength beneath his clothes. Black chest hairs curled out of his T-shirt. I rose up on my toes to kiss him.

Just like that, the stresses of the day melted away. The fear and horror flowed out, like water down a drain.

He kissed me, gaining confidence and exploring my lips thoroughly. As much as I wanted him in this moment, I hesitated and stepped out of his embrace.

"This is weird, you know. You're Kevin's friend."

"So?" he said, rubbing my upper arms.

"So, last time I saw you, you were in a soccer uniform."

"Huh? We've seen each other plenty since high school. I always make an appearance on Christmas, and the neighborhood block party, and your dad's Fourth of July barbecue . . ."

I put a finger on his lips to stop the list where our paths had intersected over the years. I didn't want to admit I'd noticed him at these places.

I started talking fast. "You know that hutch in the dining room at my dad's? That place is a time warp. The framed pictures go on there and don't ever change. Sean's college graduation picture; my confirmation, for crying out loud. You're there, next to Kevin, in your red and white soccer uniform, that year your team was All-State."

"Oh, the hutch. Now that you mention it, your confirmation dress was hot."

I shot him a look.

"Well, we've both grown up a bit since then," he said.

There was something in his pants that looked very grown-up.

Buster stroked my face. "Can't two adults have a good time?"

Adults having a good time. Is that what he was promising me?

"I want to be clear." My voice cracked as he nuzzled me. When he pushed my head up with his lips and kissed my throat, my knees let go. He lifted me off my useless feet, putting a leg between mine, pinning me gently to the wall. The plaster was cold and rough on my bare skin. Someone moaned.

"Dewey, I've been interested in you for a

133

long time now."

"How long? Not like junior high long, I hope?" I croaked the words out as he worked up to my ear. "I don't think I could live up to an adolescent crush."

He stopped and grinned a wicked smile at me. "I've always been attracted to older . . ."

"Be very careful."

I drew back my hand as though to hit him, and he caught me by the forearm, laughing. He pushed my arm up over my head, held it there, and kissed me. He brought my other arm up over my head, his hands tightening around my wrists with new ferocity. He leaned and spoke into my ear, his warm breath pushing into my neck. The tip of my ear tingled. New erogenous zones were popping up all over.

"I've always thought you were beautiful, Dewey."

I gasped at the feel of his body pressing into mine. I couldn't remember the last time a guy had made me feel pretty.

I broke free and pulled him into my bedroom. At the foot of the bed, he crushed me into him and I felt him swell. He gripped me through my boxers. Constant waves of sensation washed over me, and I gasped for air. His kisses traveled down my body and I felt a jolt each time his hot lips contacted my flesh. I could feel the lines around my body blur, my boundaries vanish in an instant. I couldn't tell where he began and I left off.

I wriggled out of my boxers; tore at his T-shirt. I felt myself nearing an edge, ready and willing to tumble into a lovely abyss.

Everything faded; the day's dreadfulness, the struggles of the last six months. I felt a puddling in the middle of me. A tight spot in my chest that had been there for months dissolved. It was as though Buster had reached inside me and kneaded that spot until it softened and spread.

NINE

When I woke up, the sun was shining and I was alone. For a moment, I thought I'd dreamed last night, then I felt the soreness along my jaw, scraped raw from Buster's unshaven face. I stretched like a pampered cat, feeling every nerve ending sing. Buster had tended to my body like no one else ever had, and I'd enjoyed every minute of it.

There was a note on the pillow. "Lesson number one." A pencil sketch of a guitar punctuated the sentence. I felt myself grin.

Greedily, I ran through the possibilities for a repeat performance. I could get free today. I didn't have much to do at the quilt show without the computer. Being the fourth woman in a three-man booth meant I was more of a hindrance than a help. Buster was going to be there. Late last night, he'd said he was going to be interviewing witnesses in the hotel conference room. Setting up on-site had solved the logistics of getting all the out-of-towners over to the police station.

I sank back on my pillow. I had never taken a guy into my bed so quickly. What had I been thinking? Buster was in the middle of an investigation. Claire was dead — a terrible tragedy for her and her family, and all I was thinking about was getting Buster back in the sack.

And then there were Sanchez's accusations that I murdered Claire.

Talk about your rude awakening. I felt my gut wrench.

On my way to the shower, I heard my neglected cell phone beeping irritatedly in the living room. I retrieved the messages. The first three were old, from Kym, yesterday. I wasn't looking forward to facing Kym after our blowup. I knew she would do anything to stop me from computerizing. But she wouldn't want me to sell either. She just wanted me to do things her way. I punched the delete key without listening to any of her messages.

The next was a brief call from Dad, repeating what he'd told Kevin — he'd be home Sunday, in time for take-down. The sound of his voice made me tear up. I could have used some of his strong silence right about now.

The last was from Justine. "Hey, Dewey. I

heard you found Claire. Please come to my room tomorrow morning. Room 511. I need to talk to you."

I would like to talk to her, too. I felt a connection with her. Being the show's organizer, she probably had a good sense of who might be interested in buying the shop.

And I wanted to ask her about Claire.

Had she seen anything when she left Claire's door? I glanced at my watch. It was only eight thirty. I had time to shower, dress, and get over there, see Justine, and still get to the booth before the show opened at ten.

After I talked to Justine, I would look for a potential buyer for the shop.

I hustled through my morning routine. When I got to the point where I usually made my bed, I could see the dent Buster's body had made in the side of the bed that usually was empty. I liked the way it looked and left it unmade.

The Dixie Chicks blasted out of the CD when I turned on the car, singing about needing a boy like a hole in the head. Like a wild goose chase. Were they right? Did I need a boy like Buster like a hole in the head?

I entered the hotel from the lobby connected to the convention center and went into the elevator. Without thinking, I pushed a button. I was lost in thought, bouncing between moments with Buster last night and wondering what Justine would tell me. The door opened. To my surprise, I was looking right into the conference room where Sanchez and Buster had questioned me yesterday. I glanced up at the number above the elevator door. Six. I'd pushed the sixth floor button instead of the fifth.

The elevator began to close. I put my foot in the way to stop it when I saw Buster's broad shoulders through the glass doors of the conference room. He was seated at the table, talking to a gray-haired woman. I stepped out of the elevator and got closer to the door, sidling across the hall like a crook, just to get a closer peek. It was weird to have butterflies in my belly over Buster.

His gray suit coat was strained across his back as he leaned forward. From the admiring smile on her face, his earnest manner was impressing the hell out of the woman across from him. Hair curled over the collar of his dress shirt. I got lost in the blue-black wave of his hair, until the elevator door dinged open behind me.

Sanchez was in deep conversation with a uniformed officer in the elevator car. Instinctively, I went in the opposite direction, pushing open the exit door to the stairs before Sanchez could see me. I let the door close behind me, my heart pounding.

The last thing I needed was for Sanchez to think I was snooping. Even I knew that the murderer returns to the scene of the crime. I had not meant to do that.

I charged down the stairs to the fifth floor. As I pushed open the gray door with the number five stenciled on it, I stopped to catch my breath, listening for noises above me. I held the door slightly open, ready to slam it and run if anyone came after me. After my heart stopped racing, I realized no one was after me. I leaned against the door, pushing against the stitch in my side.

Once in the hall, I tried to shut the door, but it wouldn't close all the way. Looking down, I saw a small notebook wedged in the door hinge. I pulled it out and the door hissed contentedly and closed. I continued out onto Justine's floor and found room 511. I knocked, then thumbed through the book idly as I waited for Justine to answer.

It was a spiral notebook, the size of a small index card. I was surprised to see the name of Freddy's shop on the top of one sheet, with pencil drawings below. Flipping through, I found pages dedicated to other

140

familiar names from the quilt show. It looked like someone had been making cryptic notes about what they saw at the Extravaganza. There were no words, just drawings and letters.

I'd seen Justine in this stairwell yesterday. These were probably her thoughts about their clients. She must have developed some kind of code so as not to offend anyone if she lost the notebook. Smart move, considering where I'd found it.

I knocked again, and when there was still no answer, I glanced at my watch. With Sanchez one floor up, I could not hang around the halls of the hotel. I didn't want to stand here and bang on an empty door. Been there, done that. Got the blood on my T-shirt.

Justine was probably already downstairs. I made my way back down to the quilt show. Inside the lobby, the crowd waiting to get in looked even bigger than yesterday morning. It was déjà vu all over again with one exception — there was no sign of Justine. I spotted Eve standing at the head of the line, where Justine had been yesterday, ready to collect cash. Eve was wearing another version of the JustEve shirt, this one teal with black lettering, and black Dockers. From the looks of the red-eyed young woman in the information booth, biting back tears, Eve was in a coordinating black mood. I hurried over there.

"Hey, I was looking for Justine," I told Eve.

"You just missed her."

I disregarded her scowl and offered the notebook. "Maybe you could give her this for me."

"Why?" Eve said, barely glancing at it. She twisted away from me, watching the burgeoning crowd.

I raised my voice. "Eve, I found this in the stairwell by your room. I think it belongs to Justine."

I poked the notebook toward her hand, trying to get her to take it reflexively.

She lifted her hands up, away from the book, looking at me like I was a lower life form. "Dewey, I don't have time for this. Get lost."

I stuffed the notebook into my pocket, feeling at the same time rejected and humiliated for caring. A few feet away, the same officious security guard was on duty, standing with his feet spread. The way he rushed me out last night came back with a sting.

The rent-a-cop watched me approach through slitted eyes, hiking up his pants with the inside of his wrists as though ready to rumble. This guy loved to throw his puny weight around. Our family station wagon had had a "Question Authority" sticker on the rear bumper most of my childhood. No way was this little twit going to play his power games on me.

He parked himself in front of me. I was wearing my ID badge. What was his problem?

"Excuse me." I bent down and looked him in the eye.

He didn't move. His face strained as he maintained his quasi-military stance.

"Remember me?" I asked.

"I do."

"Good, then you'll let me in?"

His eyes flicked to the long line behind me. I could hear the waiting show-goers breathing as though part of one organism, like a giant Chinese New Year dragon float.

"Show me your badge," he said.

I couldn't believe he was giving me grief. What does he want me to do — take it off and hand it to him? "You let me in yesterday morning."

"You were with Claire Armstrong. You said you had an ID," he hissed, his eyes darting between me and the waiting crowd. He was losing his cool. "You're a vendor."

"What if I'm not? What if I'm just a loser,

coming in on a famous person's coattails?"

Someone nudged me from behind, tugging on the cord around my neck, pulling the badge out from my shirt, making it visible. "Just show him your badge, Dewey."

I hadn't realized my badge was under my shirt. I turned to see Freddy, still wearing his sunglasses. He snapped his badge into view like an FBI agent.

He leaned in and whispered, "Not a good idea to make enemies with the guy who controls the ingress and egress."

"I didn't realize that's what I was doing." I pulled the ID badge the rest of the way out of my T-shirt and pointed it at the security guard, who stepped back.

Freddy smiled at the guard and steered me down the main vendor aisle, empty now of traffic. He was wearing a polyester shirt, all turquoise and pink whorls, that made him look like he'd just stepped off the Partridge Family bus. I had to wonder if these clothes were ones he'd worn in his youth or if he paid big bucks at a vintage store. Either way, it was a look he should have stopped wearing thirty years ago. The absurdness of his shirt drained the fight out of me.

He walked on the balls of his blue Keds, bouncing up and down in front of me, waving to folks in their booths as we passed. Everyone had a greeting for him, and he bestowed a smile on everyone as he passed. If there had been a baby available, he'd have kissed it.

"You're pretty chipper for a person with all that scotch in him," I said.

He pushed his glasses down to let me see his bloodshot eyes.

"Ouch," I said.

"It's all about the flash, girl. Fake it 'til you make it. Act like a million bucks, even when you feel like shit."

"Your outfit is enough to give me a hangover."

He nudged me with his elbow. "You missed a good time last night. Shouldn't have left so early. Turned out to be karaoke night. Ryan did a credible version of 'Me and Mrs. Jones.' "

"Sorry I missed it." Not. Whoever Ryan was, his karaoke couldn't have competed with Buster's guitar.

"Have you seen Justine around?" I asked. "She called me."

"Not today." Freddy rushed over to his booth where one of his employees was starting up a sewing machine. He stopped her. "Hey, don't pull on the hoop like that. You'll break it."

I'd heard of these high-end embroidery units that cost thousands of dollars and used computer technology to stitch out designs. Freddy got the machine going and I watched it fill in the yellow petal of a daisy. Look, Ma, no hands.

Within a few moments, that petal was finished and Freddy stooped to change to a new color thread. The show had opened, and people were flooding the aisles. I needed to find my way to a potential buyer.

"Can you help me find someone to buy Quilter Paradiso?" I pulled the notebook out. We were interrupted by a woman with tight gray curls wearing a hot pink T-shirt that said, "Don't Even Think About Touching My Fat Quarters." Freddy bent his head to her stooped height. He answered her question about the price and kissed her hand. She walked away, her hand trailing along the body of the sewing machine the way a teenager caresses his first car.

"You ready to find a buyer for the store?" Freddy asked.

I showed him the notebook. "Think this'll help?"

Freddy looked at the book. "What is it? A list of vendors? Not everyone is in here. Look, this person isn't even in business anymore. Use this."

He handed the notebook back to me, and grabbed an Extravaganza brochure from the table. He snapped open the newsprint brochure, folding the pages to reveal a vendor list and map of the show.

"Remember talking to them last night? The Freitas sisters with the hand dyes?" He took a fat Sharpie out of his pocket and circled several names. "Go see them. Here's the Youngs, that couple from Canada who specialized in custom machine quilting. Their daughter works at Google, and they're considering relocating. If they had any Google stock at all, they'll have money to burn."

He ran down about ten names of people we'd met in the bar last night. I was amazed at his total recall of these people and their lives. I was struggling to put faces with the names. I stashed the notebook in my back pocket.

"Enough," I said, taking the brochure from him as he circled another name. At least a dozen had thick black lines around their names. "The show is getting crowded already. I won't be able to talk to people if they're waiting on customers."

"Suit yourself. Good luck," Freddy said, waving me off.

I turned the corner and an image of Claire

brought me up short. For a moment, I thought I'd conjured it up. But no, her picture was printed on a white T-shirt floating ethereally in mid-air, putting her smiling mouth right at my eye level.

A chill ran through me as her image shimmied when a shopper passed by.

This was too creepy for words. Seeing Claire's face like this felt like a violation. I would hate it if someone took my mother's face and put her lopsided grin on a T-shirt. Who thought this was a good idea?

I peered into the booth. A large sign in the back said this was Nanny's Notions. I'd just seen that name somewhere in the notebook, or maybe the brochure.

The tables were filled with items printed with Claire's image. T-shirts, lapel pins, aprons, even a mouse pad. The picture had been bootlegged from the cover of her latest book. Someone must have been up all night making this stuff.

The vendor was a large woman, her butt dewlapped over the sides of a tall stool. She glared at me, slurping a cup of coffee.

"If you want a shirt, you'd better get it now. I expect to be sold out by noon," she said.

The crassness of someone profiting in such a crude way from Claire's death was appalling. Myra should be told. Claire must have had lawyers who could put an end to this. I grabbed my phone before I remembered I didn't have Myra's number.

I turned my attention back to the woman in front of me.

"Did you get the company's permission to use her likeness?" I said, trying to sound like I knew all the ins and outs of copyright violation. The woman was not fooled. She waved off my objections with her coffee cup.

"Cutie, if I waited for permission in my life, I'd still be in a trailer park in Fresno."

"That's disgusting."

"You're wrong," she said. "It's my tribute to her. Claire meant a lot to me. She helped me get my business started."

What would Myra's reaction be to coming across this? Would she see it as a tribute or insult? I had to put Myra's problems aside and get on to my own business before the show got gridlocked. I gave the vendor what I hoped was a withering glance and walked away.

I looked up and down the aisle. My mother had always talked about the people she met at these shows, but I hadn't paid any attention. I hadn't known then that one of those names might hold my future.

I felt a jolt of anger run through me that

my mother had died and left me with such big shoes to fill. I was not up to the task, I could barely find my way around this place. She had been intimately familiar with the show and the people. There was so much I didn't know.

I shook myself. She might have left me with a mess, but my mother had taught me the only way to get an unpleasant task done was to get started.

Checking Freddy's list, I saw the Freitas sisters' booth was several aisles over. Closer was another name on his list. I approached a grandmotherly-looking woman who was talking to a bulky man in a booth piled high with antique quilts. The seventy-something man was wearing overalls decorated with frayed-edge calico patches. He had yellowy-white muttonchops, reminding me of one of the cranky old Muppets that sat in the balcony. Why would Freddy send me here? I could only hope these two old people had younger partners somewhere.

As I waited for the woman to finish giving the overalled man his list of jobs for the day, my attention was snagged by an old quilt hanging across the back of the booth — a tree design formed by hundreds of equilateral triangles on a butterscotch-colored background. What kind of woman had spent her nights, bent over an oil lamp, piecing together those tiny pieces? Intellectually, I knew the answer — one who had worked all day in the fields, tended to her children, and still had the time, energy, and inclination to create something beautiful before bed. I felt like such a slacker. I resolved to go home tonight and, instead of watching another *True Hollywood Story* or *Forensic File,* install the crown molding in my dining room.

Just past the tree quilt a sign in the back of the booth read "Youngstown Antique Quilts." I looked at Freddy's list. I was in the wrong booth. I was looking for "Young's Quilts." Dammit, I was wasting time.

I was suddenly drawn into the man's chest as he bear-hugged me. I gasped as the cold metal buckle from his overalls pressed into my cheek. He pushed me away, holding me at arm's length, then yanked me in for another clench. The quick glimpse of his smiling face told me he meant no harm, but I wasn't sure I wouldn't get whiplash.

"Look at her, Noni, just like her mother." The man had tears in his eyes.

Noni smiled and touched my arm, extricating me from her husband's grasp with practiced ease. Her hand was as soft and

151

light as a cream puff, and she smelled of lilacs.

"Hello, sweetheart. Don't mind Chester, he's harmless. We knew Audra, you see, and it's such a joy to see you. Having you here is like she's still with us."

My eyes filled with tears. Noni produced a handkerchief from her apron. Lace-edged and embroidered, the hanky was too pretty to use. Chester embraced me again. I leaned away, dabbed at my eyes, and handed Noni the now wet cloth.

"I'm so glad you stopped by," she said, patting my arm. She acted as though she'd been expecting me. "I've got something for you."

She turned away from me, rummaging under the table until she came out with a large box, about the size and shape that boots come in. Chester was beaming at me, his cheeks squashing his eyes into little slits. I smiled back, wondering what would be in the box. Noni opened the lid to show me an old quilt, the fabrics worn but still colorful.

"I found this at an estate sale last fall," she said, her hands smoothing the quilt. The back of her hands were freckled deeply, with bumps where her veins bulged. I felt sad looking at them. My mother's hands would never get so fragile looking.

"As soon as I saw it, I knew it was just what your mother wanted."

"My mother?"

"You know how she loved any quilt with Flying Geese," Noni said.

Did she? I wasn't even sure what a flying goose was. I hesitated. Should I touch it? I knew the rules about never touching quilts. Oils on the skin were toxic to old fabrics, but I felt like I wanted to bury my face in this quilt. Noni saw my hesitation and took the quilt out and handed it to me. I cradled the folded bundle.

I ran my hand over the crinkled quilt, tracing the path of the peaks. "Is that what this is called — Flying Geese?"

"That's the name of the smallest unit there." She pointed at one section, a rectangle with a colored triangle in the middle. "The block is called by another name. Could be 'Flying Carpet Ride'."

"I think it's 'Corn Rows,' " Chester put in.

"You may be right, dear," she said.

The quilt was very old-fashioned, not my style, but the brown-and-pink color combination was appealing. I turned to Noni, returning her sweet smile. I had no words for what I was feeling. The quilt was dredging up emotions in me that I hadn't had before. I was bereft, yet comforted. Alone, but not lonely. Feelings of home and belonging seemed to permeate the fibers.

"Your mom told me that when you were little you wanted a quilt like this," Noni said.

"I did?" I had no recollection. And no one to ask. This was not something my father or brothers would remember.

"She said you were reading her copy of 'Quilts in History' and saw a picture of a quilt you loved."

This rang some faint bells. "Oh yeah — I was planning my wedding to Ricky Schroder and insisted Mom make me a quilt just like the one in the book."

I hadn't thought about that quilt since that summer, but with Noni's gentle nudges, the memories came flooding back.

"Mom told me she would piece a quilt for me, but I didn't want that. I wanted an old one, like the picture in the book. After several days of serious pouting on my part, she'd promised I'd have one when I got married."

My throat swelled shut as I realized my mother would never watch me get married, as I'd imagined so many years ago. The tears flowed again. Noni put her arm around me, handing me a new handkerchief, this one with pink roses embroidered on the corner. I laughed at her seemingly endless supply. She pressed it into my hand.

Noni patted my shoulder. "The quilt is yours, my dear. Take it and have a wonderful life. That's what your mother wanted for you."

A wonderful life sounded good. Would the quilt ensure that?

"Let me send you a check. An antique quilt like this must be worth a fortune." A fortune I didn't have, but I couldn't see myself giving up this quilt.

Chester held up a meaty hand. "We wouldn't hear of it," he said, his voice thick with emotion.

Noni concurred. "No, dear. We bought this quilt as a gift for your mother, to thank her for all the business she's brought us through the years. We'd be honored if you would take it."

What could I say to that? I didn't trust myself to talk.

Chester bussed my cheek. "Let me put it back in the box for you."

The box was surprisingly light, as if over time the batting in the quilt had been replaced with air.

Customers were demanding his attention. "We'll see you soon," he bellowed.

Noni drew me in for a hug. She looked fragile, but her arms held me tight.

"Thank you both so much," I said. "Make sure you stop by the booth sometime this weekend."

That was the first real conversation I'd had about my mother since she died. At the store, everyone tiptoed around me; talking ceased when I walked into the room. I felt myself relax a little. The knot in my stomach had started to loosen. A place in me, maybe it was the daughter place, was opening.

I was starting to sense that the quilt show was not a place trying to leech my mother away from me, but a place where I could add to my mother's stories.

With another reading of the map, and several false starts, I found my way to the Freitas sisters' booth. The tall, curly-haired one was restocking their pine shelves with neat bundles of hand-dyes. The array of colors was dazzling. The two sisters were dressed in flowing garments made from their fabrics, and they greeted me with the same toothy smiles.

After pleasantries, I said, "I'm getting serious about selling my mother's shop."

The tall one nudged the shorter. "Spooky, huh?" To me, she said, "We were just talking about you."

I looked from one to the other questioningly.

"We're thinking about making you an offer, Dewey. We have some questions for you."

"But not now," the shorter one with the bangs said. "We're about to get hammered with customers. The booth was crazy busy yesterday."

"Want to get together after the show closes?" I suggested. "About five thirty?"

"Sure, we'll be in the bar. Meet us there again."

The bar reminded me of the overheard conversation between Eve and Justine.

"Great. Hey, I've been looking for Justine this morning. Have you seen her? Eve wasn't very helpful."

They exchanged a look. These two had a secret and were ready to spill. "You left before the fireworks last night."

"Fireworks? I heard there was karaoke," I said.

"Not that. Justine came to the bar about midnight," Cully said.

"Straight from the card club. Tail between her legs."

This *was* news. "Did Eve flip out?" I asked.

"Oh yeah. She was ready to kill Justine."

Eve had said Justine played to de-stress. "I thought she was cool with Justine gambling," I said.

The tall one looked around before confiding in me. "Justine got on a losing streak and lost everything, including the bank deposit."

I caught my breath. "Wait a minute. She was supposed to take money to the bank. She didn't?"

"Nope, she went straight to the card club. And she had all the cash from the gate."

"How much are we talking?" I asked.

"Think about it," the tall sister said. "All of yesterday's admittance fees. Most of the attendees pay cash to get in. Running credit cards takes too long. We had more than two thousand people here yesterday. At fifteen dollars a pop, do the math."

I did the math quickly.

"Thirty thousand dollars? Gone?"

TEN

Thirty thousand dollars. I left the Freitas sisters and headed toward the QP booth. Threading my way through the crowded aisles, I wondered how much money the Extravaganza had taken in today. There was a lot more cash floating around than I'd ever imagined.

Maybe the notebook was a record of Justine's gambling debts. As I walked, I looked through it.

A drawing of a simple quilt block was repeated over and over. It was a rectangle with a triangle bisecting the length. I traced it with my finger. Easy to draw. I wasn't sure of the name, but it was similar to blocks in the antique quilt I'd been given.

There was no mention of gambling wins or losses. Maybe the book was just what I'd originally thought — a record of vendors that JustEve dealt with.

Near the middle, I found a sheet with the

QP name on the top and the number ten with several letters alongside. Ten? Was that good? Maybe on a scale for good vendors, we'd scored a perfect ten. Maybe it was the number of years we'd been doing business with JustEve. Whatever it meant, this was Justine's private property. I closed the book guiltily.

When I got to the booth, Kym was on her hands and knees. She had pushed aside the calico skirts and was half under the table. She poked her head out to grill me.

"I need more promotional QP bags. Do you know where they are, Dewey?" she asked.

"Me? I didn't pack that stuff, you did. In fact, if you remember, you insisted that you were the only one who could be trusted with that job."

Kym rolled her eyes. "I wouldn't need so many bags if people wouldn't use them for their own purposes. They should only go out to the customers, everyone," she lectured. Jenn looked innocent. Ina was struggling to keep a straight face. "The customers who spend over two hundred dollars in one sale. And only those."

Kym was looking right at me. How did she know I had taken a bag home with me last night? I arranged my face in a neutral position.

"We have plenty of those bags, Kym," I said. "Vangie can bring us some from the store if we need them."

Kym made a face and continued to rummage through the plastic bin.

I approached Ina. We exchanged grins behind Kym's back. "Do you know what a Flying Geese is?"

"Sure, it's a quilt block," Ina said.

"Like this?" I pulled out the notebook and opened it to a random page. I didn't recognize the name of the vendor on the top, but there was a row of the rectangular quilt blocks underneath. I pointed.

Ina said, "Yeah, that's the block. You see a whole row of them in a border or they can be put together in different combinations to make quilt blocks."

"I heard my mother liked them."

Ina nodded idly, taking the notebook out of my hand and flipping pages. "What's this book?"

"I'm not really sure. I found it near Justine's room. I was thinking it might be hers. And now that I heard she stole the money . . ."

"What?" Ina asked.

"Justine took the JustEve bank deposit — thirty thousand dollars," I whispered. "She

161

stole the admission money and then gambled it away."

Ina made a perfect O with her mouth. She held up the notebook. "So you're thinking she's done this before and kept some kind of record?"

I nodded. "Maybe."

"Found them!" Kym gave me a smug grin and came out from under the table. I couldn't tell if she'd heard me tell Ina about Justine. I tucked the notebook back in my pocket.

"Thanks," I said, taking a bag out of Kym's hand. She gave me a nasty look. "I need one right now. This box is kind of awkward to carry."

"What's in there?" Ina asked.

I pulled the box open to reveal the quilt. "Noni and Chester from Youngstown Quilts gave this to me."

"They gave you a quilt?" Kym stood up.

As I unfolded the quilt, Jenn and a few customers gathered around us. I knew from show-and-tell at the store that antique quilts were like newborns, impossible for women to resist. Kym didn't appreciate the shift in focus from her and cut in front of Jenn, running her hands over the quilt. I wanted to tell her to get her fingers off my quilt, but I restrained myself, just moving the quilt slightly so her hand fell off.

"Mom bought this for me," I said.

Kym cut in. "How did your *mother* buy a quilt?" she said snottily. She was determined to step on any happiness I might have.

"Well, she didn't actually buy it. That couple in the antique quilt booth, Chester and Noni, had been on the lookout for one like it for her. They just handed it to me," I said.

"No one ever gave me a quilt," Kym muttered.

Ina stroked it. "Beautiful. I think the block design is 'Wild Goose Chase,' Dewey."

"I'd call it 'Geese in Flight,' " Kym put in. Jenn pointed at her and nodded her agreement.

Ina wouldn't take the bait. "You know how it is, quilt patterns have lots of different names."

"I can't remember all the details," I said, "but when I was a kid I saw one like it in a book."

A customer grabbed Kym's attention. Jenn followed her, and the other customers drifted off, pulling fat quarter packs off the shelves and touching the bolts.

Ina and I refolded the quilt. "I know how being here drags up memories of other shows, of Mom," I said to Ina. "You'd been

163

together for what, fifteen years . . ."

"Nineteen," Ina corrected.

"Sorry about yesterday. That was rough. Kym and I shouldn't have fought like that in front of the customers." My voice faded as I struggled to apologize.

"Kym's always been a bit too big for her britches. With your mom gone, she likes to throw her weight around. She's already hassled me today about my attire. Tough toenails, I'm too old to wear petticoats and go without my sneakers."

Jenn crossed in front of us to get a ruler for a customer. Ina stifled a laugh.

"Check out her hair," Ina whispered.

Jenn was dressed like Kym in an old-fashioned long skirt and high neck ruffled blouse, but her ponytail was tied back with a soccer ball printed scrunchy. Ina coughed out a little laugh.

"Should I tell her?" I said.

Ina shook her head. "Don't you dare," she whispered.

"Ina, what if I was thinking about selling QP?"

Ina's face fell. "I figured that was what Claire was after. I saw you two talking yesterday morning."

Why was I surprised? Nothing escaped notice at the quilt show. "Claire said my mother was going to sell. Why would she do that, Ina?"

Ina looked away. "Audra hadn't made a quilt in years." Her voice was rough and low as though she was telling me a shameful secret.

"What do you mean? She loved to quilt. She owned a quilt shop, for crying out loud." I was thinking fast, trying to remember the last quilt Mom'd made. There was the Double Wedding Ring for Kevin and Kym when they got married, but I couldn't picture another.

Ina said, "The shop took up too much of her time. She'd stopped quilting and she wasn't happy about that."

Claire had thought the shop had gotten too big for Mom to handle. Freddy talked about the dangers of working in a field you loved. Now Ina was saying Mom hadn't sewn enough. Everyone had a different idea as to why Mom would sell.

"Do you think selling is a bad idea?" I asked. "I've had some other inquiries. I don't know what to do. You know I'm no good at managing the shop."

Ina pulled me in for a fierce hug. "Do whatever works for you, Dewey. Your mother wanted you to be happy."

I nodded into her chest. Ina released me

with a quick pat. I gently folded the quilt into the box and placed it in the QP bag. Last night Claire's friends had remembered her with humor. Talking about Mom with Noni, and now Ina, had felt good.

I stashed the bag under the counter and clapped my hands together, trying to dissipate the emotion I was feeling.

"You know what, Ina, enough grief already. My mother loved working this show."

"That she did."

"My mother was a fun person."

"That she was," Ina agreed.

"And," I said raising my voice so Kym could hear, "My mother always said no real quilter would allow a small thing like death to get in the way of buying fabric."

Kym took the bait. "Your mother said no such thing," she sniffed, handing her customer her receipt. Jenn glanced at Kym, who set her mouth in a straight line. Jenn frowned in echo.

I winked at Ina. She caught my drift and threw a convivial arm around my shoulder.

"Listen, kiddo, your mother and I missed a funeral once because there was a quilt shop on the way to the cemetery."

"You did not," Kym cried, keeping a careful eye on the two customers browsing the booth.

"It's not like we missed the church service, just the burial," Ina finished, barely suppressing a giggle.

"I never heard about that," I said. "But she used to tell this story about this wake, for some big remodel customer Dad had in Los Altos Hills. Dad always joked that the guy dropped dead when he got the final bill. Anyhow, Mom ducked out before the priest said mass because Thai Silk was having a big sale. She got back just as Dad started looking for her, having spent two hundred dollars on dupioni." I felt the tears coming again and laughed harder to keep them at bay.

"Do you think that's appropriate?" Kym hissed, moving closer to me while looking over her shoulder at the customers. All around us, friends were spending time together, laughing, having a great time. I was tired of missing out.

"Put a sock in it, Kym. New policy at Quilter Paradiso. We're going to have fun in this booth. I declare the period of mourning for Audra Pellicano officially over. She wouldn't want us moping around here."

"This *was* her favorite show, and we always had a good time," Ina said.

"So, if you don't have anything funny to say, don't say anything," I said.

Kym made a moue of disapproval. Jenn clucked in response. I didn't care. Almost immediately, customers filed into the booth, already attracted by the new vibe. Ina went over to help out, leaving Kym and I standing next to each other.

"You look like hell," Kym said, trying to brush my bangs out of my eyes. I dodged her touch.

"If that's supposed to be amusing, you're off to a bad start."

"I'm dead serious."

"Yeah, well, I didn't get much sleep last night." I pushed a hand through my hair, even though I knew by doing that I was risking a cowlick.

"Visions of Claire instead of sugarplums?" she asked.

Did she know what she was saying? Had Kevin told her about my dream? He wouldn't.

"Hey, what's this about you and Buster?" Kym asked.

My stomach sank even further. It would be awful if she knew about me and Buster sleeping together. She'd either go into full-on matchmaker mode and plan a double date, some cheesy limo tour of Napa, or she'd advise Buster to run while he could. Either way, I didn't want her input.

I pointed at the band aid with pink hearts on the elbow she'd cut on the blade yesterday.

"You're ruining the ambiance. Couldn't you find a historically correct bandage?" I said, trying to stave off her prying. "I could rip up some muslin . . ."

"Dewey, it's all over the show this morning that you found Claire's body and spent the afternoon with Buster and the police. When were you going to tell me?"

So that's all she knew. Good, I'd keep it that way. "I can't talk about it. Police orders."

"Speak of the devil. Buster!"

He was standing in the middle of the aisle, watching me. I felt heat rise on my face and smoothed my hand over my hair. Had he come to see me? I tried to read his expression — was that regret?

Before I could react, Kym raced out of the booth, throwing her arms around Buster's neck. He looked over her shoulder at me sheepishly. I was glad she couldn't see me, because I felt my face split into a big grin as Buster smiled like we had a secret.

She pushed him away, inspected him and wolf-whistled. He did look good, dressed in a charcoal-gray suit with a raspberry-colored shirt and narrow black tie. His leather belt had a San Jose Police Department buckle. The brightly colored shirt complemented his black hair and set off his blue eyes. I'd never wanted to date a guy who spent more money on his wardrobe than I did, but I had to admit, clothes did help make this man. Of course, I liked the way he looked without them, too. I blushed, remembering his touches.

"Where've you been?" Kym trilled. "Kevin said you were working here, but I haven't seen any sign of you."

She straightened his tie, although it didn't need it.

He tore his intense gaze off me and answered Kym. "Been a little busy."

"Of course you have," she said, patting his chest as though investigating Claire's death was a job akin to picking up garbage. "You must come to dinner Saturday night." She leaned in with a flirty grin. "It's Bunko night."

"You play Bunko?" I was unable to contain my glee. Bunko was a simple dice game, favored by Kym and her friends who couldn't master backgammon. Alcohol was usually involved.

"No . . ." Buster shook his head.

"He keeps Kevin company while we play," Kym said. "I invite a single girl once in a while to make life interesting, but most of my friends are married. Unfortunately."

I wondered why I had never been included in her invitations. She must not have thought me suitable for Buster.

I turned to him. I needed to tell him about seeing Justine outside Claire's room. "Last night, I forgot to tell you . . ."

"Last night?" Kym asked, her face suddenly looming between the two of us. Her eyebrows were arched in a comical way.

"Yeah, I was at Dewey's last . . ."

I shook my head, but Buster was either blind or incredibly stupid.

"For guitar lessons," I jumped in.

"You're learning to play?" Kym was skeptical.

"I'm trying to surprise Dad for his birthday. Buster agreed to help me. You can't tell anyone."

"Dewey, you're as musical as a tree stump," she said. "You couldn't find middle C with a map."

I pulled a face at her.

"I came to tell you your laptop is still at the lab," Buster said, ignoring Kym.

Kym was like a toddler, insisting on including herself in every conversation. "Why do the police have your computer, Dewey?"

"I had it with me yesterday," I said.

"We remove everything from a scene, Kym," Buster put in. "It's procedure."

"Your laptop was in Claire's room? Dewey, you didn't tell me any of this," Kym pouted.

I pulled up my ready excuse. "I can't talk about that."

"She's part of an ongoing investigation, Kym," Buster backed me up. "She's not free to discuss what happened yesterday."

Kym's eyes darted back and forth from my face to his. I tried to keep my expression neutral, not allowing my face to show how much I wanted to touch him. Standing this close was creating whitecaps in my gut. Kym kept a proprietary hand on his sleeve. I wanted to pluck her fingers off him. Or maybe pluck her eyes out.

"It's okay," I said, bringing the discussion back to something I could handle. "I don't really need the computer anymore. It doesn't work anyhow."

Buster looked at me questioningly.

"It's my fault." Kym used her baby talk. "I bwoke it."

"Yeah, she crashed the hard drive," I said, embellishing freely. "Lost all the data. I'm going to have to start at the beginning. Re-enter all the inventory, the bills . . ."

"Lost the data? There are recovery programs, you know," Buster said. "The lab . . . I'm sure we could help."

I cut him off. "Oh, no. I'm pretty sure, this time, the data is gone for good."

I was practically winking at Buster, but he wasn't getting the hint. Last night, he'd anticipated my every need. This morning he was totally missing my signals. Maybe Kym was causing static interference.

I pointed at Kym. "Yep, she ruined my computer. Could you shoot her for me?"

"Kevin might be a bit upset with me," Buster said, looking from me to Kym, still unsure of the dynamic. I tried to give him a "tell-you-later" look, but he just looked confused.

Kym's neck twisted as Lark Gordon entered the booth.

"Good morning, Dewey," Lark said.

I said hi as she walked past.

"Lark Gordon said hello to you," Kym hissed, following Lark with her eyes. Buster was forgotten for now. I smiled at him, grateful Kym's attention had been diverted. He touched my hand, brushing the pulse point on my wrist, sending blood coursing to meet his fingertips. I masked the gasp that escaped with a fake cough. So, no regrets.

"When did you meet her?" Kym demanded, turning back to me.

I dropped my hand away. "Last night. She wanted to film me for her show." I was winding Kym up, but I couldn't resist.

"What do you mean? You didn't refuse, did you?" Panic caused Kym's voice to break.

Buster started to move off. He could finally see trouble brewing.

"I'll see you later?" he whispered as Kym stared at Lark's back.

I nodded. He backed away and hollered goodbye to Kym. Facing down murderers was a piece of cake next to facing down Kym.

"In fact, I did," I said, answering Kym's question.

Kym groaned. "How stupid can be you be, Dewey?"

I started to tell her Lark wanted to talk about Claire, not Quilter Paradiso, but Kym had already moved away.

"Nice decorating job," I heard Lark say.

That was all the encouragement Kym needed. "My idea. Hi, Lark, I'm Kym Pellicano, Dewey's sister-in-law. I've worked for Quilter Paradiso longer than she has. Let me show you around."

Kym pointed out the coordinating sets of

174

fat quarters she'd cleverly stuffed into canning jars. They moved on to the vintage cooler filled with old-fashioned soda bottles containing bits of fabric.

Kym could have her delusions of grandeur. I stepped into the aisle to see if I could catch a glimpse of Buster walking away. Eve came out of nowhere, pointing her pencil at me, nearly knocking me over.

"You need to be in the auditorium dressing room by five tonight. Do you know where that is?"

I watched Buster's head bob over the sea of women and ignored her.

"About a size 12?" she continued, looking me up and down. "I thought you were smaller, more like Kym." She licked the pencil lead and made a note.

I caught a glimpse of Kym smiling, the first spontaneous smile I'd seen on her face in days, and knew her delight was at my expense. She was even ignoring Lark, her eyes on Eve and me instead.

"What is this about?" I asked, starting to panic. Anything that made Kym smile that way couldn't be good for me.

"The fashion show tomorrow night," Eve said. "Kym's been in it for the last four years; she said you'd model this year. Tonight's the dress rehearsal."

"Me?"

"You said you wanted to be more involved," Kym singsonged, widening her eyes in fake innocence.

So that's what she'd been talking about. Last week when we were discussing the show schedule, she'd told me to keep Saturday night free. I glared at her. She knew I hated getting dressed up. Modeling meant makeup and heels, maybe even pantyhose. I wasn't sure I owned a pair.

Eve looked at me, her face contorted. "No one told you? Dammit, Justine told me she talked to you." Eve's voice broke.

"Well, she did leave me a message." That must have been why she wanted to see me this morning. "I went up to her room, but she didn't answer."

"She's not feeling well right now."

I'd be sick, too, if I'd stolen money and gambled it away. Nor would I blame Eve if she kept Justine under wraps. How could Eve trust her again?

"Tell me more about this fashion show," I said. I didn't like the way Eve looked me up and down, still making notes. I'd missed those girly lessons handed out in junior high. My mother had been oblivious to the way she looked, dressing in the long denim skirts, sandals and tunics that had been popular with her quilt friends. My father cared about my fashion only to the extent that the clothes covered me up, and my brothers were only concerned that I get out of the bathroom we shared as quickly as possible.

"It's the high point of the weekend," Kym said. "Outlandish outfits made by fabulous textile artists. Clothes, makeup, shoes. What could be more fun?"

"A root canal, a colonoscopy, nail fungus," I suggested. Any one of those sounded better than getting dolled up and paraded in front of an audience.

I noticed with embarrassment that Lark was following our conversation with interest. I didn't want to create a scene, so I tried to tone it down.

"I wouldn't wear more than one outfit, would I?" I asked, my voice breaking piteously.

"You and Justine can work all that out later," Eve said brusquely. "Right now, all I need from you is a commitment to show up at rehearsal at five o'clock. Can I tell her you'll be there?"

I hesitated, but Eve was not in the mood for indecision.

"Just be there," Eve said. "I'm sick of fighting Justine's battles today."

Eve checked me off her list and moved on. I rubbed my eyes. I'd thought I'd be working at the show all weekend, playing with the computer. Instead, I was involved with a fatal accident and, maybe even worse, a fashion show.

Lark dumped a pile of notions and books on the table next to the cash drawer and pulled out her wallet. Kym insisted she was the only one capable enough to write up her sales slip.

"I'll see you at rehearsal," Lark said to me.

I was embarrassed she'd overheard my hissy fit. "You'll be there?"

"I said I'd help out," Lark said.

Kym blanched; she'd have sold her soul to be in the fashion show now. That was reason enough for me to be glad I'd agreed.

"I do the makeup, hair, make sure people look their best," Lark said. "I can give you a few pointers if you'd like. Got a moment to join me for a latté?"

Kym's mouth was set in a straight white line.

"No camera crew? Sure," I said.

"No cameras, I promise. Just some fashion advice. I'll tell you how to avoid getting the most uncomfortable outfit," Lark said, handing over a credit card. "There's always one top that won't stay up unless it's taped to your body. And no matter what they tell you, that stuff hurts like hell when they pull it off."

"Come on, Dewey, strut your stuff," Ina yelled from the other side of the booth, laughing.

I tried to affect a model's pose. Lark lifted my chin with a long finger. Kym pushed the credit card machine lever so hard I thought she'd snap Lark's card in half.

"Like that. You'll look thinner if you keep your chin pointed upward."

I jutted my chin.

"That's a little too Leno. More up than out," Lark said.

I tried again. Lark placed her hand between my shoulder blades, telling me to hold the tension there and tilt my chin up. Kym's frown deepened. She handed Lark her credit card slip to sign. I made a mental note to make sure that slip didn't disappear into Kym's autograph collection.

Ina said, "Now suck in your stomach, assume an air of insouciance, and you're all set."

I lost all composure, laughing at Ina's silly instructions. Lark joined in.

"Look, the fashion show is a hoot," Lark said. "Justine promised to keep the atmosphere light and breezy. By the time the show arrives, you won't be nervous at all."

"If you say so."

I waved goodbye as Lark and I left the booth.

As I passed Kym, I whispered, "Careful, your face might freeze like that."

She just glared as we walked away. As soon as I was in the aisles with Lark, I could feel the change in the atmosphere around us. People were electrified by Lark's presence. I was reminded of the buzz that had followed Claire. Lark kept a small smile on her face.

"Is it always like this for you?"

"Like what?" Lark dodged a man walking a hinged ostrich puppet with blue tufted feet.

"You don't notice the way crowds part when you walk? The silences? The glances?"

My words were not getting through to her. I could see she was so used to the star treatment, she didn't have a clue what I was talking about. It was like asking a fish about water, or a teenage boy about violence in video games. Without a word, we skirted a gang of women who'd stopped mid-aisle to stare. Lark kept the half-smile in place and never missed a step.

Suddenly a chant resounded from behind us. "What do you want?"

"Dinner!" was the answer. It was male voices.

"When do you want it?" The call and response repeated.

"Now!"

I looked around, but couldn't see where it was coming from.

"Got any idea what that's all about?" Lark asked. As I shook my head, the crowd parted and a group of men marched by, led by a pixyish woman who was guiding them with the enthusiasm of a religious fanatic.

"We've got to see this," I said. "Come on."

We fell in step behind them. They stopped in front of a booth that was already surrounded by women. By the greetings they got, I could tell at least some of these were the wives of the band of men and that this was where the impromptu parade had started. The pixie put on a wide smile and a rock-star-style headphone microphone and climbed on a platform behind a table. More people gathered around. A huge plastic banner behind her head read, "The Cutall System."

"What is that thing?" I asked. "It looks like a complicated vegetable slicer."

"About as useful," Lark said.

The vendor started her spiel. "Step right up. I have here the answer to your prayers, men. The solution to your dinner woes. I want to show you the greatest invention ever made."

A man hooted in disbelief.

"Buy your wives the Cutall System, fellas, and you will get a home-cooked meal. Think of it, guys, dinner on the table instead of your wife holed up beneath a pile of fabric. That's right, I said — pot roast and potatoes."

"Men," Lark whispered. "As a race, they're sure to fall for the toys."

The seller paused, her intake of breath audible through her headset.

"And what, you ask, is this wondrous tool? A new slow cooker? No, it's the Cutall rotary-cutting system. Get all the precision-cut pieces you need for your quilt in one-third the time."

In front of her was a box with a bright orange mat. A cartoon-purple plastic arm swiveled over to keep the fabric in place. Slots kept the ruler straight. She took up a yellow-handled rotary cutter and begin slicing the fabric at a blinding pace, without stopping her chatter.

"Cut a half-yard of fabric into two-inch strips in ten seconds. A perfect cut every time with the Cutall rotary-cutting system." She held up the pieces like strands of spaghetti. I half expected her to fling the strips on the wall.

"Do you have to buy a new rotary cutter?" a short-haired woman with red glasses asked worriedly. She glanced our way. Her eyes widened as she recognized Lark, but she quickly looked back as the hawker answered her question.

"No, not at all. Use any of your cutters. If you have this style —" she pulled out a straight-handled cutter "— just click it open, the blade is exposed, and you make your multiple cuts." She ran the blade along the fabric.

"And make sure you close it," someone yelled from the audience. Others murmured in agreement.

I thought of Claire, lying in her own blood because she'd been careless. I shook my head to rid myself of the picture.

"Or use this type," the hawker said. She picked one up with a curved handle. "The blade retracts automatically. Your choice."

"I love that cutter," a woman with a curtain of long gray hair said to her friend. "Much safer. You can't accidentally leave the blade exposed."

"I like the other kind better," her friend argued. "You just have to make yourself get in the habit of closing the cover each time.

It cuts cleaner."

"Come on, Nancy. It's the same blade, it can't cut any differently."

The demonstrator sensed she was losing her audience to a discussion on the relative merits of the rotary cutter. She rapped the side of her system sharply. All eyes turned front, and noise ceased.

"Whichever cutter you use," she said, "the system works the same, holding your fabric steady and giving accurate cuts every time. Strips, triangles, squares, whatever you need."

Her spiel was working. Lark pointed at several of the men who were reaching with thumb and forefinger into their back pockets for their wallets.

"Told you. Suckers," she said, sotto voce.

"You don't think it's worth buying?"

She shook her head. "The longer you're in this business, the more stuff like this you'll see. Some of it is worthwhile. Not sure about this particular one. It's been my experience at these shows that men will buy the expensive gadgets the women don't really want. Or use."

Heads turned as Lark's voice rose. The Cutall sales woman looked unhappy that Lark had been recognized. Next to me, I felt Lark's perfect posture get even straighter, her neck elongating. As more eyes landed on her, she stopped being herself, and became the celebrity.

"Can I have your autograph?" I heard a tiny brunette with helmet-like hair ask Lark. The Cutall spokeswoman frowned as she lost her audience again. She cleared her throat loudly.

"For the next fifteen minutes," she announced, "the Cutall system is available for $50 less than the show price. $200. That's a bargain, people!"

Lark signed the brunette's program. Another hand thrust a program in front of her. After a moment, the crowd split in two, half going to buy the new tool, the other half gathering around Lark. I was pushed out of the way by a woman in a crocheted poncho.

"Dewey Pellicano?"

A fifty-something man was standing at my elbow. He was dressed in a blue button-down shirt and khakis. I didn't recognize him. He hadn't been in the line of chanters.

"Yes?"

"I'm Colin Bergstrom. I heard that you're interested in selling your quilt shop."

Word was getting around. Probably thanks to Freddy. "That's true." I nodded.

"This is my booth." He pointed across the

aisle from where we stood. I followed him, keeping half an eye on Lark. She was surrounded by autograph seekers, looking happy and relaxed in the midst of the admiring fans. She would never miss me.

Colin was showing off his space. "My wife and I sell notions and fabric, mostly on the Internet. We've been thinking about getting rid of our online store and opening a real place."

I peered into his booth. The fabric was displayed nicely, the bolts arrayed in an enticing way. A revolving wooden display rack held notions.

"Did you make this display case? I've never seen one like it." I moved closer to inspect it.

"Yes, I dabble in woodworking. Keeps me busy between shows."

I turned the display, and the rotary cutters came into view, hanging from pegboard hooks by holes in their packaging.

Colin continued. "My wife and I live in San Jose, not far from your shop. We've just had twins, so I want to stay closer to home."

I let him talk and picked up the curved-type cutter to examine the packaging. The plastic bubble on the cardboard had to accommodate the bend in the rotary cutter. Kym only used the old-fashioned type of rotary cutter, the one with the straight handle.

I glanced at the straight-handled cutter. The two packagings were not the same. The plastic top was different. The curved-handled cutter would not fit in a package meant for the straight kind.

Sanchez was wrong. Kym had given me the packaging from the straight-handled cutter yesterday morning. But the curved-handled cutter had been by Claire's hand.

That packaging meant Sanchez was wrong, wrong, wrong. I wanted to sing it.

Colin laid a hand on my arm. I was surprised he was still there. I'd nearly forgotten him. His interest in my shop was apparent, but I was torn between talking to him more or finding Buster to tell him about the cutters. I needed to sell the shop but this difference in the rotary cutters was really important.

"So, Ms. Pellicano, when can we discuss this? I'm free now . . ."

His insistent tone brought me back. I hesitated. This earnest man with his beautifully constructed displays and his twins might be the one. The perfect new owner of Quilter Paradiso.

"I recently came into an inheritance," he said.

I shut my eyes against his perfectness.

I had to call Buster and tell him.

But what if Colin was the perfect buyer for my shop?

ELEVEN

Buster was the winner. "Colin, I can't do this right now."

He frowned. "I won't be able to get away again for the rest of the day. Not until after the show closes."

"Perfect. I'll meet you in the bar at five."

Then I remembered the fashion show rehearsal and the Freitas sisters. "Make it six. Thank you."

I shook his hand quickly, ignoring his baleful expression and glanced over at Lark. She was still surrounded by quilters. I gestured to her that I was going to leave and hurried outside to call Buster. I held my breath as I passed through the cluster of smokers outside the door.

"Hi Dewey," said a tall woman with large brown doe eyes surrounded by deep wrinkles. I recognized her from the bar last night. If I remembered correctly, she was from New Jersey and had a long-arm quilting business.

I said hi and kept moving, but I was stopped by another smoker.

"Dewey, huh? Do you work for Kym? She's out here with us three times a day."

"Wrong Kym, I'd say," I said, chuckling. I wouldn't be surprised if Kym did tell people that I worked for her, but I knew she didn't smoke.

I got out of the cigarette smoke and called Buster. He picked up on the first ring. I suddenly felt shy, realizing that with all the phone stuff between us, this was the first call I'd initiated. I didn't find my voice until after the second time he said, "Healy."

"Buster, it's me. Dewey. Got a minute?"

"I'm just wrapping up. Meet me in front?"

I positioned myself along the edge of the fountain in the middle of the drive. The gentle noise of the water falling was a stark contrast to the chatter in my brain. Had I just walked away from the best buyer for QP? I breathed in the moist air, remembering how my brother Sean claimed that positive ions in the air promoted good thinking. Sean lived in San Francisco and had a lot of strange views on the natural world. At the time, one of those late nights after a Scattergories game and plenty of Corona, I'd argued that if that were true, then people who lived near Niagara Falls would have the clearest heads ever. And a person in a positive headspace generally didn't throw himself over a huge waterfall in a barrel. Kevin had finally intervened, distracting us with his Madonna imitation.

I missed those carefree nights when we were all gathered around the big oak dining-room table, joking and playing games. I couldn't remember the last time we'd done that. Before my mother died, for sure.

I turned my face away from the mist and picked up a daisy. A display to honor Claire had sprung up since this morning, with stuffed animals, flowers, and notes covering one side of the fountain's wall. Several sprays of flowers had fallen into the water, their multicolored blooms scattered on the surface.

A similar display had sprung up on the store's doorstep after my mother's death. I took to entering by the back door so I wouldn't have to see them every day. Kym had been sad when they stopped coming. I was relieved.

A memory of my mother came to me. I was thirteen. My mother had taken me on a trip to the corporate headquarters of Esprit de Corps in San Francisco. I was only becoming aware of clothes beyond sport shorts and tees, and Esprit was the only brand name I knew. I figured I would get a cute sweater. Instead, we took a tour of their collection of Amish quilts that hung on the brick walls throughout the offices. The huge, somber-colored quilts covered with an elaborate quilted feather pattern were of no interest to me. My mother told me that I was in the presence of greatness, but I was unbelievably disappointed. When she told me the quilts were made from the same fabric that the Amish used for clothing, my only reaction had been pity for the poor girls my age who had to go to school without the benefit of jeans. The further information that the Amish didn't go to school past eighth grade only deepened my inability to relate. My mother had gotten disgusted with me and we'd left, distant as only a teenage girl and her mother could be.

After that, by mutual agreement, I'd stayed away from quilt shows and she'd given up trying to teach me how to look at quilts. A year ago, the Seventeenth Annual Northern California Quilt Extravaganza was the last place I would have expected to be.

Buster pulled up in a bright blue pickup truck with tinted windows, riding high on huge wheels that came nearly to my waist. I hadn't realized what he'd parked outside my house last night. And left there until early this morning. Not very discreet. My neighbor Alice would have something to say next time I saw her. She kept better track of my visitors than I did.

He jumped down, leaving his door open, and met me on the sidewalk.

"Kym cut you loose?" he said.

"I'm sorry about this morning."

"No apologies necessary. It just took me a while to catch on that Kym was playing her usual games. Okay if we take a drive?" he said, nodding toward the truck. "I need to gas it up, and I could use a little lost time. Budget restraints. Got to watch the over-time."

My stomach growled so loudly we both heard it. Buster grinned. "And we could get some lunch."

When I agreed, he opened the door, then turned and put his hands on my waist, as though to give me a boost into the pas-senger seat. I waved him off. I liked the feel of his strong fingers on my waist, but I hadn't been picked up since I was two.

"That's okay, I can manage." I scooted away from him and climbed into the seat. Once inside, I felt silly, like a kid in a chair too big for her. I looked down to make sure my feet were touching the floor. Just barely.

I tucked one leg under me to regain some sense of control over my lower limbs.

"Sorry, force of habit," he said as he closed the door. "The only person who usually rides over there is Mom, and she's so tiny I have to pick her up and set her on the bench."

"Nice view," I said. "A Mini Cooper must look like a Matchbox car from up here." Now I just sounded like a dork. I took a deep breath.

He stopped to take off his jacket and lay it carefully behind the driver's seat. He climbed in his side and we both buckled up. Buster's wide shoulders filled the truck nicely. He didn't diminish like some men do in a large truck. The Hummer effect, Vangie and I called it. The larger the car, the smaller the male driver appeared.

Glancing in his side mirror, he pulled out.

As we waited at the first red light, he massaged the back of his neck. "Kevin's told me over the years that these quilt shows are a big deal, but I had no idea how many people attend."

"I know what you mean. I hadn't been to this show in more than ten years. It's huge."

"I'll tell you one thing, these quilting women love to talk. About everything except what I need to hear," he said.

"Couldn't you break them down, sweat the truth out of them?" I asked. "Isn't that what you homicide dicks do?"

He raised an eyebrow and laughed. It was fun to make him laugh. His whole face lit up. "Since the Governator," he said, "our rubber hose budget ain't what it used to be."

"Give me a break. You're talking to a bunch of middle-aged women. Turn on the charm."

"Oh, does that work?" He smiled a sexy, slow-forming grin that seeped across his face and set up a tap dance in my stomach. This time it wasn't hunger.

"Don't look at me. I'm immune," I said.

"So I noticed last night."

"It wasn't your charms I was after."

He wisely changed the subject. "Here's what I learned this morning. Claire was the sweetest, most caring quilter in America, no, on the planet. Evidently, she was the patron saint of quilting." He stopped a beat and grinned again. "And many of these women have single granddaughters of marrying age."

"Really, you've got these little old ladies pimping for you?" I joked to cover the fear that one of them might be perfect for him.

"How about a little sympathy? I'm just

195

trying to find out about Claire, and I'm not getting anywhere. However, if I was looking for a great home-cooked meatloaf, I'd know right where to go."

I laughed. Buster was the kind of guy you took home to Mother. My problem had never been bringing a boy home to my mother — it had been my brothers who scared away all but the most intrepid.

"No one thinks Claire was murdered?" I asked.

"Not unless you count the redhead who thought she'd been killed by terrorists trying to upset the American public by murdering a quilting icon."

"Seriously?"

"I swear. I thought I was doing a service to the community putting away murderers. According to some of the women I met this morning, I really should have been arresting longarm quilters."

"Do you have any idea what you're talking about?"

"Don't even get me started on the danger of raw-edge appliqué," he said.

"Now I know you have no clue what you're saying."

He threw up his hands comically. I grabbed the wheel, then saw he was steering with his knees. I brushed his thigh as I pulled back, felt the electricity. My mind went to places it shouldn't. I tore my gaze out of his lap. Sex in this truck was not an option.

I stole a glance at his face to see if he felt the sexual tension in the air. I'd thought acting on my impulses last night would have dissipated the chemistry between us, but I was wrong. Instead, the attraction thrummed between us like a guitar string recently struck. After the string stops, the air is full of promise.

Buster peered up at the red light. His forehead was wide, maybe even a little wider since his hair seemed to be moving back. Deep lines on either side of his mouth and around his eyes only added interest, like beads on a quilt. I remembered a much younger man, all soft cheeks and smooth skin. I preferred the hard planes. His face held all the experiences of the last dozen years — good, bad, pretty, and ugly. I wanted to find out the stories behind the wrinkles.

He pushed his glasses up on his head and scrubbed his eyes. I felt a moment of guilt for keeping him up most of the night and giving him scratchy eyes.

"Been a tough morning?" I asked.

He squinted. "I'm kind of fascinated by

the rotary cutter. I think Claire cut herself accidentally, but if someone did commit murder with one of them, it would be hard to trace. You were right about how ubiquitous they are," he said. "There are five hundred quilters registered at that hotel and at least that many rotary cutters. If this were a murder, that would be a helluva lot of trouble for the investigators."

I tried to interrupt. "Listen, that's what I found out."

As he reached to shift, our fingers touched and we both blushed at the sparks that resulted. I snatched my hand back.

"The problem with the rotary cutter," he continued, talking quickly as his cheeks reddened, "is that the slash is not unique. Any cutter could have made the cut. With a stab wound, you can identify the knife. I can pretty much prove that a bullet came from a specific gun barrel. But the rotary cutter — hundreds of them all alike. It's crazy."

"Buster, I figured something out."

"It's not that easy to get a fatal cut, you know. She had to have hit that artery just so."

"Listen!"

He heard the urgency that time and looked at me expectantly.

"Sorry. I was thinking out loud."

I waved off his apology. "The cutters — there are two types, a curved-handle one and a straight-handle one. The one next to Claire's body was the curved-handle type. They look nothing alike, although they use the same blade."

"Dewey, we have the cutter. We know what kind it is."

"Buster, dammit! Listen to me. The one I opened that morning was the straight-handle kind. The curved one wouldn't even fit in that package."

"You're saying there's no way the cutter next to Claire's body could have come out of the packaging we found in your back-pack?"

"Get it? Sanchez was out of whack." I couldn't help but gloat. I wanted to do a happy dance right in the truck, but I restrained myself. "He was wrong. I'm off Sanchez's list of suspects."

"Sure."

I was disappointed he didn't feel like dancing, too. "You don't sound very impressed."

"I never thought you killed Claire."

"What about Sanchez?"

He shrugged. "We're about ready to declare it death by misadventure. The ME said the femoral artery, the big one in the

199

thigh, was cut. It wouldn't take long to bleed out."

"Claire was alone when she died. Just cut herself terribly and bled to death." I was saddened by the idea that Claire had not been able to save herself.

We stopped at another light. The street was lined with tall, stately palm trees. I sighed as we didn't move. Long waits at traffic lights were a fact of life in Silicon Valley.

"Hey," Buster said, trying to see my face. "You don't think I'd be out here with you if I seriously considered you a suspect, do you?"

"I don't know . . ."

"Trust me, Dewey, I would not jeopardize my job."

"Thanks a lot."

"Hold on, hold on," he said. He took my hand as the light changed and held it, eyes back on the road ahead. "That doesn't mean I don't want to be with you. I like spending time with you. But I won't do anything that looks improper."

"Maybe you should take me back then," I said, bristling, letting go of his hand, tucking mine in my front pocket of my jeans. The notebook in my pocket got in the way and I shifted it.

"No way. I promised you lunch, and I deliver on my promises," he said.

We were quiet as he maneuvered the streets. I didn't like the feeling that he thought I was leading him astray. Claire had died alone, a victim of a careless act. What else did Buster and I have to talk about?

"Speaking of quilters and quilts," he said. "Did you know your mom made me a quilt when I went off to college?"

"Way to change the subject, Healy." I had a college quilt, too. It was in my car when it was stolen. Mom never got around to making me a new one.

"I still have it. It's soft, like an old shirt. Whenever I have a cold, I wrap up and lay on the couch, watching ESPN classic."

"She thought you were special."

"She was one-of-a kind, Dewey."

"You were a big help to my family. I appreciate that." My words were stilted, but I couldn't get my lips to open any wider, suddenly feeling formal.

"I wish I could have done more."

My stomach growled again. The light changed and Buster shifted gears.

"How about that lunch?" I said, to lighten the mood. "Preferably something greasy and salty, with plenty of trans fat. I'll buy."

"I know the perfect place." He was chuckling to himself as he spun the wheel, made two quick turns, and pulled into a potholed driveway of a small fast-food restaurant. The building was peeling white stucco with an immense orange and tan hot dog on the roof.

"Hot Diggity Dog!" I exclaimed. "I didn't know this place was still open."

"Saved from the wrecking ball just last week. Want a chili dog?"

"Two. And garlic fries."

At the drive-up window, Buster placed our orders and handed the bags to me. The smell of garlic filled the truck. He smacked my hand as I grabbed a fry out of the bag.

"No fair picking. I know a great spot," he said. "We'll be there in a minute."

Buster pulled into the asphalt lot of the creek trail that wound around the Guadalupe River. Rolling down the window, I could smell the eucalyptus. He jumped out, moved a gate that said "No cars past this point," and got back in. He drove past the gate, got out and closed it, then drove a couple hundred feet up a dirt path and parked. Being the law came in handy when you wanted to get off the beaten path.

It was a lovely spot. The river flowed over shiny rocks. Less than a mile from the convention center, we were surrounded by nature. Tiny dots of miniature daisies carpeted the ground. A red-winged black-bird, the first I'd seen this season, flashed his bright color at me.

I could hear the steady pulsing of the freeway traffic, invisible from where we sat. We spread the feast out between us on the bench seat. Buster sipped greedily from his soda and I took the first bite of my chili dog. Juices ran down my chin. He reached for a napkin and handed it to me, teasing me about my manners.

We sat companionably quiet, eating and thinking our own thoughts. I felt so far away from the quilt show. Just like last night, when I was with Buster the world seemed to slip away.

He'd rolled up his sleeves to eat and his forearms looked vulnerable. The hair on his arms was dark; the wide leather strap on his watch scuffed and worn. I resisted the urge to turn his arm over and kiss the pulse spot.

I was suddenly aware of the wide plush seat that spanned the truck and the privacy afforded by the tinted windows, the isolated location. I leaned away from him, into the window, letting the air cool me down.

Sex with Buster yesterday had been like hearing a good song for the first time. I liked the music, felt the beat, but I didn't know where it was going. I caught some of the lyrics, most of the chorus, but only half heard the rest.

The second time, a song has more meaning. Anticipating the wordplay, knowing where the chord changes are going to come, enhances the experience. And yet there's still the joy of discovery — the modulation that wasn't apparent the first time, the great turn of a phrase. Today I knew some of the lyrics. The initial excitement of the unknown was gone, replaced by the thrill of what variations might be coming.

Down girl, I admonished myself. That way leads to a complicated love life. One time making love meant friends with benefits. I could live with that. What I was not prepared for was meaningful sex. Besides, I was too old for messing around in broad daylight. In a truck.

Buster leaned back on his seat. He looked satisfied, like the carbs had gotten to him and soothed his hunger. Outside, a bee, only half awake on this April day, flew erratically and narrowly missed colliding with the windshield.

"Don't you need to get back?" I said.

He shook his head. "Anyone I need to talk to is either in a class or at work. I've got a few more interviews scheduled for this evening, but we're wrapping it up."

I drained my soda and put the cup into the holder.

"I didn't want to say anything in front of Kym," he said, wiping his mouth on a napkin, "but I really came by the booth this morning to see how you were doing."

"After last night? Worried about my virtue? How quaint."

"After finding Claire's body yesterday?"

"Oh." I felt like an idiot.

"I'm sorry you had to see her like that."

I didn't want to dwell on finding a dead body. Maybe Myra was right. Talking about it only kept the horror alive. I waved him off and returned to simpler times.

"Why did you become a policeman? I thought you were going to be a fireman."

"You remember that?" He turned to me, eyes alight. A grin tugged at his lips and I looked away, afraid I might kiss him.

"Of course I remember. From the time you were six and we saw the firemen games at the Frontier Days."

"Oh, yeah, the hose roll. It was so exciting, those firemen racing down the street. Then I found out about all the equipment that a fireman had to wear. I much prefer street clothes."

I smiled. Buster's vanity was endearing.

"Dewey." His voice was soft and sweet, and I remembered how his whispers had washed over me in bed last night. I didn't want to fall under that spell again. I crossed my arms over my chest and stared out the window. A small jackrabbit, his ears comically large, paused and looked my way before disappearing into the high grass.

Buster kept talking. "About last night? I had a great time."

Kym's face swam into my psyche like a bucketful of cold water.

"I don't want a relationship," I said.

His brows lifted in surprise at my abruptness. "But we started something."

"No, we didn't really, Buster. It was a nice night, but that's all. Don't make a big deal about it. I'm not into double-dating with Kevin and Kym."

"Is that it? My being friends with Kevin has you freaked out?"

"You're practically family."

"But I'm not. You and me — not related. No shared genes, whatsoever."

I didn't mention the DNA we'd shared last night. I kept quiet, looking out the window, hoping he would move away.

"I didn't notice you having any problem with that in your bed," he drawled, his voice low. His fingers trailed across my forearm. I

206

squirmed in the seat and opened the window.

It was true, I hadn't thought of him as a family friend once since he'd taken his clothes off. Now carnal thoughts crowded in, making it difficult to construct a coherent argument.

I rolled up my window. "Let's go back to the show, Buster. We don't have time for this, either one of us. I've got work to do."

"I'm off for the rest of the afternoon."

"I'm not," I said, unconvincingly. I could be free for the afternoon, too. Without the laptop, I was just an extra body at the booth, and I wouldn't be able to talk to potential buyers until later.

He reached over and brushed a hair from my face. His fingers felt like fire. I let myself lean into his hand. It was large and strong, and he stroked my cheek with two fingers.

"Making you smile makes me happy," Buster said.

He had made me smile last night, and my body ached now for his touch. Attentive, unselfish guys are rare. Why should I refuse? All he was offering me was pleasure — how could that be wrong?

I felt my resolve crumble. My family had already demanded so much from me. I'd given them the last few months, keeping the shop open so that they could feel like life was just the same as before Mom died. I seemed to be the only one that noticed things had changed.

Buster noticed; he was in tune with my feelings. Maybe it was that empathy that made him a good cop, allowed him to read right into my soul, and know exactly what I needed.

My lips bent into a smile just to please him. He moved away from the steering wheel, pushing his leg against mine. Buster kissed the pulse on my neck. My body shuddered.

"I will never hurt you," he whispered.

Buster pulled my T-shirt over my head. The sweet fresh air from the open window hit my bare skin like water on a parched throat. He folded the shirt and lifted my head, gently tucking the fabric behind me. I pulled off my chinos and felt the scratch of the velour seat under me. The discomfort heightened the sensations flooding my body. I tangled my hands in his hair, pulling him closer to me.

I needed a soft place to fall and Buster was it.

TWELVE

"Do not go to sleep, Buster." I rubbed my painfully tingling left arm and pushed his head off my shoulder. My mouth was dry, and I could taste hot dog at the back of my throat.

"I need to get back to the show, now."

One of us had knocked over the leftover lunch bag. An overpowering stale garlic stench rose up. I grabbed a bottle of water from a six pack on the floor and drank greedily, catching the water in my hand as it spilled down my chin. I pulled on my pants.

I jostled Buster again. His probing cop eyes were closed, the worry lines in his forehead relaxed. He looked more like the kid I remembered playing soccer on Hayes Street.

A plane roared overhead. I heard a pile driver pound the earth rhythmically. A few moments ago, all I'd heard was our breathing. Noise by noise, the world intruded. I wiped my wet hands on the seat cover and looked at my watch. We'd been gone for two hours.

"Buster, move it."

He opened one eye. I stifled a laugh. Shifting in his seat, his elbow bumped the horn. The sharp blare set off a flurry of mourning doves across the path in front of the truck.

"What's the time?" His voice was thick. I plucked his glasses off the rearview mirror and handed them to him.

"Four thirty. I have to get to rehearsal. Move this truck out of here." His keys were still in the ignition, so I reached over, started the engine, and rolled down my window. Fresh cool breezes flooded my overheated skin. I pulled down my T-shirt, feeling a frisson of excitement as the cloth pulled over my tender breasts.

He planted a kiss on my cheek. "Man, you stink."

"I don't smell that much, do I?" I said, fighting an urge to sniff my armpits.

"My favorites, garlic and sex."

I handed him his shirt. "It's not bad enough that I have to model in a fashion show; I've got to do it smelling of garlic? Geez, Buster."

"A fashion show?" He pulled the shirt over his undershirt and I silently grieved as the star tattoo on his shoulder disappeared.

"Don't say a word," I warned, slipping his tie under his collar as he buckled his belt.

"Fashion show screams Kym," he said.

"Believe me, I am not happy about it."

"Maybe I'll come. When?"

"Don't you dare. I'll probably be outfitted in some dorky patchwork jumper with huge pockets. With lace."

He leaned against the back of the seat, still dreamy-eyed. "Maybe you'll get to wear something slinky."

"Not that kind of lace. These are quilting fashions, not Victoria's Secret. Come on, let's get out of here."

I checked my cell for messages. He reached over and grabbed it, the phone tiny in his palm.

"Hold on, hold on," he said, warding off my reaching for the phone with his left hand. He typed on the keypad.

"What are you doing?"

"Putting my cell number in here. Right up front. Look, I'm the first one in your address book."

I looked. He'd put his name as #Buster so he would stay at the top of the list.

"Cute."

"Just want to make it easy for you to reach me. Anytime. Middle of the night . . ."

"And why would I call you in the middle of the night?" I asked. Buster brought out my inner flirt.

Grinning, he revved the engine. "Maybe your cat's up a tree?"

"I don't have a cat."

He thought for a moment, eyebrows comically furrowed. "Or your pilot light goes out."

"I have an electric stove." I was enjoying this game.

"An itch you can't scratch," he said, reaching for my back.

I moved out of reach. "I can get a back-scratcher at any dollar store. There's only one reason a woman calls a man in the middle of the night," I said.

"Yes?" he said provocatively.

I gave him a blank look. "A loud, unexplained noise."

His face fell. Not the answer he was looking for, but he was a good sport. "That's okay with me, too."

I reached for the gear shift. "Back to reality."

"Wait. Did you ever use a rotary cutter to cut linoleum?"

"Huh?"

He smiled quickly. "I've been thinking about those cutters. There must be other

212

uses for them. I'm replacing the floor in my mother's tiny bathroom and I've got a bunch of small cuts to make. That thing might come in handy. You said there are two different types?" he prompted, shifting back into neutral.

He was obviously trying to prolong our time out here. I couldn't blame him. I was so relaxed. I pulled my legs under me, sitting cross-legged on the seat, closer to him than my door. I knew something about home improvements.

I began, "There's the straight-handle kind. You pull down a lever on the safety cover and the blade comes out. Cut, then push on the lever to hide the blade again."

"Okay, so the blade doesn't retract until you close the cover."

"Right. The newer one, the one with the curved, ergonomic handle, has a trigger in the handle. As you press the handle, the blade opens. If you're not holding the handle, the blade disappears into the safety mechanism. But I don't think they're designed to be used on linoleum."

"So you let go of the handle . . ."

His head came off the back of the seat, his eyes wide. He cursed and flung the gearshift in reverse. The truck spun gravel as he backed down the trail, his arm flung over the seat. He got out and opened the gate, flung himself onto the seat, and drove the truck through without closing his door.

"Want me to get the gate?" I asked when we reached the other side, but he was already out of the cab. When he climbed back into the driver's seat, he spoke with new urgency.

"Are you sure?" He turned to me, his blue eyes flashing. "As soon as you release the handle, the blade is no longer exposed, right?"

I thought back to the earlier demonstration. The saleswoman had been using the ergonomic one. "Yes, why?"

He pulled too quickly onto the street, bouncing me. My head banged against the window as the truck slid around a corner. I scrambled for my seat belt.

"Hey, slow down. What's the hurry all of a sudden?" I said, fighting panic.

He kept his eyes on the road, changing lanes without signaling. Something I'd said had caused this sudden need for speed.

"What is it? Why do the different types of cutter matter? What does that mean?" I asked.

"Murder."

I heard bells ringing. A red-striped wooden arm began its descent across the roadway in front of us. A loud horn sounded. Buster goosed the accelerator toward the railroad crossing.

I yelled. "You'll never make it!"

He shot me a look and hit the brakes hard, thrusting me forward. I broke my fall with hands braced on the dashboard. The bumper stopped just shy of the tracks as a freight train began its slow procession.

Buster threw the truck into park and pounded the steering wheel. "Shit, piss, fuck," he said.

"Nice talk," I said, rubbing my wrist.

"Sorry, but this train takes at least six minutes to pass."

I peered down the length of the train, then at him. "You said murder. Why?"

"I didn't say that." He tapped a nervous rhythm on the dashboard with his thumbs, keeping his eyes straight ahead.

He could deny it, but I'd heard him. "Yeah, you did."

I watched as his face shuttered. The cop was back with his game face on. The one who acquired information didn't give any out. Our lovely interlude was over.

"Drop it, Dewey. I'm not about to talk to a civilian about an ongoing investigation."

Civilian? I bristled at the tag. I crossed my arms and looked out the window, focusing on the rotary cutters to keep from feeling how belittling his remark was.

I was the only one who knew what Claire's body had looked like, besides Myra. I allowed the picture of the hotel room to form in my mind. The bedcovers lying partly on the floor. The blood. The curved-handle cutter lying next to her.

My heart sank as I tumbled to what Buster had already figured out. "If she had dropped it while using it . . ." I voiced what I didn't want to know. "The blade would have closed before the cutter ever hit her. Someone deliberately cut Claire."

I turned slowly to him, the horrible truth descending between us like a curtain on a bed in an old black-and-white movie, keeping us apart. In the blink of an eye, his job had changed from explaining a fatal accident to catching a murderer. And I truly was a civilian, an unnecessary burden. Or worse, a suspect.

He sat higher in his seat, his shoulders stiff. He glanced in the mirror and pulled his tie up, knotting it with a vicious tug. The transformation was complete. From Buster, friend and lover, to Benjamin Healy, homicide detective.

Murder changed everything.

The train continued on, sounding like

bottles knocking against each other. Metal-barred cars carrying chickens trundled past. Feathers floated in the air. Fifty cars must have gone by already and still no caboose in sight. I pulled on the confining neck of my T-shirt. I wanted out of the truck.

"Buster, you know I didn't do this, right?"

He nodded once, without looking at me.

I didn't do it, but someone did. "What about the fashion show? I mean, everyone is going to be there. Do you think it's safe?"

"You'll be fine, Dewey." Buster rapped his fingers on the steering wheel, beating out a tuneless rhythm. "There'll be lots of people around, right? Chances are Claire's death has nothing to do with the quilt show. Murders like this are almost always committed by the people closest to the victim. We'll talk to her husband again."

He'd lapsed into copspeak. Claire had become just another victim, her loved ones viewed as potential suspects. I could see him grow distant, probably figuring out his next move. I wanted to keep him here with me. In my mind, I reenacted my route to Claire's room. I remembered I'd never told Buster about seeing Justine in the hall just before I got to the door.

"Buster, Justine was there and she owed Claire money," I offered, watching his face.

"She stole the cash from yesterday's admittance from the show. Eve was furious last night when she found out."

"Stop," he said softly. His hands had stilled and he unconsciously brought one up to run through his hair. He looked straight out the windshield, shoulders hunched, elbows leaning on the steering wheel.

"No, listen to me," I said. "I know you have to talk to Claire's family, but there is something going on at the show. Money is missing."

The notebook might hold a clue. Maybe Justine had made notes on her gambling. I arched my back to get my fingers into my pocket. Buster grabbed my arm, stopping me.

"Dewey, it's a quilt show, for crying out loud."

I pulled my hand away. "There's plenty of cash around."

He shook his head, his expression hard. I didn't like this look.

"I could ask around," I said. "Everyone thinks of me as just my mother's daughter. I bet I could get people to open up, tell me what they know."

He looked at me, incredulous. "You've got to be kidding me, Dewey. What do you think this is — some kind of game? We're talking about murder, remember?"

"Remember? I found Claire's body, didn't I? Do you think that's easy to forget?"

"That entitles you to sympathy, not —"

"So you feel sorry for me? Is that what this has been about?" I flung my arm out of his grasp, pointing at the seat between us. " 'Poor Dewey, she found a dead body, I think I'll cheer her up.' Instead of holding your hand out in sympathy, you haul out your —"

"Dewey," he warned. "You can't bring Audra back."

My heart stopped. "My mother? What does she have to do with this?"

His voice was soft. "I've seen this, Dewey. A cop can't get the bad guy he's chasing, so he transfers his rage to the next poor slob in his sights. It doesn't make for good police work."

"My mother's death has nothing to do with Claire's," I yelled. Buster put a restraining hand on me, but I shook it off. I reached down and pulled on my socks so hard, I nearly put my big toe through the seam. I jammed my foot in my sneaker and brought my foot up to tie my laces. Buster frowned at my shoe on his upholstery. I brought my other foot up and silently dared him to say anything.

"Don't take this personally, Dewey. This is my profession."

"Why should I take anything personally? I have cable. I've seen *Moonlighting*. I know once the sex happens, the relationship is over."

"Don't make this about us, Dewey. You don't know anything about my job."

"Hey, coming out in your big blue truck was your idea. Just get me back to the show. I've wasted enough time this afternoon."

I wasn't about to tell him that I was always on the lookout for a tan Camry with a dented front-quarter panel. Did he have any idea how many tan Camrys were on the streets of San Jose? He had no clue what it was like to be unable to go to the mall without first circling the parking garage for the car that killed your mother, or to drive for miles on your day off, sometimes south to Paso Robles, sometimes north to Napa County, just driving and looking at license plates. Catching glimpses of drivers, trying to picture what the guy looked like. Looking for the last thing my mother saw before she died.

He started to protest, but I waved him off. Sex with Buster had been a really dumb idea. I felt stripped bare, vulnerable in a way I wouldn't have if we'd kept our clothes on.

"What do you know about my mother's death anyway?" I muttered under my breath.

I jumped out of Buster's truck before he brought it to a complete halt by the fountain in front of the convention center. I didn't want to give him the chance to help me down from the high seat. My speedy exit was hampered by a blue-haired woman dragging a bulging canvas tote on wheels, moving at a slug's pace, blocking the sidewalk next to the truck.

After several false starts, I finally got around her and hurried inside, feeling Buster's eyes on my back. I looked for signs to the fashion show dress rehearsal. The signs led me past the quilt show, down the hall, and farther into the convention center.

What a fool I'd been. As angry as I was at Buster for tossing off my interest in Claire's murder as some kind of game, I was madder at myself for thinking that he and I could exchange bodily fluids without any consequences. I felt like an idiot. Sex. There was always a price to be paid.

I'd been away for hours. How could I have let the afternoon get so far away from me? My face flamed at the thought of Buster and I entwined in the front seat of his truck.

Gone was the feeling of relaxation, now I could only think of everything I needed to do. I had an appointment at five with the Freitas sisters and another at six with Colin Bergstrom. I would tell Justine I was out of the fashion show. There was no time. Even if I found a buyer tonight, I'd still have to get the computer back from the police and get all the files up to date. I wanted to run the new system at the show for at least one day so I could show the new owner how well it worked. I needed to make the inventory balance. I still had those invoices from WGC to reconcile. I had no time for a fashion show. Justine would just have to understand.

A sign pointed to the auditorium to my left. I walked a long way down a corridor. This auditorium was far away from the convention center, and no other events were being held down this way. The hallway widened and I saw the auditorium doors. I passed the closed doors and continued looking for the backstage area.

I slowed at the thought of facing Justine. Buster might not think she was capable of murder, but I wasn't sure. Had Claire been alive or dead when Justine walked away from her door?

A hand snaked out of the doorway and grabbed me.

"You're late," Eve said, jerking me into the dressing room.

My heart pounded. "Where's Justine?" I gasped. After the way she treated me this morning, Eve was the last person I wanted to deal with.

Her eyes glittered and she ran a rough hand over her hair. Her skin was pale; dark pouches had formed under her eyes since I'd seen her earlier.

"Is she in here?" I said, trying to peer around Eve. I could only see an array of half-dressed women, milling about a room nearly twenty feet square. Clothes were everywhere — on the floor, on the backs of the chairs, hanging from a long rack. The scene was like a G-rated, middle-aged, well-fed episode of *Las Vegas Showgirls.*

"She's around somewhere," she said, not looking at me.

I reached for the notebook but stopped. Something in Eve's tone made me realize Justine was not here. "Didn't she show up?"

Eve gave me a look that said this was her business and she would tend to it. "Not a problem. I've got everything under control."

"I'm missing the matching cloche," someone yelled.

"Look in the hamper over there," she shouted, her eyes darting around the room as her attention scattered. "Some stuff hasn't gotten unpacked yet."

"What a zoo," someone muttered.

A pretty woman with mahogany skin dashed by in a full skirt and a jogging bra, shouting about a missing bustier. Eve checked her clipboard and directed the woman to the back of the room.

First Justine had stolen money from Just-Eve; now she'd blown off the fashion show. No wonder Eve was in such a foul temper. I began to say something sympathetic, but she held up her clipboard as though warding me off from treading on her personal life.

"Go find your outfit, Dewey. We're running late. The lighting people are complaining because they can't get in to focus the lights. The stage is locked up tight, and no one can find the key. Everything's behind schedule."

"Listen, I can't be in the fashion show. I've got appointments to keep."

Eve stiffened and frowned. She flinched as the soundtrack from *West Side Story* blared suddenly and the group began singing along with the lyrics about feeling pretty, oh so pretty. Lark had said Justine liked to keep the atmosphere lighthearted. Eve obviously didn't do fun well.

"What time is your appointment?"

"Five."

"You're not going to make it. You need to be here for rehearsal." Eve was not backing down. I could see she wasn't going to let me go.

"I've got to be out of here in an hour," I said.

"Find Lark. She'll give you your selection."

I reached for the notebook. Buster hadn't wanted it. I didn't want to be responsible for it any longer.

"Okay, but Eve, wait. Take this notebook from me, please. I don't want to misplace it. If it's not Justine's, put it in your lost and found or something."

I reached in my pocket. As soon as I did, I realized the notebook was no longer there. I'd lost it and I had a good idea where — Buster's truck.

Eve saw the confused look on my face and dismissed me, pointing toward Lark. She moved away to settle an argument over shoe choices. The notebook was in Buster's hands now. He was the detective — let him figure out what it meant.

Along the wall to my right were wooden

cubbyholes. Street clothes, gym bags, purses hung from old-fashioned brass hooks. The opposite wall was bisected horizontally by a continuous countertop, with large mirrors above it. Globes were spaced about a foot apart, creating bright pools of light underneath.

Lark motioned me over, pulling a hanger off the free-standing rack at the end of the counter. The outfit shook as if it was alive. It was made up of nothing but pink feathers ranging in hue from Pepto Bismol to Barbie Mustang to Mary Kay Cadillac. Without the hanger, I wouldn't have guessed it was attire.

I shrank back in horror. "How many flamingoes had to die for that dress?"

Lark tch'd. "It's a marvelous piece. Each feather is hand-stitched to the base. It's very *Sex and the City*."

"More like cat in the birdcage."

"Find something to wear," Eve commanded, from across the room where she was tugging on a recalcitrant zipper.

Lark put the pink monstrosity back on the rack and pulled out another outfit. I blinked; she had to be messing with me. Was this her idea of a joke? The top was a bandeau bra and the skirt consisted of thousands of ribbons sewn onto a waistband. Ribbons of all

226

colors and sizes, but none more than an inch wide. Anyone walking in the skirt would expose their private parts each time they moved. The title card read *Rainbow Coalition.* Jesse Jackson would be so proud.

What had I agreed to? What kind of fashion show was this? I looked around. As the models pulled on clothes, the answer became too apparent. The outfits in this fashion show were outlandish. Laughter erupted as a woman in a space-age foil dress struck a pose. I saw a woman in a red flapper-style dress, her hair pulled back with a sequined headband. In the corner, a woman was checking herself in the mirror, tilting a hot pink and neon green two-foot-tall Cat-in-the-Hat hat just so. It matched her swing coat and turtleneck dress. As I watched, she thrust her feet into coordinating shoes, covered in pink and green beads.

I had to shut my eyes. It hurt to look at this stuff. Kym had to be laughing her ass off right about now. There was no way I was going to wear one of these creations in front of an audience. Lark tugged at my belt buckle with one hand, pulling my T-shirt out of my waistband with the other. "Let's go. Time's a-wasting."

I grabbed a handful of my shirt and

stopped her. "No way, I'm not going to do this."

Lark tossed a glance at Eve, who handed a jewel-encrusted belt to a tiny Asian woman and threw me a don't-make-me-come-over-there look.

"You're here, Dewey," Lark said. "Lighten up, have fun."

I didn't see how that was possible. I released my T-shirt and tried to relax. I felt a tap on my shoulder.

"Wear this." Myra was standing behind me. She was dressed almost the same as she was yesterday — another navy suit, this one with pinstripes. She looked like the lone peahen in a room full of peacocks.

To my relief, she was holding a pretty ensemble in shades of blue, green, and purple. The jacket looked to be of normal hip length, pieced of many small quilt blocks. The dress was sleeveless with a gored skirt, done in alternating bands of color. I could have kissed her.

"That's not part of the fashion show," said Lark, her face screwed up in disapproval as she took the hanger from Myra.

"This is a Claire Armstrong original," Myra said haughtily.

"I don't care who made it. There's a lineup already in place," Lark said. "You can't insert new outfits in willy-nilly."

"I want it in," Myra said. "That's the least we can do to honor Claire."

I hadn't seen this assertive side of Myra, and I admired her loyalty.

A whistle blew, shrilly cutting through the noisy chatter of the dressing room, ending all conversations, including Myra and Lark's standoff. They glowered at each other. The more I looked at Claire's outfit, the more I could see myself wearing it.

From atop a chair, Eve let the whistle fall back on her chest, cupped a hand around her mouth, and yelled, "The keys to the stage door should be here shortly. I want you completely dressed and lined up, at the stage entrance, in ten minutes." She pointed to a small red door cut into the wall at the far end of the counter. A brass plate read "Stage."

Her comments caused a flurry of activity as the models finished dressing.

I reached for Claire's outfit.

"Not so fast." Lark held the dress away from me, a game of silky keep-away. "I'll need to get Eve's permission for you to wear this."

I grabbed the jacket sleeve. "Tell her I wear that or I'm out of here."

Myra demanded my attention, tapping my

free arm. She said, "I've got something to tell you. Come with me."

She was pulling me away from Lark, away from the dress. "Hold on, I need Claire's entry," I said.

Myra took two steps toward Lark and snatched the hanger away from her. "Here."

Lark protested, but Eve waved her off, and Myra thrust the dress at me.

"Eve's got bigger troubles than whether or not you wear this or something else. Just put it on," she said, pushing aside a pile of street clothes, clearing an empty spot at the counter. "I've got other news."

I grabbed the dress and turned my back on Myra, stepping quickly out of my shoes, jeans, and T-shirt and pulling the dress over my head. The garlic smell coming off my clothes transported me right back to the truck. I stuffed down my sense of shame with great effort, unable to stop a red blush from crawling up my neck.

The dress slipped on easily, the silky fabrics cooling down my hot skin. I looked at myself in the mirror. The dress complemented my coloring without washing out my skin. The fabric pieces were intricately shaded, the tones enhancing each other. It had taken a great eye to pull all these fabrics together in such a cohesive way.

"How did Claire do this?" I asked, fingering the hem. "Did she make the fabric or what?"

Myra nodded, picking up my pants off the floor and hanging them on a nearby hook. "There's silks, cottons, rayons, over a hundred different prints in that skirt. She just sewed and sewed pieces together to make new fabric, then cut that apart and sewed again. The jacket is miniature quilt blocks. It took a lot of work, believe me."

I examined the jacket before pulling it on. "What about these buttons? I've never seen anything like them."

The buttons on the jacket were unique. Round with a center core of blue, the holes were surrounded by tiny green leaves and purple flowers. The colors in the buttons matched the fabrics of the jacket exactly.

"Fimo clay. Claire made them from scratch. You've got to have an edge if you want to win first prize."

She grabbed my hands. Her palms were freezing. "Never mind the dress now. Let me tell you my news."

I could tell she was excited. Her pale skin was highlighted with two high spots of color on her cheeks.

"It's official," Myra said, clapping her hands. "I can buy Quilter Paradiso."

"You buy Quilter Paradiso?" That was the last thing I'd expected to hear.

"I talked to the lawyers this afternoon," she said. "We're going to execute the sales contract that Claire had drawn up with your mother."

"A contract? I didn't know they'd gotten that far."

"Claire's attorney knew all about it."

"But I didn't know you wanted the shop," I said. "I lined up some other people to talk to. I've scheduled appointments."

Myra zipped me up. "Well, now you don't have to. I think Claire wanted me to have it," she said wistfully. "That was her intent all along. She was buying your mother's store for me."

The idea that I could stop looking for a buyer started to take hold. The shop would belong to Myra. No more worrying about the inventory, or making payroll. No more agonizing over what lines of fabric to buy. No more Kym. I felt lighter. I straightened my shoulders. I didn't need to meet with Colin after all, and missing my drink with the Freitas sisters didn't matter. I could let our family attorney handle the details. I could be finished with Quilter Paradiso.

I held out my hand. "Okay, Myra, you've got a deal." We shook. Myra smiled and I returned her grin. I'd call my old work buddies on Monday and start networking for a new job.

Lark brought me back to earth, jerking me onto a small step stool. "Let me put up the hem, Dewey." She was armed with a pin cushion strapped to her wrist.

"I'm done here," Myra said, patting my forearm. "I'll go see if Eve needs my help. I can't wait to see you on stage in Claire's outfit. You're going to be quite a sight."

Lark knelt on the floor, gave the skirt a fierce tug and, taking pins from her mouth, began rapidly turning up the hem. I glanced at her in surprise.

"I didn't know you knew how to sew."

"You see any needle or thread? I'm pinning, not sewing, Dewey," she growled. "If it was up to me, I'd use scotch tape. Hold still."

Chastened, I held my hands down at my side, and tried to stand motionless.

"Keep your chin up. Remember what I told you."

We were interrupted by two shrill blasts of a whistle.

"Line up," Eve's voice cut through the noises of the crowd. She clipped her syllables like a cheerleader. "Your outfit should have a number. Get in numerical order."

Lark let me go reluctantly, the pins in her mouth twitching as she spat out one more and jabbed it in the hem. She gave me a hand down off the stool.

Eve bent down to hear what Myra was telling her. From the vantage point of her chair, Eve pointed across the heads of the models at me.

"Dewey, you're first."

"First? No way!" I cried. "I don't know what to do." I felt silly, with everyone's eyes on me without even leaving the dressing room. What would it be like in front of an audience?

"That's why we're having a rehearsal," Eve said. "Myra's right. As long as you're going to wear Claire's work, you should be out in front. I'm not messing again with the lineup. Get over here. All you have to do is walk across the stage without tripping."

The models were already bunched by the closed stage door, jockeying into position. Wending my way to the front, I stepped on a mermaid's tail and heard a yelp. I apologized.

"I'm on first, sorry. Excuse me, I need to get by."

Lark called out, "Chin up. Shoulders back, don't look down whatever you do."

I gave her a feeble wave.

Eve handed me a pair of shoes. I slipped them on and she pointed me toward the stage. "Walk slowly, one foot in front of the other," she said.

Another chorus of "I Feel Pretty" started in the back of the room. She turned to the rest of the models, waiting in a line behind me.

First on meant first off. That was some consolation. Maybe I wouldn't be late meeting Colin Bergstrom and the Freitas sisters. I should let them know I'd agreed to sell to Myra.

"Okay, everybody, ready to strut your stuff? Just because this is only a rehearsal doesn't mean you can't vamp it up. Be outrageous."

That was the last thing I wanted to be. I just wanted to get across the stage upright. The shoes pinched with each step I took. I felt sick. One of Lark's pins had worked loose and was poking me in the calf. I felt a trickle of sweat travel between my shoulder blades. Kym was going to hear about this.

I looked around for Myra. She was standing in the back of the dressing room and gave me a thumbs up. That made me feel better.

"Ready with the spot? Lark, get ready to open the curtain," Eve said into her walkie-talkie. "Okay, Dewey, go, go, go."

I felt my heart pound. Eve opened the door and pushed me out onto the stage. I hesitated, and she shoved me hard, like a commander pushing a parachuted rookie out of a plane.

I took several baby steps. Small footlights lit only the area directly in front of me. Myra was expecting me to do Claire's outfit proud. I sucked in my stomach and took another small step. Inhaling, I mouthed Lark's words. Chin up, don't watch your feet. I took two more steps.

A noise from the doorway behind me froze my progress. I looked. Eve was wheeling her arms, urging me on. Faster, she mouthed. I picked up the pace and moved closer to center stage. A bright spotlight came on from behind the audience, blinding me. I shielded my eyes without thinking and heard Eve holler, "No!"

Damn it, I was doing my best here. What did she expect? I'd told her I had no experience onstage. "Sorry, it was just so much brighter . . ." I turned to apologize, to explain to her that I hadn't been prepared for the light but I would do better next time.

Eve was hurtling toward me. At my feet, she crumbled to the floor and began crawling. What was she doing? She passed me

236

and I looked to see where she was headed. The stage was brightly lit now. I blinked, sure I was not seeing what I was seeing. Suddenly my eyes cleared and I knew I was looking at another dead body.

Justine lay in the middle of the stage, a large pool of dark blood underneath her head. The blood had spread around her but stopped, the jagged edges forming a red mantilla around her blood-darkened hair. Holding my own breath, I looked to see if her chest rose, but I saw no sign of life.

I closed my eyes, refusing to believe it. When I opened them again, Justine had not moved.

I looked back at the rest of the models, who had been shocked into complete silence. I saw Lark standing head and shoulders above the others. For a long moment, I held her eyes, refusing to acknowledge that Justine was laying three feet away from me, dead. Maybe if I never looked . . .

"She's hurt!" a woman in a feathered hat shouted.

"Call 911," someone else yelled.

No one moved. I couldn't leave Eve alone. I took the several steps to where she was kneeling alongside her fallen friend, her tears spilling freely.

"Justine," Eve keened, the word taking

more syllables than I would have thought possible.

My second body in as many days. I was getting to be an expert.

I put my hand gently on hers. "Don't touch anything, Eve."

"But she's hurt." Eve's words were followed by gully-washing tears.

"She's past being hurt."

Eve turned her sorrowful brown eyes to me, the pain so deep in them I had to look away. I reached for my phone, then remembered it was with my clothes. "Someone call the police," I yelled. "She's dead."

The crowd of models remained huddled in the doorway on the edge of the stage. The woman in the flapper dress shook, her fringe flying vigorously. Just a few minutes ago, they'd been a lighthearted group, singing and bitching about too-tight waistbands.

Everyone was looking at me as though I should know what to do. And I did. I knew I had to keep everyone together until the police came. I tried to find Myra, but I couldn't see her. She shouldn't be alone.

"Lark," I hissed. She took several tentative steps closer, keeping her gaze on my face, off Justine's body.

"Keep everyone in the dressing room. Make sure no one leaves. The police will want to interview them," I said.

She nodded, herding the models back into the dressing room. I heard their voices rise excitedly, quiet shock replaced by the compulsion to talk about what they were experiencing.

I remembered the #Buster on my phone.

"And tell Myra. Tell her to bring my cell phone. She knows where it is."

Eve pulled on Justine's bangs, smoothing the hair on her forehead. I looked away, unwilling to look at Justine's flat, staring eyes. Nothing, I learned again, was as empty as eyes with no life behind them.

I wanted to move away. "Eve, honey, we've got to leave," I said gently.

"No," she roared. "I'm not going." She moved closer to Justine, cradling her shoulders. I knelt, keeping a distance, reluctant to get bloody again. Eve stroked Justine's cheek over and over. Her face told me she knew her friend was beyond feeling, but she was unable to stop.

"She was a good person, Dewey. Even after everything she did, I still loved her. And she loved me."

"I know she did." I shifted, my knees stinging from the cold wood stage.

"Listen to me," Eve pleaded. I sat back on my heels, Claire's skirt covering my legs, the pins in the hem digging into my thighs.

"We never should have moved out of San Francisco," Eve said quietly. "I thought we'd have a better life in Reno. But Justy was lonely there. It was harder to make friends than we thought it would be. I had my garden, but Justine, she needed people. She tried golf, tennis, but she got bored."

Eve struggled to replace Justine's sandal that had fallen off. Her bare foot was white as marble, vulnerable and cold. I swallowed hard.

"At first when she started going to the casinos, I didn't mind. I was glad."

I looked back at the stage door. The models had migrated back to the entrance in a knot. Lark was not with them anymore. I couldn't leave Eve alone, and no one was coming out to spell me. I shifted my skirt so the pins weren't sticking me as much. It would be a while before the police arrived, even with Buster and Sanchez in the building somewhere.

Eve continued, her voice insistent and low. I felt like she'd been waiting to tell someone this story for a long time.

"At first I didn't know where she was going. Justine always handled our finances. We were short some months, but she always had an explanation. The truck needed a transmission, or she'd made a deposit on a hall in Lancaster for the spring convention. She always had a reason."

Eve grew quiet, and I thought she was finished.

"I followed her to the casino one night," she said, her voice thick with emotion. "Justine was at the blackjack table, playing for thousands of dollars. The dealers knew her well, brought her White Russians and coffee. She loved White Russians."

Eve dissolved into tears. I patted her while she rocked back and forth, wordless sounds coming from her mouth. Where was Myra with my phone?

A movement on the stage caught my eye. Was the killer still here? I started. Eve sensed my urge to flee and grabbed my hand, keeping me at her side. My heart in my throat, I tried to make out what I saw. My eyes adjusted to the darkness and I could see the gold fringe fluttering on the American flag that stood in the back corner of the stage. Her rocking had caused a cross breeze, making the fringe move and settle. Nothing alive, just shiny gold fringe.

My breathing returned to normal, and Eve lessened her grip. I scanned the stage, trying to assure myself that that was all that I'd seen. I spotted something familiar on the floor near the back of the stage. One overhead light was illuminating the little orb.

A button. From here, I could clearly see the brightly colored flower in the center. Just like the one on the jacket I was wearing.

I pulled the jacket around me. A chill went through me. If Sanchez saw this, he would suspect me of murder — again. My heart fluttered. I had to get that button.

THIRTEEN

Two EMTs arrived, easing Eve away from Justine's body. I heard them muttering about gunshot wounds. Lark came out and hugged Eve, dragging her toward the dressing room, as the emergency workers bent over Justine. I backed away, gathering the skirt around me, sat back on my heels, and glanced at the crowd regrouped at the stage door. All eyes were on Eve. I scooted backward, away from the front of the stage. No one noticed that I was moving away from them. In the semi-darkness of the downstage, I put my hand out, fingers scrambling, reaching until I found the button. I scooped it up.

To my right, on the opposite side from the models, I felt for an opening in the curtain. To my great relief, I found one and, still crawling backward, slipped through.

I stood, letting the curtain close around me. I pulled off the painful shoes. I was in a dim, musty space off stage left. My bare foot bumped into something hard and I nearly tripped over a metal dolly. I bit my lip to avoid crying out in pain.

One hand out, I felt my way toward the red glow from an EXIT sign at the end of the hall. I closed my other hand around the button. The sharp edges dug into my palm.

No way was I going through an interrogation with Sanchez believing I had something to do with another murder. Hours of questions I had no answers to. I knew there would be consequences later, but I didn't care. My throat closed. I felt as trapped as a squirrel in a forest fire, with the same overwhelming urge to flee.

I pushed the exit door open, waiting for alarm bells, only breathing normally when none came. I was outdoors, on a small concrete dock. I couldn't see the street from here, but I could hear the air brakes of trucks stopping at a nearby traffic light.

I had come out onto the loading zone for the auditorium, similar to the one we had used to set up Wednesday night — the mundane working end of the convention center.

I tore the jacket off and compared the buttons to the one in my hand. An exact match. I counted the buttons down the front. Five, all intact. No buttons were missing off the jacket. No sixth buttonhole, no little threads indicating a button had fallen off. I patted the dress down. It had a long zipper in the back. No buttons on the dress, not as fastener or embellishment. Where had this one come from?

My mind spiraled back to Justine's dead body. I had to keep the button away from Sanchez. I didn't need anything to point me to the scene of the crime.

I walked along the concrete pad. A stenciled sign on the back wall read "No jumping off the dock." Did people really commit suicide off loading docks? Was this loading dock the Golden Gate Bridge of Silicon Valley?

I scrubbed at my eyes and dragged the fingernails of my left hand through the hair at my temples. The pain reminded me this was not some nightmare I could wake up from. People were dying around me. First Claire, now Justine.

I reached for my phone to call Buster before remembering I didn't have it. What would I tell him anyhow? That I was running from another crime scene? That I was withholding possible evidence?

A shiver ripped through my body. Most of the area was in deep shade, and the air was cold. Moving toward the sun, I saw steps that led down to the drive — steps to freedom. Somewhere around this maze was the way out, a path that would lead me to the parking garage and my car and my real life. Away from death, away from murder. I would make a run for it.

I had reached the top step when I heard footsteps behind me. I stopped short, left foot dangling near the edge, and felt the hairs rise up on the back of my neck. A tickle set up in the small of my back. Was Sanchez coming to get me?

Not knowing was worse. With trembling knees, I forced myself to turn. Myra was framed in the doorway, holding my phone. I yelped with relief.

"I'm so glad it's you," I said.

"Are you okay? I saw you leave. I wanted to make sure you were all right."

"I'm going home. Let them come and get me."

Despite my tough talk, my legs were wobbly and I didn't trust them to navigate the stairs. I sat down on the top step.

"Here we are again," Myra said as she came alongside of me, handing me my cell. The two of us sat facing the ugly stained driveway. I felt so stuck.

"Yeah, another day at the quilt show,

another murder," I said.

"What do you mean?"

"The EMTs said Justine was shot," I said.

"But Claire had an accident, Dewey."

Me and my big mouth. I'd forgotten that Myra didn't know Claire had been killed deliberately.

"She tripped and fell with the cutter in her hand," she persisted.

I grasped my cell, wishing I could call Buster. The button in my hand reminded me I couldn't.

"What? Do you know something? Tell me," Myra said.

She deserved the truth. I laid my hands in my lap. Without looking at her, I explained. "I was talking to Detective Healy earlier about the different kinds of rotary cutters. He realized that the type of cutter found by Claire was the safety cutter."

A look of recognition passed over Myra's face, and then another. She was familiar with rotary cutters and got the meaning immediately.

"So she *was* murdered?" she said, sounding strangled.

"Someone," I continued, "had to have held that cutter and cut her with it."

Myra exploded up. She took several long steps away from me, then wheeled back at me. Her face was contorted with anger. I felt sick that I'd been the one to tell her.

She was walking close to the edge of the dock. There was no guardrail here, just the edge of the concrete and then the drop. I looked down — it would be a nasty fall. I was afraid that with one slip of her foot, she would go over.

I pushed myself off the step and approached her tentatively. I put a hand on her elbow. She pulled away from me and, off balance, teetered near the edge. I felt my own feet get unsteady. I stiffened my knees to hold my ground.

"Just watch your step, Myra." I backed up, afraid we would both fall. Myra was still standing too close. I hoped my words would be enough to settle her down.

"Look, I'm sorry if I upset you. I know this is craziness. It's not fair that Claire's gone and now Justine. It's not fair at all."

I felt the cold seep up through my ankles from the damp concrete floor as her eyes bore into mine.

"Dewey, now another person is dead. Don't you see?"

"I get it, Myra. Probably the same person killed both of them. Maybe if someone had figured out who killed Claire earlier, Justine would be alive."

Could that someone have been me? If I'd talked to Justine earlier, told her I knew she had borrowed from Claire, that I'd seen her walking away from Claire's door, would she still be alive? I would never know.

But who killed her? Maybe her partner had been mad enough to kill her. It would take passion to shoot Justine, and Eve had plenty of reasons to be angry with Justine. I remembered her scathing toast of Claire in the bar.

"Did you see Eve around the auditorium before the rehearsal started?" I asked.

Myra looked at me quizzically. "What are you thinking?" she said.

"What if Eve confronted Justine about stealing and ended up killing her?"

"Do you really think that might have happened? Whoa." Myra stopped to think, her brow furrowed with concentration. "I wasn't around earlier. I was at the lawyer's this afternoon, and I had to get the dress; it was back at my loft. I had only just gotten to the fashion show when you saw me."

I felt the button in my hand, pressing into my palm. I was going to be imprinted with the detail from the design if I wasn't careful. I tried to relax my fingers.

"Myra, this button . . ." I held my hand open for her inspection, moving the cell aside. "It matches the ones on Claire's jacket."

Myra picked it up and looked at it. "Yes, it does. Where did you find it?"

"On the stage. Way back. But there are no buttons missing on the outfit. I checked."

"So what? Claire usually put an extra button on the inside seam. It must have fallen off when you knelt down."

"But it was so far away. I found it way back, almost to the back of the stage."

"So it rolled." Myra studied the button as though she could figure out its trajectory.

I flinched as the door banged open again. I jumped out of the way of the swinging metal, and Myra steadied me. Sanchez took a step outside.

"I need you two back inside. Now," he said.

I heard disdain in his voice, through the veneer of courtesy. His face was locked down tight. As he held the door open, I caught a gleam off his manicured nails.

"I won't go back in there." I was surprised how weak my voice sounded. In my head, that statement had been strong.

Sanchez held the door open wider. He looked past me, his eyes scanning, taking in all of the dock and the driveway beyond. A car went by and he studied it, not turning from it until the sedan was out of sight. When his eyes finally lit on me, I could see his eyes were narrowed with barely controlled rage.

"Ms. Banks," Sanchez said to Myra without looking at her, "please go inside. There's an officer waiting to escort you to be questioned."

Myra gave me a feeble wave, fist closed over the button. I relaxed, the button out of Sanchez's clutches for now.

I sensed his impatience with me, his thin lips growing tighter. He frowned, the parallel lines carved deep into his forehead, reminding me of furrows left in the sand, except that these were permanently etched on his brow and wouldn't disappear with the tide. Buster was on his way to having those same lines.

I didn't know how to change this man's mind about me. I thought of myself as a good and honest person who captured spiders and released them. He saw me as a liar and murderer.

"What did you think you were doing, leaving the scene like that?" he said.

"I don't want to go through this again. I won't. I can't."

"You do not have a choice. This is an official police investigation, and I will not

251

tolerate your interference."

"Buster . . ." I began, before I remembered Buster would not help me.

His eyes locked on me and his voice grew even deeper. "I'm aware of your personal relationship with Detective Healy. I understand you lured my detective away from his duties this afternoon."

"I did not lure —"

He cut me off. "How convenient that you kept him away for hours while someone else was murdered."

"How was I to know Justine was going to get killed?"

He stared at me, the stare of a leopard trying to paralyze his prey.

I realized what he was saying. "Oh come on. You don't seriously think . . ."

"What am I to think? According to Healy, you haven't looked at him in the twenty-odd years you've known each other. Suddenly, you find him irresistible and you choose today to seduce my detective. What am I supposed to think?"

How dare Buster tell his partner we'd been together. Was he truly that suspicious about my attraction to him? My cheeks flushed with embarrassment. It was mortifying to think this cop knew details.

"Stop. You've got no idea," I said.

"You lead my detective away from the convention center, in the height of an ongoing investigation, and keep him away. Another person dies. If you're not killing people, maybe you're protecting someone. Tell me, who?"

My mouth fell open. I tried to conjure up some courage. The courage of the falsely accused.

"I've got nothing to hide." Again, my words sounded weak. Sanchez was draining whatever strength I had.

"We'll see, Ms. Pellicano. We'll see. It would not be that difficult to switch rotary cutters next to a dead woman."

We returned through the hall I had used to escape. I was beginning to understand that talking was not my best option. I clamped my lips tight. We were getting closer to where Justine's body had landed. A nerve in my thigh twitched painfully. I did not want to go there.

"Follow me."

Sanchez opened a door and led me across the apron of the stage, in front of the closed curtain. I could hear low voices, feet scraping, and other indistinct noises as people tended to Justine. I could only imagine what they were doing behind the curtain. I shut down my imagination so I wouldn't conjure up any images.

Lights embedded in the carpet led our way down three steps to a flat area in front of the stage. We stopped, facing the red-velvet tiered seats. My back was to the spot upstage where I'd found Justine's body. In the back wall, I could see a high window where the sound and light people were housed. The auditorium looked like it was ready for the next keynote speaker, maybe a financial guru: "buy real estate with no money down," or a spiritual lama, extolling the virtues of compassion. People sat in these seats in the hopes of changing their lives. Tonight, lives had been changed, but not for the better.

As my eyes adjusted to the dim light, I could see the fashion show models scattered in the seats. Contrasted to the blue-suited police that were standing on the periphery, they looked ridiculously overdressed in their wild outfits. From chic to silly was a short distance.

I felt exposed, standing next to Sanchez as if I were some kind of teacher's pet. I tried to smile at the other women, but no one would catch my eye. Their expressions were uniformly grim. I sensed resentment toward me as though I, as the common denominator between this death and

Claire's, was somehow responsible for the evening's turn of events.

Sanchez spoke into the silence, his words thick with authority. "Thank you for your cooperation. Please wait here until we call you. Talk to no one. The officers will be taking your statements shortly."

I looked around the room. Someone, maybe even someone in this room, was killing off people. The only thing that I could see they had in common was quilting. And money.

Sergeant Sanchez turned on his heel, gesturing for me to follow him. As we went through the doorway into the dressing room, I saw Buster. He had his back to us, huddled with a group of patrol officers. His shoulders stiffened as I passed by.

Eve was sitting on a stool in front of the still-lit makeup bar, her face white and crumpled. Her eyes were downcast, focused on the cuticle she was picking at. By some signal I didn't see, a policewoman joined Sanchez and me.

Sanchez spoke. "Ms. Pellicano, we will need to take that outfit you're wearing."

My anger flared. "Again with the clothes?"

Eve glanced up. My outburst didn't warrant a glance from Buster.

"You know the drill. There may be trace

evidence on your skirt," Sanchez said. "Please allow Officer Hall to accompany you to the rest room. Are your street clothes here somewhere?"

I nodded, reluctantly pointing toward the hook where I'd left them.

The blond officer followed closely as I gathered my clothes and headed for the bathroom. I had to pass through the doorway where Buster stood, the pile of clothes smelling of garlic in my arms. Tears sprang to my eyes as the horrific turn the day had taken hit me anew. A half-sob escaped from my lips. Buster never looked my way, his head bent to a small woman in an outfit made of tulle.

The policewoman held the door open, searching my eyes. I pulled my shoulders back, and sucked in a deep breath.

"This is the second time in two days that my clothes are going to the police," I said, trying to make a joke. She kept a poker face. I wondered if I could shock her by telling her about the times I'd taken my clothes off voluntarily with Buster.

She told me to keep the stall door open and didn't look away as I began to undress. I laid the phone on the floor.

I fiercely attacked the buttons on the jacket, suddenly anxious to be free of everything associated with the doomed fashion show. The top button snagged and I tugged at it, nearly breaking the threads that held it on. I handed the officer the jacket. I reached over my head and grasped the zipper on the dress, pulling it part way down. I asked the policewoman to help me with the zipper. As she unzipped me, I let the dress fall to the floor.

She asked for the cell.

I didn't want to let go of the phone. "Can't I make some phone calls and let people know where I am?"

She nodded. "One."

We left the bathroom and stood in the hall outside the dressing room. I could hear murmurs from officers working on the scene. I called Dad's cell. After two rings, a mechanical voice informed me that customer XJ-70 was not available. Figures. Dad had never wanted the phone in the first place.

Who else could I call? The booth was closed for the night; I didn't have Ina's cell number in my phone. Vangie was out of the question; the store would be too busy and her attitude toward the police would not be helpful. I dialed Kevin.

"Punk?"

"Yeah, Kev. It's me." I had to talk around

the lump in my throat. He hadn't called me that in a long time. It was a shortened version of Punky Dewster, that had sprung from his little-boy crush on the star, Punky Brewster. I'd gotten the love he felt for her in that nickname. That one word made me realize how much I missed my little brother.

"There's been another death — at the fashion show. Justine Lanchantin was shot dead." The words came out, tumbling over each other.

"Slow down, I didn't understand a word you said."

I took a breath. I cradled the small phone. This was Kevin. Once upon a time, I could tell him anything. I needed him to be that brother again. I had to take a chance and see if he would step up.

"Justine Lanchantin is dead," I said.

I heard a whine in the background. "Kevin, come here."

"Hang on, Kym. She died? Another accident, Dewey?" Kevin sounded incredulous.

"No." I heard Kym demanding to know who was dead. He repeated what I'd said.

"Dewey, is Ben there?" Kevin asked.

Buster? "He's here."

Kevin's voice was thick with relief. "Good, stick with him. He'll know what to do.

Promise me you'll stay close to him."

I thought of Buster's face, closed off as he pursued his investigation. "Sure, Kev." There was no point in telling Kevin how it really was between us.

Kym was asking questions. I hung up quickly. It had been a mistake to call him. I thought I would get some strength from him. Instead, I felt completely alone. I handed the phone over to the policewoman and prepared myself to be taken back to the auditorium, girding myself to sit for hours, waiting to be called in and questioned. I sighed with the unfairness of it all.

We stepped back into the dressing room. Sanchez was helping Eve to her feet.

Sanchez crooked his finger at me. "Come with me."

"Where are we going?" I asked.

"Mission Street. To my office."

My heart thumped in my chest. "Why do we have to leave? Can't you just talk to me here?" I protested.

Sanchez's face was hard as he shook his head. "Two deaths in the last two days. That calls for you and Ms. Stein to come to my office where I can talk to you properly."

He pointed out the door. My stomach muscles clenched as though protecting themselves from a blow.

"Healy!" Sanchez called. "I'm taking these two ladies to my office. I want to talk to them in relative quiet."

Buster turned and nodded. I thought his expression was unreadable, then I realized the message was loud and clear: I was on my own.

Eve and I got into Sanchez's car without exchanging a word. Eve seemed fragile, so unlike the woman I'd seen in action yesterday and today. Her outfit looked like something culled from several of the fashion show items. She wore red pants with a shiny satin stripe down the leg and a black low-cut sweater. We stopped at a light on First. I admired the front yard of a large craftsman-style bungalow on the corner. It was full of wild and unruly plants just like I hoped my lawn would be someday. My heart sunk as we started up again and passed the big sign stuck in the hostas — "Bad Boy Bail Bonds." Would one of us be needing their services tonight?

I glanced over to see if Eve had noticed, but she was staring out the opposite window, her body crammed against the door as far away from me as she could get. I reached out to her, brushed her arm lightly.

She recoiled. "Leave me alone, Dewey," Eve said.

Sanchez looked at me in his rearview mirror, frowning. His phone rang and he answered it. A fire truck screamed by, horns blowing as it slewed through the intersection.

I settled back on the seat.

At the police station, Sanchez led us to a large office space with cubicles that reminded me of every high-tech company I'd ever worked in. Standing in the midst of the gray speckled panels and blue computer screens, I had a surreal sense that I belonged here.

Other officers were scattered about the room, talking on the phone, working on the computers. No one looked up as we passed.

"Stay put," Sanchez said, directing me to a desk in the far corner. "I'm going to seat Ms. Stein in the Witness Interview room. I'll be right back."

Eve went off without acknowledging me. I looked around. This office was where Buster came to work each day. I knew immediately which desk was his when I saw the Metallica coffee mug. I averted my eyes, unwilling to look any deeper. The top of Buster's desk, like the rest of his life, was no business of mine.

Sanchez came back, patting the back of the chair convivially, inviting me to sit. He smiled. Out of the estrogen-laden atmosphere of the quilt show, he seemed able to shed his macho image. The cock-of-the-walk act fell away.

He settled into his chair behind the desk, centering my cell phone in front of him on the bare wood. His shoulders were pulled back, his head held high. I knew a lot of Filipinos who had served in the U.S. military. Sanchez certainly had the bearing.

His sideburns were cut in a straight line across his cheek, longer than what was in style. Not a single hair strayed past the designated line. I wondered what the cost was of always being so vigilant.

Sanchez turned to the desk drawer on his right, pushed a button, and told me he was taping our conversation. He said the date, time, my name, and his. The interrogation started quickly.

"Tell me why the deceased, Ms. Lanchantin, called you."

"I don't know."

"She did call you; it's in your call logs."

"I'm not denying that," I said. "I just never talked to her. She left me a brief message. I assumed it was about the fashion show."

"Did you return her call?"

He knew I did. That had to be in the logs,

too. "I did, but she didn't answer."

"Where were you at 3 p.m.?"

He knew exactly where I was. I answered reluctantly. "Having lunch, outside the building."

"Do you know why Ms. Lanchantin was at the auditorium this afternoon?"

"She was in charge of the fashion show. Rehearsal was at five." While we were all jammed into the dressing room, fretting over which dress to wear, Justine was laying alone on that stage. I only hoped that she was past our help by that time.

Sanchez pressed on. "Who knew she was going to be there?"

"It seemed like common knowledge."

"What do you remember seeing when you walked on stage?"

I talked fast, trying to get it over with. "I didn't see anything at first. I was nearly to the middle of the stage before I saw her body." I was unable to go on, my voice caught in my throat, feeling like a stone was lodged in my gullet.

"Continue," he said.

His tone forced me to swallow hard, but I couldn't finish my answer. He switched his tactics.

"What time did you leave the convention center this afternoon?"

"I guess around two. I wasn't really looking at the clock."

"And before that? Where were you?"

I was starting to panic. I was with Buster after two, but if Justine was dead before that, could I account for my time? I couldn't remember what I'd been doing.

"Do you think she was killed earlier?" I asked.

"Her time of death is still a question."

His cold tone got to me. Justine had been reduced to a time of death. A victim, a puzzle to be solved. "Do you ever get used to it?" I asked him, a question that started out sarcastic but ended up pleading.

He studied my face for the meaning behind the question. "You've had a violent death in your family, correct?" he said.

Hairs on the back of my neck stood up. I didn't want Sanchez to speak about my mother. As awful as Claire and Justine's deaths were, their murders were tiny tears, little rips compared to the gaping wound left behind by my mother's accident.

"Audra Pellicano, hit and run last year," he continued.

Her name on his lips froze me, and I gestured for him to stop, but he wasn't looking at me. He was looking at a picture on his desk.

"Have you been able to explain to your friends how that changes you?" he asked. "How you feel like a foreigner — no, more like a solo navigator trying to circumvent the globe without a sextant. You must keep moving, but you're in the dark."

I could see it was a black-and-white photo of a man and a boy. Sanchez's face told me this wasn't going to be a happy tale. I didn't want to hear it.

"I have nothing more to tell you," I said. "Let me go home, please."

He ignored my outburst. "You're no longer Roy; you're Roy-whose-dad-was-killed-in-a robbery-at-his-appliance-store. There's a stigma permanently attached to you."

"Your friends drift away, don't they?" he continued, each word searing my heart. "They can't grasp what losing someone to a sudden violent death means. And God help you, you don't want them to know; you wouldn't want them to suffer the way you did. But the fact that they don't know means you have no one to talk to."

I thought about my father, and the times we hadn't talked about Mom.

Sanchez was relentless. "People are afraid to speak of the dead, and that leaves you in an untenable spot. Unable to think of anything but the deceased, but unable to tell anyone."

The truth of his words grabbed me like a rip tide, tossing me at will. He was right. I had not expected to be so isolated. At first people hung around, lingering too long when all you wanted was for them to go home so you could curl up in a corner and cry. The neighbors, the college buddies, the old family friends cooked for you, took back your library books, picked up prescriptions. Then their lives made demands on them. The dog needed to go to the vet or the car needed its 30,000-mile checkup and, slowly, errand by errand, they went back to their lives, and you went back to yours. Except yours was no longer there.

That was what Myra would discover, and now Eve. Already her life had irrevocably changed. Instead of grieving for her partner, she was being questioned by the police.

He was looking at me now. He kept his distance, leaning back in the chair, watching to see what he had churned up in me.

I wanted out of here, away from Sanchez's probing eyes. What did I have to give him? What could I tell him so he would let me go?

"I saw Justine the morning of Claire's death," I blurted out.

Sanchez's forehead creased. "Go on."

"When I first went up to Claire's room, I noticed Justine walking away from me. She went down the service stairs."

"I don't remember that as part of your initial statement."

I shrugged. "At the time, it didn't seem like anything."

Sanchez's lip twitched. "If Justine was involved in Claire's death, it was very important."

"Well, sure, now it looks important. I'm just saying, at the time . . ."

"Never mind. Is there anything else?"

"No."

"Are you sure?" Sanchez bit off his words.

I let the sarcasm fly. "It's kind of hard to be sure when you don't know what matters."

"Listen to me."

"I'm not trying to be difficult," I interrupted, suddenly realizing that if I allowed it, I would be here for hours as Sanchez plumbed my memories for everything surrounding the deaths. He would never be satisfied. I threw my shoulders back and straightened my spine.

"I'm done. That's all I have to say. Let me go home or charge me."

FOURTEEN

The streets of San Jose were packed, cars moving at a crawl even though it was after midnight by the time Sanchez's officer returned me to the convention center to pick up my car. He gave my cell phone back as I got in to drive off. I hadn't seen Eve again, and Sanchez hadn't told me where she was. I had no idea how she was coping. Was Sanchez telling her his sad story, trying to get a confession out of her?

Right by the arena, I was forced to stop short to avoid hitting a group of concert-goers. I crept forward slowly. When Dad taught me to drive, his contention had been that teenagers were like deer. If you spotted one on the side of the road, you could be sure there were others just waiting to jump in front of your car. I didn't get up to full speed again until I was beyond the next traffic light.

What passed for conversation with my

Dad always involved my car. Most Sunday afternoons, he took my Acura out for a drive to see how the engine "sounded." When I protested that he never took my brothers' cars out for a road test, he just grumbled. He'd usually be gone for an hour, sometimes longer if the car was due for maintenance. I knew he was checking the tire pressure, topping off the oil. The gas tank was always full when he came back. To thwart him, I used to gas up on Saturday, but I'd quit fighting him about these afternoon rambles after my mother's death.

Sanchez's story about his father had stirred up a longing to see mine. I'd allowed him to take his fishing trips, separate himself from me and the boys without much of a fight. I'd let him stop talking about my mother. That was going to end. As soon as he was back, I was going to tell him my favorite memories about Mom. When I was finished, I would make sure he told me his stories. All of them.

Away from downtown, traffic eased and I was home in a few minutes. I let myself in the back door. Inside, I threw my keys on the kitchen counter. The message light on the phone was blinking. I felt the familiar fluttering in my stomach that meant Buster had called. I pushed the button, but to my complete disappointment, Kym's voice came out of the machine.

She wanted to know about Justine's death. She'd wrung everything he knew out of Kevin and now was starting in on me. I deleted her mid-message with a firm press of the button.

Buster's old messages remained on the machine. I was tempted to replay them, let his strong voice fill the empty space, but Buster's silence tonight at the auditorium told me all I needed to know. I was either a suspect or a sick hanger-on who wanted to tie myself to the police investigation to avenge my mother's death. Either way, he wanted nothing to do with me.

I stood in the hall between the kitchen and bedroom, trying to get back the feeling of sanctuary my house had always given me. Tonight, the plaster walls felt cold. Buster's voice had brought warmth to my space. I'd ruined that source of security, his voice no longer calming, now only a reminder of our shared two-day history. Buster was unwilling to take on Sanchez on my behalf. And why should he? We didn't have a relationship; we had sex. It wouldn't hold up to a date and real conversation.

I needed to get rid of Buster's messages and stand on my own. Before I could talk myself out of it, I pushed the erase button. "Message deleted," the mechanical voice said. I hit the red button again and again until all of Buster's soliloquies were gone. I felt dizzy — the sense of being alone in the world finally hitting me.

In my bedroom, the still-rumpled bed sheets reminded me what a long day it had been, starting out on such a high note and ending with death and suspicion. I could not face sleeping in my bed tonight. I found my sweats on the hook in the bathroom and put them on.

On the couch, I wrapped the fleece throw around me. The heavy softness enveloped me, as yielding as my mother's cheek when she'd lain beside me whenever I had cramps or a cold.

I closed my eyes, but Sanchez's accusing face loomed. I wondered if his story about his father was true or just a cop trick to get me talking. I was beginning to understand that putting words together into a cohesive narrative was an essential skill for a detective. Buster was a good storyteller, too. I knew that from his messages.

With great effort, I shifted my mental focus to the store. Myra's offer to buy Quilter Paradiso was the one bright spot in my life. I tried to concentrate on that, but the sale of my shop seemed cursed. Every time I tried to sell the shop, someone died. Would Myra be next?

I shook off thoughts of voodoo. The shop was not under some kind of curse, afflicting all who approached it. That was just silly. Look at Kym, she thrived at the shop. Unless she was the one doing the cursing . . .

I laughed out loud. Sanchez was wrong. The real trouble with violent death is that you began to make up scenarios, reasons why it happened. Explanations where there are none. Pretty soon you were thinking your white-bread, squeaky-clean sister-in-law was murdering people. Ridiculous.

At dawn, birdsong woke me up before I realized I'd been asleep. A niggling problem rose to the surface with false urgency. Where had I left the pink and brown flying-geese quilt that Chester and Noni had given me?

I'd dreamt about the woman who made the quilt, and awoke feeling bereft. Someone in her family had treasured that quilt enough, so that even now, a century-and-a-half later, it was still in perfect condition. And I couldn't even remember what I'd done with it. I sank back onto the couch pillow, retracing my steps yesterday morning. I was glad when I finally remembered that the quilt was safe at the booth, locked up in the convention center. I'd left it behind to go for a ride in Buster's truck. I should have stayed with the quilt.

It was too early to go to the show and get it. I would go find the quilt history book I'd seen as a kid. I showered and pulled on yesterday's jeans, with a fresh QP T-shirt.

In the backyard, I found the little notebook propped up on the picnic table. A note stuck to it read "Thought you might need this in your quest for a new owner. B."

Buster had discovered the notebook in his truck and returned it to me in the night. I must have slept more soundly than I thought. I hadn't heard his truck or seen the headlights that surely would have shone through the living room. And Buster hadn't knocked on the door to let me know he was here. Shaking off a creeping sadness, I tucked the notebook in my pocket and continued to the store.

I parked along the Alameda and entered through the front door. It was not quite eight, so not even Vangie was here. I breathed in the unique smell of the shop, a combination of wood polish and fabric sizing. I wanted to stay within the familiar walls. I wouldn't go to the quilt show. Ina, Jenn, and Kym could handle the booth.

Without the laptop, and now that I'd found my buyer, I didn't have much to do at the show. I'd just stay here today.

A lump formed in my throat as I realized I would be the last of my family to own this building. I shook myself. Dwelling on things I couldn't change was deadly. Action was the only way out.

I found the *Quilts in History* book in the big classroom. The summer I'd spent reading this book under the pear tree in the backyard came back to me as soon as I opened to the page with the reprint of a nineteenth-century ad for Coats and Clark thread. I had pored over the pictures of quilts, reveling in the stories of their makers. Hardship and honor. Making clothes for a large frontier family had seemed like fun to me then.

I'd nearly worn out the pages, thinking they held a blueprint for how to be a woman. In those days, I'd thought I would be just like my mother when I grew up. I'd been wrong.

The quilt I remembered was near the middle of the book. The caption read, "Wild Goose Chase quilt, circa 1855." That settled the question of the name of the quilt. Ina had been right. The colors and fabrics were just like the quilt I'd received from Chester and Noni. I could see the wide variety of prints, stripes and paisleys that made up the blocks.

According to the book, when Harriet Strauss of Stamford, Connecticut, became engaged, she made the requisite ten dowry quilts. But her beau had gotten gold fever before they could marry. He traveled west, and she stayed at home, piecing the eleventh quilt, the Wild Goose Chase quilt, making hundreds of small blocks, by hand. The smallest ones were the rectangle flying-geese blocks, measuring 3 inches by 1 1/2 inches. I couldn't imagine putting together such tiny bits of fabric.

The fabrics were not just pieces of old clothes, but new fabric bought especially for this quilt, an extravagance for her farming family. Her fiancé didn't return for five years. According to the book, her parents begged her to give up on him and marry the local parson. She refused, piecing the blocks, but not quilting the top until he returned. She finally quilted the top in Denver where the young family settled a year later.

I re-read the description. The quilt was made up of flying-geese blocks. According to Noni, my mother had loved flying geese. Now that I knew what one looked like, I would look for quilts that contained them.

I heard voices. To my surprise, Kym walked past the door to the classroom on her way to the kitchen.

Kym's voice sounded loud, even for her, in the morning quiet. "I told you I would take care of things. Now that Claire's gone, everything will go back to normal, Vangie."

Vangie? I stopped reading, my finger holding my place. Why was Vangie here? The only time Kym had criticized my mother was when she'd hired Vangie back. At least once a week, Kym brought a reason to fire her to my attention. Vangie studiously avoided Kym. Why the sudden tête-à-tête?

I wanted to hear what they had to say to each other. I quietly reshelved the book and tiptoed back to the doorway.

"What about the other woman who died?" Vangie asked.

"Justine? She was just in the wrong place at the wrong time."

"That's harsh."

"I can't help that. Our only concern is Quilter Paradiso and keeping things just as they are. Agreed?" Kym said.

I positioned myself where I couldn't be seen and peeked into the break room, just in time to see Vangie set down a bag of bagels from Noah's and two cups of coffee.

This was not a random meeting.

"Kym, Dewey's serious about selling the shop." Vangie's back was to me as she cut into a bagel. She was wearing a QP T-shirt and jeans and her usual motorcycle boots. Kym sat at the table facing me, the stiff collar of her period blouse framing her face. She took the lid off the coffee cup and blew gently into the steam. Her bright pink nails showed up anachronistically against the brown paper cup. Her hair lay on her shoulders, streaked with expensive highlights that her historical counterparts never dreamed of.

"I won't let that happen," Kym said. "This shop is part of my family."

I knew that QP meant family to Vangie, too, but she was brave enough to stick up for me. "But selling is Dewey's decision."

"Where would you be without QP? Out on the street, that's where. Jobs aren't that easy to find, you know. Especially for someone with a past," Kym said.

Uh-oh. Kym had to be bluffing. Only I knew the real extent of Vangie's visits to the wrong side of the law.

Vangie was quick to shift the focus from her. "The store is Dewey's," Vangie said. "Why can't she do what she wants with it?"

"Look, Audra made a mistake leaving the

store just to Dewey. If she hadn't died so suddenly, I'm sure she would have changed her will to reflect my involvement in the shop."

"But Dewey is her daughter. Do you really think Audra would have excluded her?"

Kym waved her off. "Look, Dewey can be the owner. I can accept that if she'll go back to her high-tech job and let me run the store. Problem solved. And if you help me convince her that's the best solution, I'll take care of you."

"That's what you want — to be the manager?" Vangie asked.

"Don't you get it, Vangie? If she sells or if she stays, either way, Dewey is on her way out. As far as I can see, you have only two choices. You can either stick with me or take your chances with a new owner. What's it going to be?"

When Vangie didn't answer, Kym went for the jugular.

"You need this worse than I do. Who's going to hire you with a felony on your record?" Kym said, her sweet smile still plastered on her face.

Vangie stiffened, hand poised over the split bagel with the long bread knife in her hand. We'd both thought her criminal record was a secret.

Vangie turned and saw me in the doorway. Her face was guarded, but her eyes sparked, reminding me that she had survived much rougher characters than Kym. I took a step forward, about to reveal myself, but she warned me off with a look and a wave of the knife.

"Hey, Kym," Vangie said. "When were you going to tell Dewey about those calls from Claire Armstrong?"

Claire had been calling me? I looked from Vangie to Kym and was rewarded with a look of complete astonishment on Kym's face. Not surprise about the calls, but surprise that Vangie knew about them.

Kym sputtered. "I never got any calls from —"

"Oh yes, you did," Vangie said. "Claire called yesterday morning after she saw Dewey at the show. Said she'd been trying to get to Dewey for months, but she couldn't get past you."

My fists clenched into hard little balls. Kym had been manipulating things behind the scenes, keeping me in the dark about Claire's offer to buy the store. Claire must have come down to the show specifically looking for me Thursday morning. I stepped into the room.

"I didn't know she wanted to buy the

store," I said. "When were you going to tell me?"

At the sight of me, Kym tightened her lips and crossed her arms tightly across her chest. She glared at Vangie. Vangie relaxed. She poured some of her coffee into a cup and offered it to me. I signaled no thanks.

"Try to see it my way," Kym said. "I've put my heart and soul into this place and it's not fair that you can just up and sell it anytime you like."

I saw red. "It's *your* fault I want to sell the shop. If you'd have just tried to get with the technology, things might have been different. I'm just not interested in being here unless the store gets computerized."

Kym rolled her eyes. "That's because you don't understand quilting or our customers. You don't know the first thing about quilting."

I shrugged, wondering why that hurt. I knew I was not a quilter, but still the words stung. "You may be right, but that's not the issue. The fact is the store is mine, and I can sell it if I want to. My brothers, my father, you — especially you — have no say. It's all up to me. And I say I'm finished."

"How can you sell the store when the precious computer says inventory is missing?" she said.

Vangie tensed, stopping in mid-sip. Kym's eyes flashed with victory. She tore off a tiny piece of bagel and ate it.

I wasn't backing down. "Is that the reason you crashed the computer? Did you think that without the accurate inventory I couldn't sell?"

Kym tossed her hair over her shoulders, first one side, then the other. "Kevin told me I didn't wreck the laptop, that it would take more than just turning it off to lose all the data. You lied to me."

"He's right, the computer's not broken. That doesn't mean you haven't been doing everything you can to undermine me."

"Exactly how have I been doing that?"

I glanced at Vangie. She was watching with interest. "Tell me why you've been sending $550 a month to WGC when we've never received any merchandise from that company."

"WGC? That's what you 'found'?"

To my total disgust, she used air quotes around the word.

"Wise up, Dewey," Kym said. "That's the money your mother borrowed."

I looked from Vangie to Kym. I couldn't believe what Kym was saying.

"Mom borrowed money, yeah right." I let the sarcasm drip. "For what?"

She shrugged. "It's no big deal. Your mother had borrowed from Claire before."

"Claire?" Now I was just confused. I looked at Vangie but she just shrugged. "What does Claire have to do with this?"

"WGC is Claire's company, Dewey," she said.

Kym caught my look of confusion and continued with the air of someone who loved to be right. "Claire uses that company to collect the money she lends to quilters. Been doing it for years."

My head spun. My hand went to the notebook in my pocket. I *had* been on the right track. But the book wasn't a list of Justine's gambling losses, it was a record of who owed money to Claire.

"You know, Dewey, it kind of hurts my feelings that you thought I'd do anything to harm Quilter Paradiso," Kym said.

Kym didn't look in the least hurt. She looked like she was enjoying herself, like she always did when she knew something I didn't. She drained her coffee and jumped up from her chair, pulling down the lace-trimmed cuffs on her shirt and smoothing her skirt, ending with a hair flip. "I'm glad I could clear that up for you. Let me know if there's anything else you need."

Without another word, she dropped her

coffee cup in the garbage, grabbed her purse and her keys, and left.

I sat in the chair she'd vacated, the seat still warm from her body, pulling the notebook out of my pocket.

"Why did Mom borrow money from Claire?" I asked Vangie, even though I could see she didn't have a clue.

I laid the notebook on the table and opened it. The answer was in these pages. Maybe if I understood the significance of the markings, I could figure this out. Vangie looked over my shoulder.

"What's that?"

"I found it the other night. I thought the notebook belonged to Justine, but it must be Claire's. A ledger. A list of accounts. Something."

I flipped through. Before I got to the QP page, I found the page with Justine's name across the top. Below were several groupings of flying-geese blocks with letters alongside. I couldn't see it yet, but this was the proof that Justine owed Claire thirty thousand dollars.

I handed the notebook to Vangie. "What do you think?"

Vangie licked her finger as she turned the pages. "There must be forty names in here, Dewey. Do you know who they are?"

"I recognize some as vendors from the show."

Vangie's brow furrowed as she studied the pages.

"What?" I asked her.

"Think about it, Dewey. If Claire was lending out large sums of money, anyone that owed her money had motive to kill her."

I looked at Vangie. "You mean anyone like me."

FIFTEEN

The answers to the questions about Claire's lending and why my mother borrowed money from her were at the show. Freddy, Myra, Eve. Someone had to know what these markings meant in the notebook. There was still more than an hour before the show was scheduled to begin. I would try to talk to them before things got crazy.

The Wild Goose Chase antique quilt was at the show, too. I needed to have it home with me.

"Have a nice ride yesterday?"

The wrinkled smoker, Pam, was standing outside squinting into the early morning sun as I approached the convention center. Her skin looked like an interior decorator had done a faux-crackle finish on it; fine lines crisscrossed the strong planes of her face. I turned my face away as she exhaled.

"Saw you yesterday getting into that shiny truck. Just wondering if you had a good time," she said.

I bristled. "Not that it's any of your business."

"Well, it is, kind of. I had a side bet with Myra that you and that cute cop are more than just friends." She picked a piece of cigarette paper off her tongue.

Clearly the smoking had hardened Pam's arteries to the point where she was suffering from short-term memory loss. Myra hadn't even been around yesterday afternoon.

"Officer Healy and I just had lunch, so you lose the bet," I lied. "I'll be sure to tell Myra when I see her."

"Go ahead. There she is." Pam pointed her cigarette past me. I brushed by her as I spotted Myra waving at me from inside. She was pushing a dolly through the still-deserted atrium. I joined her.

"Show must go on?" I asked.

Myra rolled her eyes. "Eve's insisting the schedule remain the same. I didn't want to add to her angst this morning, so I'm heading inside to set up for the lecture later on."

Myra leaned on the pile of quilts, a little breathless. "So what happened at the police station? Was Sergeant Sanchez mean to you? Did he put you in a holding cell?"

"We talked in his office," I said. "He was

very polite. He finally figured out I didn't have anything to tell him, and he let me go home."

"That's good. Be sure to come to my lecture. I'm going to make a very exciting announcement."

Alarm bells sounded in my head. "You're not going to talk about the shop, are you? I'm not ready for you to say anything about that."

"You'll just have to attend and see," she said coyly.

"Hold on, we have some conditions to talk about." I needed to talk her into keeping Vangie.

"Just be there." She started to push off.

"Wait, do you know anything about WGC?" I asked.

She held up her hands as if to say, "No."

I decided to tread lightly. If she didn't know about Claire's sideline, I didn't want to be the one to tell her. I'd been the bearer of enough bad news for Myra this weekend. "Someone told me that Claire had a separate company named WGC."

"That's preposterous," she snorted. "Who told you that?"

She didn't know. She was going to be devastated when she found out.

I tried to cover up. "Never mind."

287

Luckily for me, Myra was concentrating on her own agenda. "I've got to get going," Myra said. "We're setting up in the alcove back by the prizewinners. See you at two."

Myra pushed the cart toward the quilt show. The door was open and unmanned, and she was out of sight in a minute.

"Sweet mother of God, girl, what's with you and finding bodies?" Freddy came into view. He was moving quickly, but he stopped and slung an arm around my shoulder.

"Don't remind me. Justine had been dead the whole time we were in the dressing room, just lying on that stage."

"Man," Freddy shook his head and squeezed me. I cleared my head of the vision.

"Going inside?" he asked. "Walk with me. I'm giving my staff a pep talk in about three minutes. I've got to move at least six embroidery machines before tomorrow night."

"Freddy, tell me about borrowing from Claire. Your name's in here." I held up the notebook.

"What is it?" he asked, angling his head to get a better look.

"That's what I'm trying to figure out. You borrowed from Claire, right?"

A pained look crossed his face. After a quick glance around, Freddy plucked the

288

notebook from my hand. His voice got rough.

"You don't know what you're talking about."

He moved swiftly, his hand gripping the notebook so tightly, his knuckles turned white.

"Freddy, wait up." He was already ten feet away before I put my legs in gear.

I started after him but felt a restraining hand on my back. I turned. Behind me, his head just barely grazing my shoulder, was the security guard.

"Sorry, can't let you pass." The scrawny security guard linked his hands across his chest, trying to appear bigger than he was. The blue shirt with pockets and epaulets didn't help — he looked more like a Boy Scout than a police officer. I reached for my badge and realized I didn't have it — again. Day three of the quilt show and I was in the same place. I could tell by the smirk on his face that he was enjoying my discomfort.

"Don't do this to me," I begged. Freddy disappeared from view without looking back, carrying the notebook with him.

"No ID, no entrance." He stepped in front of me.

"You're really not going to let me in?" I asked. "You know I belong in there."

He smiled. Payback's a bitch.

I stared at his back, imagining myself laying him out with a knock to the head. It was tempting. I controlled my anger and tried to think.

Where was my ID? I'd had it yesterday afternoon — Buster'd taken it off my neck after I'd caught the elastic band on the volume knob of the truck radio, nearly strangling myself during our tryst in the truck. I forced myself to think past that moment, to what came after.

I'd come back to the quilt show late, and gone straight to rehearsal. Putting on Claire's outfit, I'd taken off my ID. I didn't remember picking it up when I'd retrieved my street clothes. The badge must still be on the hook in the dressing room. I headed that way.

The corridor to the dressing room was deserted. A picture of Justine walking this way yesterday filled my mind. I felt her presence in the silence. Before the fashion show, this hall must have felt as quiet and empty as it did right now.

My stomach fluttered, and I regretted every scary movie I'd ever seen. I could just skip getting into the show. I wouldn't need the ID if I just went home now. But the Wild Goose Chase quilt was in the booth, so I pressed on.

A noise up ahead made me stop in my tracks, heart pounding, as I envisioned entering a murderer's lair. I was giving myself the creeps. When the silence deepened, I convinced myself I was alone and started walking again. I had to get into that show, talk to Freddy, and get the notebook back, and there was Myra's lecture. What was her surprise? I needed my badge. Now.

Eve had said she didn't care about Justine's gambling, that she was okay with her partner blowing off steam. But that was before she stole from their company to keep her habit going. Had she done it before? Eve had to be mightily ticked off about that.

Suddenly, my path was blocked by yellow crime-scene tape. The doors to the auditorium were to the left, just past the tape, and the dressing room lay beyond that. I'd thought I'd be able to continue down this hall to get to the dressing room. I hadn't considered crime scene tape.

I looked around, saw no one. I could find a police officer to let me in. Or I could just get in there and get my badge. I tugged on the tape to see how well it was secured. To my surprise, the end came off easily. Before I could form another thought, I pulled the tape away from the wall, took two steps inside the boundary, then pushed the end back in place. Thankfully, it stuck, looking like it had never been moved. The difference between the crime scene and the rest of the world was just a few steps.

I would duck into the dressing room and get the ID badge and leave. No one would have to know I'd been there.

I went past the closed doors that led to the auditorium and through the arched doorway into the dressing room. Several lights were still on, casting weird shadows on the counter. A rack of clothes stood in front of the lockers, the outfits hanging forlornly on the hangers. In the morning light, their sequins, feathers, and glitter were glaringly inappropriate, like a Las Vegas showgirl walking down the Strip in broad daylight.

There was no sign of my badge.

I turned slowly, straining to see through the clutter. An abandoned eyelash curler lay on its side, looking like a medieval torture device. Promises of beauty unfulfilled. The echoes of us singing "I Feel Pretty" reverberated in my head. Last night, this space had been full of life, now it was sad and empty.

I spotted my ID card lying in the middle of a pile of makeup dust, the edges red with powdered rouge. I scooped it up and wiped the dust off on my backside.

"Hold on."

The sound of Buster's voice behind me sent a chill down my spine and I shuddered to release it. This was not the sweet rhythms on my answering machine. This was pure cop. He sounded too much like Sanchez for me. I palmed my ID and turned.

Buster was framed in the doorway, legs spread wide apart as though to block my escape. His eyes were dark, like the ocean on a stormy day. He was pushing his ball-point pen open and closed. Each measured click set up an answering drip of acid in my stomach.

He came toward me, holding his hand out, palm up.

"Give it to me."

I handed over my badge. The smiling picture, taken Wednesday night when all I had to worry about was getting through the weekend without killing Kym, mocked me.

"What do you think you're doing here?" he said, his fist closing over the badge. "This is a crime scene, Dewey."

"I needed my badge."

"Are you trying to give Sanchez a reason to throw you in jail? It wouldn't take much, believe me. Why do you think he took you to the office last night? One wrong word and you'd have been put in custody."

"You don't actually suspect me . . ."

"Do I think you killed Justine or Claire? Of course not, but you're not making my life any easier."

I started to protest, but he silenced me with a look and walked me out of the dressing room, his hand rough on my upper arm. Once we were in the hall, on the other side of the yellow tape, he let go.

"I can't get into the show without the ID," I said. "That frustrated security guard playing his power card won't let me in. I didn't think the dressing room was part of the crime scene."

"Dewey, this is a police investigation. Leave it alone." He placed my badge in my hand. I felt his fingers tickle my skin and pulled my hand away before I could feel anything more.

"Come on, you know I was with you when Justine died."

"Yeah, I know. Therein lies the problem," he said.

I arched an eyebrow at him. "Problem? I thought we were having fun."

"While you and I were out having *fun,* someone got killed. On my watch. Not cool."

"Sanchez seemed to know a lot about our

time together."

He was shaking his head. "I never told him."

"He knew that we knew each other before."

"That came up when we were at the Armstrong scene."

"He practically accused me of sleeping with you to get away with murder."

Buster shrugged. "Sanchez is testing you. He thinks if he puts people under pressure, he gets the truth."

"You don't?"

He shrugged. "Not always. Sometimes scared people say dumb things. Things that could make them look guilty."

Was Buster saying I had said dumb things, but he could understand why? I looked into his eyes and tried to read what was in there but I came up short.

His guarded expression made me mad. "You're the same, Buster. You and Sanchez. You can't trust anyone. Including me."

"Come on, Dewey, this is my job. I don't get in your way of doing your job."

"Oh, no? What about taking my laptop? All my store stuff is on there."

"All right, all right. I'll get the computer back to you today."

It wasn't much as far as peace offerings

went, but I'd take it. "Thanks."

His phone rang and he snapped it open, striding away from me. He handled that thing like it was a weapon in his arsenal. I found myself imagining what he looked like with a gun in his hand.

He was quickly engrossed in his call, so I walked the rest of the way to the atrium alone. I got into the show unmolested; the skinny security guard barely glanced at me, now that my badge was around my neck.

I went down the aisle to find Freddy and the notebook. When I approached his booth, he looked up from a sewing machine demo in surprise.

"Where've you been? I thought you were right behind me." He looked at me, squinting his eyes as if he wasn't sure I was here now.

"So tell me about Claire."

"Quiet," he hissed. He pulled me farther into the booth, shielding me from his customers and sales help. He held up the notebook, using his long arms to keep it just out of my reach. He whispered harshly, "Everyone used her."

"What are you talking about?"

His eyes narrowed. I felt the hair on the back my neck stand up. "Do you think that starting a business was easy? We all needed money, especially in the beginning. Banks wanted nothing to do with quilt shop owners whose business experience consisted of bake sales and raffle quilts. Claire saw an opportunity."

I waited for more, my breath caught in my throat. Freddy gestured and I flinched. Surprise crossed his forehead and he softened his tone.

"Throw a rock from here," he said, "and you'd hit at least three people who borrowed from her at one time or another. Not so much lately. I told you, times have changed. Now the banks are crawling over each other to give out money."

"Like the woman with the T-shirts," I said. "Nanny's Notions. She said Claire gave her her start." Was this what she was talking about? And the toasts in the bar, didn't some of them mention money?

"Like me, last year. I had a great deal on embroidery cards coming from Southeast Asia. All cash deal. I had to act fast. Claire gave me the dough. I used it, paid her back a month later. Fourteen grand, plus interest. End of story."

"Why all the secrecy?"

He glanced around and lowered his voice again. "She charged interest like a Soprano. Last time I looked, usury was still a crime."

I thumbed through the book. "So all these people in here . . ."

Freddy's face turned pensive. "I just wish Claire hadn't been so flipping ready to lend me the money. Turned out the DVDs were worthless. I lost the fourteen grand investment. Still had to make good to Claire, though. She didn't care that I'd been ripped off. She just wanted her money back."

"DVDs? Were you going into the music business?" I was confused.

Freddy chuckled. "No, knucklehead, DVDs of embroidery designs."

He pointed at the sewing machine. Chugging along, the needle was rapidly filling in the spaces of a lime-green cartoon character.

"That's what makes those things go. The designs are on CDs. Download to your machine, and you're good to go. I was buying DVD technology, very cutting-edge. Too cutting-edge. Turned out the discs weren't compatible with the machines on the market now. I have a storage unit full of crap. Fourteen-thousand dollars worth of shit."

I flipped open the book to Freddy's page. On his page, next to the fourteen flying-geese blocks, was the notation DVD.

TLA, Three-Letter-Acronyms. The high-tech world was full of them.

I flipped to the QP page in Claire's note-

298

book. There were the ten flying geese, but it was the notation alongside that suddenly made sense. Next to our name, Claire had noted POS.

At my old job, the letters could have stood for Pissy Operating System, or possibly Piece of Shit. But I knew immediately what they'd stood for. Point-of-Sale system. The computer program that contained every sale, all our customer information, and the inventory.

The kind of business application that should cost thousands of dollars. Ten flying geese. Ten thousand dollars.

I knew in a flash the real story — that my mother had purchased this system when I was laid off, to put me to work. Mom had borrowed the ten thousand dollars for this software. She hadn't cleared the purchase with Dad or he hadn't agreed to it, so she got the money from Claire.

A week later, she'd been mowed down by a drunk driver.

"Dewey," Freddy said. From the exasperation in his voice, he must have called me several times. I looked up from the book.

"I gotta go," I said. "I need to have a talk with my sister-in-law."

Sixteen

I headed for the booth. Did Kym know why Mom borrowed the money? Why hadn't she told me?

The doors had barely opened to the show, but our booth had a half-dozen people in it. Word about Justine being shot was obviously not out yet. Eve was doing a good job of keeping it quiet. Or maybe it was the way Sanchez wanted it.

Ina was writing up a sales slip, and several people were waiting to check out. A stack of bolts sat at the cutting station, ready to be cut.

"Where's Kym?" I asked, more abruptly than I'd intended.

"Haven't seen her yet," Ina said.

"I pissed her off pretty good this morning. She's probably punishing me by being late."

Ina looked worried. "Jenn's not due until one. I'm going to need help."

I softened my tone and Ina's forehead relaxed. "I'll stay. But I've got to go to Myra's lecture," I warned.

"Okay," Ina said, thrusting a rotary cutter and ruler at me.

The booth had a steady stream of customers for the next two hours. Kym didn't appear and I didn't have much time to wonder where she was. In the first lull, I grabbed a bottle of water for myself and one for Ina out of the cooler beneath the table. Under there, I spotted the QP bag that held the Wild Goose Chase quilt, and resisted the urge to take it out. I'd be sure to take it home later.

I'd barely opened the top of my water when I noticed a pile of reproduction fabrics on the cutting table.

"Quarter yards of everything, please," a wiry red-haired woman in a "Don't Call it a Stash, it's My Life" T-shirt said.

I tried not to sigh. It would be no fun cutting nine inches, over and over again, but I'd learned quilters liked variety. With an effort, I pushed myself off the table I was leaning on.

"Finish your water, hon. I'm in no hurry," she said.

I sucked down the rest of the bottle gratefully. She added another bolt to the top of the pile.

"I've got the whole day. I told my doctor I had to attend the Quilt Extravaganza. He said okay, as long as I don't overdo. So I'm taking my time."

I half-listened to her chatter, keeping an eye out for Kym as I cut. What did Kym know about Mom buying the POS system? Was it the reason she resented me so much?

The customer made more trips to the back of the booth, carrying bolts one at a time. I now had fifteen bolts in front of me, and I had cut only two pieces. This job was going to take forever. I caught Ina's eye. She shrugged and nodded toward the line that was forming in front of her at the cash register. I smiled bravely at her.

"Besides, he's the one that told me to get a hobby," the lady continued. "Wrote a prescription and everything. 'One hobby taken with passion, as needed.' Like it was some kind of anti-puking drug or something."

These fabrics reminded me of the Wild Goose Chase quilt, and I thought of Harriet making her choices as she added to her quilt. I looked up from the pink paisley I had on the mat.

"Who's this quilt intended for?" I asked.

"A new daughter-in-law. My son is getting

married for the third time."

I must have looked startled, because she laughed. "Hey, it's family. What can you do? I figure maybe this one will stick around." She waited a beat and caught my eye. "Or not. Either way, I'm too old to worry about it. So I make her a quilt and hope she sticks around long enough to give me another grandchild before I kick the bucket."

She spoke so easily about dying. I looked closer at her face and saw she had no eyebrows. Her hairline was uneven. The oddly colored hair was a wig. I finally saw the pink ribbon lapel pin she wore. She saw the realization in my eyes.

"Yup, breast cancer. Survivor, so far."

"I'm sorry," I choked out, feeling guilty for even thinking about complaining about her quarter-yard cuts.

She smiled at me, a smile so genuine, so real, that it felt like a gift. I couldn't help but smile back.

"I only know one thing for sure — I'd be already dead without quilting. D-E-A-D. Some days all I can do is fold my fabric. Hell, who am I kidding, there are days all I can do is look at my stash, but it's enough to get me through to the next treatment. And the next wedding. That's what matters."

In the midst of this speech, Kym quietly entered the booth. She avoided my gaze, fussing with her apron. I turned my attention back to the woman, who was still talking.

"My will stipulates that my mini-group gets my stash. If I leave it to my kids, all this fabric will end up at a garage sale, selling for ten cents a yard."

"That would be awful," I said, remembering with a twinge that I hadn't cared what happened to my mother's closet full of fabric six months ago. I'd let Dad deal with it. I wondered now what he'd done with all the boxes.

"Well, I'm not dead yet. So bring it on." With that, she ran out of energy. She leaned heavily on the table, a tired but satisfied smile on her face.

I brought over a folding chair so she could sit while I finished cutting.

"You're a doll," she said. "Take some advice from an old broad on her way out — enjoy each day as it comes."

"I'll give it my best shot," I replied.

"Look what happened to that poor Claire Armstrong. She never expected to die like that. You never know."

Or Justine. I felt my gut twist.

I turned my attention back to the task at

hand, sorting her quarter yards by color, arranging the small fabric pieces in a pretty array. I gave her one of our special tote bags, even though she hadn't spent the requisite two-hundred dollars.

When the woman left, Ina brought me a soda while Kym took over at the register.

Ina said. "What are you smiling about?"

"That woman has breast cancer, but buying fabric made her happy," I said in wonder.

Ina gave me a sideways hug. "Quilting helps people cope with tough times. Meeting people like her makes me glad I work in a quilt shop."

"Me, too." For the first time, I felt the truth of that statement. "Me, too."

"I'm grabbing lunch," Ina said. I looked at the clock. It was just before one. Ina and I had been working for nearly three hours without a break.

"Take your time," I said. "Kym's here now and there's Jenn."

Kym approached. "Why did you give that old lady a tote bag? She didn't spend enough," Kym said.

"Because I wanted to." When she gave me a spiteful look, I added, "Because I'm the boss, and I could."

She didn't like the sound of that, and

began to flounce away. I stopped her, and asked, "Do you know why my mother borrowed that money from Claire?"

Her face twisted with anger. I wasn't sure if she was mad at me or my mother. After all, the POS system was what brought me to — and kept me — at the store.

Before I could get an answer, Lark came into the booth. Today she was dressed in flowing pants and an unconstructed jacket made of handpainted silk, the colors of the ocean. Her high-heeled sandals were delicate with tiny pearls on the crosspiece. Kym sidled up to her, smiling obsequiously.

"Lark, I brought more of those batiks you liked from the store," Kym said. "Let me show you."

Lark ignored her and approached me, her eyes searching my face. "You doin' okay? That was nasty last night. The police kept me there until after nine. I didn't see you."

"I'm okay," I lied. I didn't want to talk about Justine's death. "Go ahead, check out the batiks. They're awesome."

I watched as Kym led Lark to the other side of the booth. Kym and I would talk later.

"I'm off," I said when Ina returned just before two. Kym was still cutting fabric for

Lark, keeping her back to me. "I'm going to grab lunch and go to Myra's lecture. I'll be back."

I took a yogurt from the cooler and ate quickly before I headed to the back of the hall to the alcove where the award-winning quilts were hung. I skirted the edge of the crowd, looking for the room where the lecture would be held. The far wall of the alcove had been opened, revealing another room. I could hear Eve yelling. This must be the place. I followed the sounds of her voice through the quilts.

"I can't believe you waited until now to set up those stands. Get a move on, people. You've got ten minutes."

I passed through the doorway and saw Eve, arms crossed, barking at several of her workers who were struggling to set up quilt stands. These were portable stands, smaller than the ones in the main exhibit. A skinny boy in a knit cap and a struggling mustache pulled up the side rods that telescoped from a tripod base. He grabbed a pole, threading a quilt on it, and slotted it into the cross bar. Two quilts had been hung. Myra's dolly sat to the side with its large pile of quilts. I counted at least nine more that needed hanging.

I tapped Eve's shoulder. "Can I help?"

She shuddered at the unexpected touch and turned. Her eyes were red-rimmed and puffy. I wondered how long Sanchez had kept her last night. She looked like she had gotten no sleep. Of course, with only an empty hotel room to go back to, she probably hadn't.

She hugged her ever-present clipboard. I felt sorry for her, despite her treatment of me. I knew about using work as a distraction from grief. Mostly I knew that it only worked for a while.

"Sorry if I startled you," I said.

She shook her head, barely glancing at me before turning back to the scene in front of her. "Come on, Adam, quit showing off."

I moved out of the way as a young man in precariously low-slung jeans struggled to move a wooden podium into position. I was afraid to watch, in case his pants made the short descent off his flat butt to the floor.

Adam set the podium down and helped the other kid to tighten the screws that keep the horizontal pole in place.

"Can we talk?" I asked. "Do you have a moment?"

"Do I look like I have a *moment?*" she said harshly.

I couldn't be put off by Eve's brusqueness. Justine was the template for all of

Claire's lending business. The more I knew about how Claire operated, the better I could figure out what Mom had borrowed and protect myself from Sanchez's suspicions. I plunged in. "Eve, you knew Justine borrowed money from Claire, right?"

Eve remained stone-faced. She tightened her arms across her chest, but said nothing.

I had to break through her silence. "I saw Justine that morning, you know. She was in the hall outside Claire's door."

That was a hit. I saw in Eve's eyes that she hadn't known I'd seen Justine. Had she already considered the notion that Justine might have killed Claire?

"Claire Armstrong was a leech, preying on the weaknesses of others," she bellowed.

Her blast backed me up a step, as though her words had physical force.

"She's the reason Justine gambled. She kept giving her money."

"Tell me," I said.

With an annoyed gesture, she did. "We borrowed startup costs from her long ago. We paid that money back, but when Justine started gambling, Claire popped up again. She insinuated herself into our lives, always ready with an easy loan."

Eve fought back tears. I placed a hand on her shoulder, but she shook it off. "Justy got in too deep. She couldn't pay the money back as quickly as Claire wanted."

"Did Claire threaten her?"

"I've got a lot to do," she said, moving away from me. "Come on, you guys. Look alive!" she shouted at her workers.

"I heard you with Justine on the phone Thursday night. Was Justine afraid? Is that why she stole from you? To repay Claire with the admission money?"

Eve turned to me, and again I saw the face that made her underlings cry. Her fists came up; her body was contorted with rage.

"My . . ." I began. "My mother borrowed from Claire, too. I know how you feel."

She threw her words at me. "No, you don't. You do not."

She struggled to speak. I watched as her facial muscles twisted with regret and loss. She spit out the words. "I refused to give Justine the thirty thousand to pay Claire back. I could have, I could have sold stock or mortgaged the house, but I thought Justine should learn to be responsible."

She made the word "responsible" sound like a horrible choice.

Her words dripped with self-loathing. "It's my fault she stole the gate. She paid Claire and then tried to repay JustEve by playing blackjack. She maxed out her credit cards at the card club. That's how her mind worked. She was sure she would win the money back. Instead, she lost it all."

I was thinking quickly, trying to map out Justine's actions over the last two days. She stole the admittance money Thursday morning. I saw her at Claire's early that afternoon — she must have been paying her debt. She went to the card club the rest of the day and into the night, trying to win back what she needed. Instead she lost everything and came back to the bar Thursday night, broke and miserable. She called me sometime before Friday morning and died that afternoon.

"Where was she in the morning?" I asked. "She didn't answer the door when I knocked."

"You must have just missed her. She came down to work, and I sent her back up to the hotel room. I couldn't let her near the cash again."

I remembered the scowl on Eve's face when I'd approached her. "You didn't see her after that?"

She shook her head. "I was swamped all day. She called me about two, on her way to set up the fashion show. Said she had found a way to get out from under. When she didn't show up, I figured she'd gone back to the card club again. She always knew the next time would be the time she would hit big. I thought she was gambling. I didn't think she was dead . . ."

"It's not your fault," I said quickly, trying futilely to block out the vision of Justine's body lying on the stage.

"The police said she could have died right after I talked to her."

If Justine died soon after two, that meant Eve had hours of that awful time when Justine was already dead and she didn't know it. That nasty, in-between time. Those minutes when you didn't know your loved one was gone, when you were still happy, or angry, or bored. When everything was the same until you found out, and then nothing was the same ever again.

Mom had been dead for two hours and twenty-three minutes before I knew. She'd already been taken to the funeral home when Kevin finally got through to me. Hours I'd been laughing, drinking with my friends, my phone buried deep in my backpack. Time she was no longer a part of my world but I hadn't known. I hated those hours.

Eve had been running her business and then at the fashion show, organizing the models. She'd probably spent that time furious at Justine, who was already dead. Eve would come to hate those hours, too.

She stopped talking, rubbing her eyes. Her body sagged into a comma shape as though it took too much effort to keep herself erect.

Did I sense relief, too? Relief that she wouldn't have to deal with a sick partner anymore.

She read the question in my eyes. She straightened her spine and looked me full on. "Justine has ruined the business, pure and simple. The cash she stole was money already spent. JustEve Productions is not going to survive this. I have to try and recoup some of the money. That's why the show is still open. I will make good on all her debts if it's the last thing I do."

A large bang startled both of us, sending Eve a foot straight in the air. The two boys were faking a duel with the pipes from the quilt stands, the metallic noise echoing in the empty space. Eve took a step toward them, her face tightened into a scowl. I put a restraining hand on her shoulder.

"Eve, wait. There are still some things we need to figure out."

Eve turned to me. "We?" she snarled.

I took a step back. "Someone killed Claire and Justine — don't you want to know who?"

Her face turned bright red, fists clenched at her side. She leaned in close to me, her voice low and shaking with intensity.

"I don't have the luxury of speculating, Dewey. Justine left me with a fifteen-thousand-dollar bill for the convention center rent, concessionaires that need to get paid, vendors who are threatening not to show up tomorrow."

Tears were streaming down her face. She made no effort to stop them. Did she even know she was crying? I'd had days like that after my mother died when weeping arrived without warning. Tears that barely touched your skin. Tears with their own agenda.

"I've got eight employees to pay," Eve continued. She ticked off each item on her fingers. "Two hundred people with tickets to a fashion show tonight that isn't going to happen. I'd love to worry about what happened to Justine. Unfortunately, I've got to clean up this mess she made."

"I'm sorry, Eve. I need to find out what happened."

"Well, you will have to do it without me. I don't care about Claire Armstrong and I'm finished with Justine Lanchantin. Finished."

Eve stalked away, barking at the workers. I backed to a corner of the room, feeling useless and in the way.

Eve said Justine had paid Claire. Where was that money? Thirty-thousand dollars, in mostly twenties, was no small bundle. Had the killer taken it?

"Dewey, lost in the quilts?"

I'd been staring at a quilt that Eve's boys hung while I was standing here, lost in thought. Lark had come up beside me silently. "Sorry, did you say something to me?"

She sighed. "Quilters at a quilt show remind me of men when a motorcycle is nearby. You think they're listening to you but all their attention is on the throbbing machine, or, in the quilter's case, the layers of fabric, thread, and batting in front of them."

Whatever. "Are you here to listen to Myra?" I asked.

She nodded. "One of your employees told me you'd be here. I wanted to make sure you were okay."

A blast of feedback shattered the quiet and I looked to see Myra tapping a microphone. She was dressed in her normal somber tones. I thought perhaps she was paler than usual. We'd all been pushed to the max over these two days.

Myra looked around helplessly and the boy in the knit cap stepped forward to help, taking the microphone and pinning a lapel mike on her instead.

Chairs had been set up in rows, facing the twelve or so quilts hung alongside the podium. I counted ten rows with twelve chairs in each row. Eve was expecting a crowd.

"Let's get our seats," Lark said. "Then we can look at Claire's quilts."

We found two empty chairs at the back. Lark laid her bag down.

"Hey, nice." I pointed at Lark's QP logo tote.

"I couldn't resist those batiks. I bought five yards of every one."

"Great." With her high profile, our bag would get noticed. That wouldn't hurt booth sales. That should make Myra, as the new owner, happy.

About a dozen quilts were hung. Lark and I strolled past the exhibit.

"Your sister-in-law told me I could find you here," Lark said.

"She did?"

"She thinks you ought to do a piece for my show."

"I bet she does." Anything to make me more uncomfortable. After the fashion show fiasco, I wasn't about to let Kym talk me into anything else.

Lark's eyes cut over to me. She started to speak, but I interrupted.

"I'm really not interested," I said.

"Dewey . . ."

"No way."

Lark turned away, obviously ticked off. I could live with that.

"So what do you think?" Myra asked, approaching us from Lark's side as we faced a quilt entitled "Soaring."

"The quilts are marvelous, Myra. Quite a body of work." I felt like a bit of a liar, not really knowing what I was talking about. Myra didn't seem to care.

I needed to make sure she didn't bring up buying my shop. I pulled on her sleeve and took her aside. Lark continued to walk past the display.

"Myra, your announcement — it's not about the shop, is it? I mean, I haven't told my employees and we need to talk . . ."

"Myra," Lark drawled. "How would you like to be on TV?"

Lark looked at me over Myra's head as she asked. I guess I was supposed to be upset that it was Myra going to be on her show, not me.

"Love to." Myra's eyes snapped across the room where Eve was tapping her watch.

Myra said, "Dewey, don't worry. Take your seats."

Lark and I were barely seated when Myra began talking. I felt my stomach start to clench. I took in a deep breath, trying to relax.

"Good morning. My name is Myra Banks. I've been Claire's assistant for the past fifteen years. If you've taken one of Claire's classes, you know me as the classroom aide. I was the one who pressed your blocks, measured your seam allowance." She paused for dramatic effect. "Unstitched your mistakes."

The audience laughed. I moved up on my chair. Would she mention QP? Lark yawned, her delicate hand covering her mouth. I heard her jaw snap as she stifled another. I felt the chill coming off her toward me.

"Claire and I worked closely over the years," Myra said. "Indeed, there were times when we worked as one person. I tell you this to assure you that nothing will change with her death. I will keep the Claire Armstrong look alive."

She hadn't been as close to Claire as she thought. She hadn't known about WGC, the lending company.

Myra took a step away from the podium. All crowd noises had stopped. There was no

318

shuffling of feet, no coughing, no asides between friends. Every eye was on her as she walked across in front of the display. She swept her hand, taking in all the quilts hanging around her.

"Instead of 'Come Quilt with Claire,' " she emphasized, "look for the books and patterns you love under the name 'Myra Creates.' My new company will be based here in San Jose."

I leaned forward, my stomach suddenly in knots. Did she mean Quilter Paradiso? I tried to catch her eye without success. I shook my head, just in case she looked my way.

Harsh whisperings started in front of me. Myra didn't seem to notice the protests. She looked at the audience expectantly, the look on her face like a toddler who's just used the potty, oblivious to the fact that only her parents cared.

"Can you believe this?" I heard someone mutter.

Myra was still smiling as though there was no animosity building in the room. She started down the line of quilts, touching each one and studying it.

"The best part of this is that even though our beloved Claire is no longer with us, her quilts will go on and on. Just look for them under my new name, 'Myra Creates.'

She was like an author on a talk show who couldn't stop repeating the name of her book. Myra didn't get that people were getting angrier by the moment. I heard someone mutter, "What was wrong with the old name?"

"Her boss isn't even buried yet. This is low."

"Taking credit for Claire's ideas. Who does she think she is?"

"Myra, you're no Claire," a woman with a Boston accent shouted from the back of the room. The way she pronounced Claire was broad and flat and sounded like an accusation.

"You've got your nerve," she continued.

Myra stood in front of a pink and blue quilt, the geese designs spiraling off the edge, and pointed. "This is a particular favorite of mine. I will re-release the pattern in the next few months."

Chairs scraped back, and people stood to leave. Myra was lost in her quilts, looking at each one as though it was the first time she'd seen it. The noise in the room was growing less and less friendly.

"Leech," someone shouted. "Fraud!"

At that invective, Myra seemed to tune back in. She turned quickly to see who said it and tripped over the foot of the quilt stand. She lost her balance and grabbed hold of the quilt to steady herself, but her momentum was too much. I heard a ripping sound. To our collective horror, the quilt gave way, tearing off the crossbar, leaving only the top border still on the bar. Myra was sent sprawling. With a quick stutter, the quilt stand tottered and fell. In what seemed like slow motion, but quicker than any one of us could react, the quilt stand fell with Myra underneath it.

Lark and I jumped up; we were the only ones who moved. We pushed the quilt and pipes away until we found Myra, lying on the floor. She looked dazed.

To my surprise, Buster appeared at my elbow. Kneeling, his eyes scanned the crowd, passing over me, assessing the situation, finally resting on Myra.

"Everyone okay?"

Myra sat up and nodded. "I'm fine. The metal bar missed me by an inch."

He looked into her eyes, checked her pulse. Finally he patted her shoulder and stood up. "Just give yourself a moment."

He quietly took charge, directing Eve's crew to move the fallen pieces out of the way.

"Is she okay?" I asked.

He nodded and pulled me aside. He tugged down the cuffs on his dress shirt and ran his finger under his collar. The leather thong peeked out of his cuff, offering me a tiny thrill. I quickly looked away.

"Tell me what happened," he said.

"She tripped and fell, bringing down the quilt stand. I guess Eve's boys didn't put them together too well. What are you doing here?"

"Looking for you."

I cocked an eyebrow at him. Had Sanchez sent him to arrest me? My hand went to the notebook in my pocket. The proof that Claire had been lending money. Possibly the motive behind the killings. Should I just give it to him and be done with it?

"I delivered your laptop to the booth. Ina told me you were here," he said, watching as Myra stumbled. In two long steps, he was at her side.

I watched him as he steadied her, feeling his hand on my back instead of hers. I shook myself.

The laptop was back. That meant I could get the booth online for tomorrow and give Myra a demonstration of the new system.

Buster was talking quietly to Myra. She seemed shook, but okay. The room emptied quickly, people seeking to distance themselves from Myra's self-involved view of the world.

Lark crossed in front of me, not seeing me, talking into the air. "Get here now."

I tried to move past her, but she grabbed my arm. Glancing up, I saw the phone receiver in her ear, looking like a strange insect that had landed there. "My crew's coming right over," she said to me. "This is big news. I'll do a show on Myra and Claire."

She was in full-on TV hostess mode. Lark let go of me to drop her cell into the QP tote. "Looks like I don't need you after all," she said. I saw confusion on her face as she opened the bag wider.

"Hey," she said. She motioned me closer. "Look at this." Her voice cracked. She had the look of someone who was not believing what she saw.

She held the bag open.

I couldn't make anything out. "What is it?" I asked.

"Cash. A lot of cash."

"What?" I grabbed the mouth of the bag and opened it farther. I could see a dozen stacks, each wrapped with a colored bank strap I knew denoted one-thousand dollars. At least twelve-thousand dollars. "Not yours?"

She shook her head.

"Where'd it come from?" I asked.

"That's what I want to know. It's in the QP bag. Is it money that belongs to your shop?"

"I doubt it." Even on our best day, that amount of cash was not something we dealt in. Most of our customers used debit or credit cards.

This was the kind of money, however, that Justine had stolen from JustEve.

"If it was QP money, we would have stamped our logo on the paper strap holding the bundle together." I looked closer. "Lark, look. JustEve is the name on here. Justine. The bank deposit that never got to the bank."

That Justine gave to Claire. There was only one way the money got from Claire's room to this bag. The killer. I took a step back from Lark.

Lark's voice rose rapidly. "What's it doing in my bag? You've got to help me. You know that detective, right? Call him over here, make him take fingerprints or something. This is not my money. I want it out of my bag now."

Lark set the bag on the chair, picked it up, then put it down again as though it contained a ticking bomb. She was coming apart. I'd have thought she was unflappable, but finding this money in her purse had frightened her. Maybe her tenure as host of *Wonderful World of Quilts* was more fragile than I thought. Or maybe she had killed Claire and Justine. I tried to remember if her name was in the notebook. She would be a good one to take over Claire's lending. She had a very high profile, knew everyone in the business, and no one would suspect her.

I took another step back. "I'll get Detective Healy."

She followed my eyes and saw Buster at the podium talking to Myra. "Do that. Get him over here."

I waved at Buster. He held up a hang-on-a-minute finger.

I looked at the QP tote. It was just like the one I'd been carrying around yesterday. A realization chilled me.

"Lark, when we were looking at the quilts," I said, "the bag was just sitting back there. Anyone could have dropped the money in."

"But why? Why would someone do that?"

A feeling of dread crept through my belly. Her bag had a Quilter Paradiso logo on it. Anyone who didn't know better might think that bag belonged to me.

First the notebook, now the money. Someone was trying to set me up. For murder.

SEVENTEEN

Lark twisted her fancy rings on her fingers, eyes over my head. "Oh no. Here comes my crew. They're ready to film Myra. I don't want them to see this."

The same camera-toting man and young woman I'd seen approach Claire Thursday morning were headed our way. Lark grabbed my arm, squeezing my bicep uncomfortably. I swallowed a yelp.

"Dewey, if my production company gets wind of this, I'll be fired. I need this job. I need to be on air. I'll never find another gig unless I'm on the air. I need to be seen."

She started toward the door, the QP tote on her arm. I stopped her with a hand on her arm. "Just wait. Buster'll be done in a minute. He can get the money tested for fingerprints or something. That would prove you didn't touch it."

Or that you did.

I couldn't let her leave. If someone was

trying to set me up, I needed that money tested. There was no way my fingerprints were on it. I made a grab for the tote, but Lark pulled it out of my range. I grabbed again. The contents spilled onto the floor, and she gave me a horrified look.

Neither of us moved, just stared at the pile of fabric now covering the money. Buster looked up from talking to Myra and questioned me with a raise of his eyebrows. I shrugged and looked down. His eyes followed mine, and I saw him excuse himself and start over.

"Drop something, ladies?" he asked.

Buster had moved silently and quickly; Lark and I were still staring at the floor. "May I?" Buster squatted down and reached for the pile. I couldn't let him destroy evidence that I needed to prove my innocence.

"Don't touch the money!" I said, ignoring the baleful glance Lark shot me. She stomped her foot in frustration. Buster looked up in surprise, drawing his hand back. Her high heel had come down too close for comfort.

"Money?" He moved aside enough fabric so the money was visible. "Explain," he said.

"The money doesn't belong to Lark. It might be part of the stolen bank deposit," I said, stuttering. "JustEve's."

Buster sat back on his haunches, his eyes moving from Lark to me and back again. "Go on?"

I waited for Lark to speak. After all, this was her deal. Lark remained silent, her lips a thin line.

"Lark . . ." I invited.

She shook her head.

I took over again. "She found the money in her tote bag after Myra's lecture. We don't know how it got in there, but it's probably what Justine stole."

"You think?" Buster asked.

"Hey, no need for sarcasm," I said.

"You find a pile of money, quite possibly the motive for murder, you neglect to tell the police, and you bust me for being too sarcastic. Come on, Dewey, what part of dumb don't you understand?"

I felt my face redden. "I didn't find it, she did. Yell at her."

"Don't go anywhere," Buster said to me, his face a wall of implacable copness. He called a uniformed police officer and asked her to stand guard over the money.

"Please come with me, Miss Gordon."

Buster led Lark to the other side of the room, away from the doorway. Several of Eve's people were tearing down the exhibit under Eve's watchful eye. She had gone to a lot of trouble for nothing and didn't look happy about it.

Myra crossed over to where I stood, leaning against the door jamb. "I can't believe that stand fell apart like that," she said without preamble. "Eve's boys are pretty useless. I should sue her. Look at my head."

She leaned forward, and I could see a bump rising. I made what I hoped was a sympathetic noise. Over her shoulder, I watched Buster and Lark.

Myra straightened. "You know, our latest book, *Quilts from Claire's Clipboard,* sold over fifty thousand copies. I think people will continue to buy my books and patterns, don't you?"

Given the muttering I'd heard in the room, I doubted that. "You may have to give people time to adjust."

"You're probably right. That's exactly what I will do. By this time next year, my goal is to have an award-winning quilt at the Quilt Extravaganza. Under my own name."

Was she kidding? I took my eyes off Buster and Lark and looked at her. She was sincere. Myra's bravado was touching. It took a certain kind of character to pick yourself up and start all over again, especially so soon after the death of her mentor. I patted her hand.

"I'm sure you'll succeed," I said.

Lark's raised voice drifted across the room to us. Buster was leaning in, attentive as she explained. Her hands moved rapidly and gracefully. She was almost as tall as he was, and I felt a stab of jealousy at her easy beauty.

Jealousy that I had no right to. Buster and I were over, and there was no going back.

Lark's crew entered. Myra's eyes followed the guy carrying the camera.

"That's my cue. Does my hair look all right? How great that Lark wants to interview me. I'll be able to get myself on TV and tell everyone about 'Myra Creates.'"

I watched her go. I wasn't sure if she was naïve, dumb, or very smart. Her ability to stay focused on her task in the middle of this chaos was amazing. Lark's entourage surrounded her. Lark joined them.

Buster crossed over to me. "You okay?" Buster said, his face grim.

Did he really care, or was this just the cop talking?

I nodded. "What's up with the money?"

"I don't know, Dewey. That's why we investigate. Tell me why that bag has your logo on it."

"It's a promotional item," I explained our policy.

"Where'd the money come from?"

"I don't know." He was silent, waiting for me to say more. "Claire was running a side business, loaning money to quilters. Justine . . ."

"How do you know?" he asked.

I handed him the notebook. "It's all in there once you know the code. I figured it out. I told you Justine owed Claire money. What if the money we just found came from Claire's room? The murderer —"

"Dewey, stop." He slapped the notebook on his thigh. "Back off. We will find out who did this and bring that person to justice, just like we will find the hit-and-run driver who killed your mother."

My temper flared. "Are you on that again, Buster?" I felt betrayed by him. My voice grew cutting. "You know you might be right. I went crazy and killed Claire, slicing her open with a rotary cutter, and then shot Justine. And next I'm going to kill Lark. Oh, and Myra."

My sarcasm was lost on him. Buster wasn't looking at me anymore; his eyes had gone unfocused, his expression grim.

"I had the bastard that night," he said quietly. "I should have cuffed him when I arrived on scene; he was in no shape to drive. Then I recognized your mother's car. I stayed with her until the ambulance came, but by then he'd disappeared."

He was talking about the drunk driver who ran into my mother's car, but all I could comprehend was that he had been with my mother when she died. Suddenly I could hear nothing. I saw Buster's mouth moving, but I couldn't take in what he was saying. I leaned in closer, cupping my hand to my ear like one of my elderly customers.

"Say that again," I demanded.

Buster drew back, his ears turned pink with surprise.

"I was there. Six months ago, I was still a patrol officer. The guy that killed your mother, I should have taken him into custody first."

"Not that part. My mother . . ."

"Dewey, I was the first one on the scene," Buster stammered. "She died in my arms."

His expression was a combination of pain and pride. Then his face fell as he realized this was new information to me.

"You didn't know?" His words were soft as though he was trying to gauge the impact he was having. I struggled to keep the hurt from showing in my face. I wanted to hear what he had to say. I knew he would stop if he thought he was causing me too much pain.

"Tell me," I said, giving him an impatient gesture, resisting the urge to grab his lapels.

He saw my need to know the truth and nodded. "She was in rough shape, but she knew me, I saw the recognition. I told your dad and Kevin. Sean and Jamie knew. I just assumed you and your family had talked about it."

The pain grew deeper and wider. All my brothers knew. And for sure Kevin would have told Kym. The idea that Kym knew this, when I did not, crushed me.

I opened my mouth, but no words could express how I felt. For the last six months, I'd thought my mother died alone. Before today, when I'd pictured my mother's death, it had been in the form of sensation — a crash, followed by a white light. A light too bright to look at — like a solar eclipse. Just a noise, light, and my mother's life was over.

Buster had laid that lie to rest. My mother was conscious, aware of what was going on. Aware enough to know she was being held by Buster. Could I bear to know that my mother had been awake, had suffered?

"I tried to tell you myself," Buster said quietly. "But I couldn't say that to your voice mail."

I didn't think it was possible to feel worse about my mother's death, but I did, my stomach turning sickeningly. The messages — that's what the messages were about. God, I was stupid. He'd been extending a hand in friendship — in family — and I'd misinterpreted it as an invitation to date. I felt my face flame with embarrassment.

Buster touched my arm gently, like a rider would a shying horse. I pulled away and tucked my hands over my chest, letting my arms swaddle me.

I took several steps away. "I'm okay." I didn't want him to touch me. I couldn't bear for him to console me. I needed to process this information by myself.

His cell rang. He glanced at the readout. I could see by his expression that the call was important. He caught up to me, flipping his phone open at the same time.

"Wait," he said to me. "Healy," he said into the phone.

I walked faster, eager to get away from him. I fought to assimilate what he'd said. He dropped back, murmuring, then clicked his phone shut.

He reached for my shoulders. I twisted away, and he dropped his hands. His eyes searched mine. I blinked to keep them tear-free.

"I've got to go," he said. "We're not finished talking about this. I'll get with you later, I promise. Be careful."

He took off at a run, leaving me wondering about everything I had accepted as truth. What had my mother gone through in her last minutes? Pain and despair, even recognition that she was going to die. I couldn't bear to think about her slipping away slowly.

I knew I should be grateful that my mother had died in the company of someone she cared about, but all I could think about was the fact that I'd been robbed of that knowledge these past six months. All because my father and my brothers thought they should protect me from the facts. My father and the boys not knowing what was important to me. Again.

EIGHTEEN

Buster disappeared through an outside door I hadn't noticed before. I went in the opposite direction, back through the award-winning quilts alcove. The room was packed with quilters, elbow to elbow, generous hip to generous hip, all chattering as they examined the best in the show. I heard Myra's name mentioned.

I headed for the main entrance to go outside for better cell reception. I would call my dad to find out what he knew. Didn't I have the right to know how my mother died? Obviously, Dad and my brothers didn't think I was adult enough to handle the truth. I could handle the store, but not the details of my mother's death.

The problem with a sheltered life was that the pain didn't lessen when you found out the bad things later rather than sooner.

His cell rang and rang, until finally his brusque voice exhorted me to leave a message. I knew that this was only a feeble stab at phone etiquette. He refused to learn how to retrieve messages. I hung up.

I called Kevin next. He answered on the first ring. His cell was an extension of his person. With Pellicano Construction booked solid and Dad gone, Kevin spent most hours of the day with the phone to his ear.

Noises from his workmen infiltrated the phone. "What's up?" he asked over the din. "How's the show going?"

I had no time for niceties. "Kevin, why didn't you tell me Buster was with Mom when she died?"

I could still hear the background noise, but nothing but breathing from my brother. His lack of reaction made me angrier still.

"Did you think I'd never find out that Mom didn't die right away?" I asked. "That she lived on, probably in pain." My voice broke. I stuffed down thoughts about how she might have suffered. Kevin had kept this from me, and I needed him to explain why.

"I can't talk now, Dewey. I'm about to go into a progress-report meeting."

I wouldn't let him put me off. "What else don't I know? Does Dad have a girlfriend on the side? Was Mom running drugs out of QP? Are you really my brother?"

"Don't be ridiculous."

I caught my breath, ragged and painful as though I were trying to breathe inside a burning room. My throat felt seared. "You told Kym."

There. I'd said it. I could probably live with the knowledge that they hadn't told me, if Kym hadn't known.

"Kym knew more about my mother's last moments on this earth than I did. How do you think that makes me feel?"

He went on the defensive. "She's my wife. I needed to tell her."

"What about me?"

"You? Miss Independence? You don't need anyone, Dewey. You never have."

"Is that what you think?" I said, the sadness leaking through my voice. He'd completely bought my act of self sufficiency. Mistaken my bravura for true courage.

"I can't do this now. I'm working," he said.

My anger rose. My brother was gone, in his place a guy I didn't recognize. All my life, I'd thought Kevin would be there for me. My little brother, but the one I could count on, talk to. Until Kym came along and got between us.

"Do me a favor. Give Dad a message. Myra Banks is buying Quilter Paradiso. We'll sign the papers as soon as we can."

I hung up and sat by the fountain, trying

to breathe but finding it hard to draw a full breath. The pressure had returned under my sternum, the one that had begun to dissolve this weekend.

I would not go back to not talking about my mother.

A steady stream of chattering women passed me, walking two by two, pulling their overstuffed rolling carts and tote bags. The show was closing. Another day of the Extravaganza over. I couldn't wait for the end.

The laptop. I pushed myself up. If I was going to sell to Myra, I needed the laptop up and running. I bucked the tide of shoppers and headed for the booth.

Once I got past the bottleneck of people exiting the show, the aisles were mostly empty. Around me, vendors were shutting down their booths for the night. I heard the scrape of coins and shuffling of bills and a strained voice counting loudly, "Twenty, forty, sixty, eighty, two hundred."

The closing routine — so normal, so far removed from the day I'd had.

Kym was alone in the booth when I got there, putting the day's receipts and cash into the mesh bag.

"Can we talk?" I began. Kevin's words had stung, but I still wanted to know everything Kym knew about my family.

Kevin told her everything, I knew that now.

Kym interrupted. "Here's the thing. I knew your mother borrowed the money."

The POS system. I'd momentarily forgotten that Mom had borrowed ten thousand dollars from Claire.

"I didn't know what she wanted it for," she continued. "I believed her when she said the software was a test program. I didn't know we were going to actually use it."

"You thought the software program was just my mother's way to get me to work in the store."

"Not permanently."

I flinched at her choice of words.

She waved me off. "I mean, I thought your mother was trying to help you out while you were out of work."

"Then I would leave, and things would go back to the way they were."

I saw tears in the corners of Kym's eyes. "With your mother gone, nothing is the same. I hate it!"

Tears flowed down her cheeks. I'd never considered that Kym might love my mother, too.

She stepped away from me, dabbing the skin under her eyes carefully with a forefinger, and grabbed her purse and the deposit bag. "I'm out of here," she said, pretending to be composed.

A huge sigh escaped me as she walked away, and I realized I'd been tensing for a scene that never came. I wasn't the only one confused and missing my mother.

I felt the adrenaline drain from my body, leaving in its wake a feeling of being slightly sick, like I'd been running full out and hit the wall.

Eve's voice came over the loudspeaker, thanking the vendors for sticking with her through the hard times. Her voice broke, and she abruptly reminded everyone that they had five minutes to close up and leave. The sound of static ended her announcement. Poor Eve. How would she get through the night now?

The laptop sat next to the cash register. I ripped off Kym's calico cover. I needed only a few minutes to see if it was up and running. Around me the vendors filed out. Some that I met earlier shouted goodbyes.

Freddy was one of the last ones out, and he stopped. "Want to go for a drink?"

I shook my head. He shrugged and went on without another word. His invitation seemed forced and I wondered if he was mad at me for exposing Claire's secrets.

In a booth somewhere a cell phone rang, forgotten or maybe purposefully left behind.

My cell beeped ominously; the battery was about to run out. I glanced at the screen. One missed call — Buster. I wasn't going to return that call. I had no idea what to say to him.

I grabbed the laptop cord. Parting the full calico skirts that were velcroed to the table next to the cash register, I reached under blindly, but couldn't feel the power strip to plug in the cell and the laptop. The floor space under the table was a jumbled mess of plastic bins.

The power strip had gotten pushed all the way to the back of the booth. I had to get down on my knees and crawl underneath the table to reach it. Misjudging, I hit my head on the edge of the table and sat down hard, rubbing the sore spot. The sharp pain brought tears to my eyes, disproportionate to the ache. I felt the tears welling and swiped at my face. I pushed the plugs in roughly.

I heard footsteps and stilled myself, adjusting the calico curtain so I wasn't visible. I felt ridiculous sitting underneath the table, but I knew I would feel sillier if that jerky little security guard found me scrambling around on the floor, crying.

I scooted backward to conceal myself better. My feet got tangled. I pulled up whatever it was I was struggling with. By the dim light cast by my charging phone, I could see it was Kym's apron. I pushed the cotton pinney off me like it was a slimy beast and heard cellophane crinkling.

I'd knocked out a pack of Winstons. What were cigarettes doing in Kym's apron? I rummaged through the other pocket and found a neon pink butane lighter, decorated with hearts. No doubt about it, the cigarettes and lighter belonged to Kym.

Tears still hot on my face, I laughed right out loud, then clamped my hand over my mouth. These were Kym's cigarettes. I wondered if Kevin knew. I doubted it. I'd never even smelled smoke on her. She must have gone to elaborate means to conceal her habit. I had a secret on her, but I couldn't enjoy it like I would have earlier.

I heard footsteps going past and froze again, holding my breath. The security guard must be on his way back out. I wanted to be sure he didn't find me so I withdrew farther back, moving something else out of the way. The smell of lavender and mothballs wafted toward me. It was the bag with the Wild Goose Chase quilt from my mother. I pulled the quilt out. I couldn't help but stroke the yielding bulk. I pictured a young married couple lying beneath it, planning their life together.

I needed to feel the quilt around me. I struggled to get it out of the bag quietly in the limited space. I felt the tears coming freely now and stuffed down a sob with a fist in my mouth. With a final yank, the quilt was out, and I cuddled it. Under the table, wrapped in the quilt my mother had bought for me, I couldn't stop crying.

The quilt was tangible proof of a true love over a century old. The woman who'd made the quilt waited for her man for years, never losing hope. The love behind the quilt spanned the decades.

This old quilt laid my feelings bare. The beauty of the quilt, the simple juxtaposition of color and texture and form, reached in and wrung my heart out.

My mother's hopes for her little girl to find love were infused in the quilt. This quilt, which my mother had never seen, never touched, connected her so deeply to me.

A week after her death, my mother had appeared in my room. It was a vision. I wasn't dreaming. I hadn't even been sleeping. I was scrunched against the headboard, watching the sunrise send watery pink rays of light on my walls. I felt a shift at the bottom of the bed as though someone had sat down. When I looked up, she was perched at the foot, smoothing my bed quilt and smiling at me. My face ached as I grinned, testing muscles I hadn't used in a week.

She patted the end of the bed where my toes had just been. I felt the heat coming off her hand. A sense of well-being washed over me. I felt comforted by her touch like I had as a child. All I'd needed then was one touch, and pain had disappeared. One kiss on the bruised knee, the sting miraculously gone. One strand of hair tucked behind my ear was enough to take away whatever hurt my brothers had inflicted.

That early morning, I felt the certainty that she hadn't left me. I knew in that moment she would always be with me. She was in her quilts. In her family. In her store.

Curled in a ball on the cold concrete floor in the convention center, I cried all the tears I'd been holding in for months. She was here in this quilt.

I wept until I ran dry. When I finally crawled out, the large room was completely quiet. Auxiliary lamps were on, dimly illuminating the aisles. Natural light leaked in through the high windows.

I folded the quilt and returned it to the bag. I would take it home and put it on my bed.

I turned on the computer. No need to hurry out now. I might as well take a few moments to make sure it booted up okay. I'd come in early in the morning and finish the setup.

The POS screen came up. I could fix the inventory easily now that I knew why money was going to WGC. I'd wipe the account off the books and pay back Claire's estate once I'd sold the store.

Another gift from my mother. Like the pink and brown antique quilt, the POS system was meant as a gift to me. Neither one was meant to come to me after her death, but that's what happened. I felt incredibly sad.

The database and point-of-sale systems looked fine, so I closed down the computer and felt for my car keys on my hip. I grabbed the Wild Goose Chase quilt and walked away from the booth. I would find my way out of here and to my car. I might have to find the security guard to let me out, but I'd try to get one of the back doors first. I needed to go home, be in my own living room, wrapped in the quilt, watching *Pride and Prejudice*.

After tomorrow, I would be done with the quilt world. I could sell the shop to Myra and get out from under the daily grind of following in my mother's footsteps. I knew now she had never meant for me to make the shop my life's work. Like Kym had said, it was only supposed to be temporary.

I turned left out of the booth, heading for the back wall, toward the dock where we'd unloaded Wednesday night. That was only three short days ago, but the difference was immense. A wide gulf between what was then and what was now.

I heard the air conditioner cycle off, a large bang when the cooled air hit the metal baffles. I passed a sewing machine that had not been shut down, the red lights on the panel glowing. My footsteps sounded loud on the wooden floor, each reverberation a reminder of how alone I was. Weird under-sea light emanated from a digital sign, casting blue stripes in front of me. Looking up, I saw the sign that read "Award-Winning Quilts."

Through there was the door Buster had used to escape earlier. My steps slowed as I passed into the alcove. Wall sconces il-luminated the space. I made my way to the back wall, but I found no door. I remem-bered that the door Buster had used was behind the panels that had been opened earlier for Myra's lecture and were now closed up tight. There was no way to exit through here.

I turned to wend my way back through the exhibit to the main hall. Several rows of quilts were in front of me.

These were the penultimate quilts — the best in their field. The Extravaganza was one of the biggest conventions in the country, attracting the most elite quilters. Tomorrow the show would be closing, and these quilts would never be assembled again. This was my last chance.

Time spent with my mother was only a memory now. I had to glean something new from the lessons she'd already given me. The thousands who came to the show found something in the quilts. I needed to figure out what drove all these people to attend.

And maybe drove one person to kill.

I walked down the first row, studying the wonderful color and designs of these quilts. As I came into the next row, I gave out an involuntary yelp. A tiger's face was staring at me, watching through jungle fronds, his green eyes glowing in the low light. The tiger had been rendered in thread, the orange and black colors intensifying the bright eyes.

I moved away, feeling as though the animal's eyes were following me. The tiger's fierce look reminded me of Eve protecting Justine. Could it be that the same fierceness had led her to murder?

I stopped in front of a quilt. The card attached said the title was *Sunbonnet Sue Does Dallas.* There were twelve blocks, each featuring a strange-looking character with a large hat covering her face. She was in profile, walking in front of images of Texas: oil wells, a city skyline, longhorn bulls. Her shape and hat never changed, just her dress fabric. I didn't get that one.

The next quilt was abstract. Like a Mondrian, blocks of color were assembled on a black grid. I admired the way the colors were rendered, but it didn't do anything for me either.

The quilts were hung in threes. Each grouping was interconnected by the quilt racks. I moved to the next batch.

I stepped back, trying to get a better view. I had seen my mother look at quilts. She usually stood back and squinted, I remembered. Blurring the lines of the quilt was important to visualize the quilt as a whole and not see the individual blocks. As she got older, she joked she didn't need to narrow her eyes; she only needed to take off her glasses.

Claire's first-prize quilt was to my left, and I turned to read the card. The quilt was made of what I knew now were flying-geese blocks, although these flew in a curved formation.

"How do you like that quilt, Dewey?"

I was startled to hear Myra's voice. I turned; she was watching me. How long had she been there? The natural light coming in from the high windows was beginning to fade, putting her face in shadow. I couldn't see her eyes clearly.

"How'd you get in here?" I asked.

"I sneaked in — the guard is fast asleep. I've been looking for you."

"I was heading home." Why was she looking for me? Warning bells went off in my head.

Myra pointed at the quilt. "Take a good look. Do you think this quilt deserved to win first prize?"

Her colorful bracelet caught the low light, throwing tiny rainbows of color onto the floor. It looked different than when I'd first seen it on her, outside Claire's room. One button didn't reflect like the others. I looked closer and saw it wasn't a button at all, but a hardened glob of amber-colored glue. Something was missing. A button about the size and shape of the one I'd found on the stage had fallen off. Myra had taken the button from me on the loading dock after Justine died. Had she taken it to repair the bracelet?

My mind raced. Pam, the smoker, said Myra saw me get into Buster's truck. That was at two o'clock, well before the fashion show. Hours before Myra said she'd arrived. Myra had lied about being in the building when Justine died.

She was the one who arranged to meet Justine.

I blurted out what I knew. "You set up a meeting with Justine at the auditorium before the fashion show."

Myra looked away from the quilt, studying me with a smirk on her face.

"Indeed I did. Very smart. I didn't think anyone remembered me coming in."

"The smokers," I said, almost to myself. "No one pays them any attention." I was embarrassed that I hadn't noticed them either. In fact, I'd ignored everything Pam said because she'd said Kym was out there with her, smoking. She'd been right about both things.

"Justine got greedy. She wanted her money back. She thought that with Claire dead, I'd hand it over. Just because she saw me argue with Claire."

I had to get out of here. I was locked in the quilt show, after hours, with a murderer.

Myra reached into her purse and thrust

something at me. I jumped back, but it was only a neatly strapped bundle of money with the now-familiar JustEve logo. Myra must have taken the money from Claire's room after Justine had repaid her debt.

"Take this. Put it in your bag." She pulled at the tote hanging over my shoulder. I shied away. I didn't want her hands touching the Wild Goose Chase quilt.

"You put the money in Lark's bag?" I asked.

"I thought it was your bag. A mistake I will not repeat."

She held out the bundle of cash. I took it reluctantly. I opened my bag. This was my chance to get my cell. I could push the buttons that would call Buster without taking it out of the bag. She didn't have to see me. As I rooted around, my heart sank. My cell was still in the charger, under the table at the booth. Defeated, I dropped the money inside.

Myra stuck her hand into her purse again. I was ready for another bundle of cash, but instead she palmed something else. I felt a sharp stab in my ribcage and looked down.

Myra was holding the gun that had killed Justine.

Nineteen

Days of speculating who had killed Claire, who had murdered Justine, had not led me to Myra. She'd hid her hatred well until now. It was as though the inside of a beautiful quilt was suddenly revealed, with twisted seams, uncut threads, points that didn't match up.

Even if the security guard made rounds, it was unlikely he would see us. We were hidden in the alcove, surrounded by quilts. I took a step away from Myra, but she stopped me, her long fingers curled around my arm above my elbow, the bracelet dangling from her arm. I tried to push her away, but she had a death grip on me. Her brown eyes were as dark as night; the whites looked unnaturally vivid. She smelled bad, like wood rot coming to the surface.

I pulled back, feeling her fingers dig deeper into my bicep, and got another steely jab in my side.

"We're going to do this my way, Dewey."

"Myra, come on. I never did you any harm. Why are you doing this to me?"

"Because you are the one. You're the one the cops will believe killed Claire and Justine."

"Not true, Myra. I was with Buster when Justine was killed."

"Time of death is so tenuous, you know. I guess she was killed earlier than they thought. Or later. You'll explain it all in your suicide note. Do you think the cops are going to look much harder once you've confessed to the dirty deed? I don't think so."

"Buster will. He won't believe that I'd kill myself."

I flinched as spittle hit my face. I wanted to lash out and hit her, but the gun was supreme right now; I didn't want to do anything to make her mad enough to use it. I held my breath, only releasing it when she began talking again.

"First we're going to go sign the contract, selling me the shop. Gee, I think the price just went waaay down. My negotiating skills are greatly enhanced by this," she said, waving the gun.

I had to keep her talking. As long as she was talking, she wasn't shooting.

"The shop? You want Quilter Paradiso?

You can have it; you don't need to hold a gun on me. I'll give you the shop."

"First, you confess to their murders."

"Listen, Myra, I'm no lawyer, but I don't think it's murder if you didn't mean to kill them. They were both accidents, weren't they? Take Claire — she dropped the rotary cutter; it fell open and cut her. Justine, you were talking, the two of you chatting, the gun went off . . ."

Myra looked interested. Was she buying my idea that she would be able to talk her way out of a murder charge? I kept going.

"You didn't mean to kill Claire, did you? She was like a mother to you."

She laughed, a cackle that cut through me, seemingly cutting my spinal cord in half, making it impossible to stay upright. I started to slide, but she caught me under the right shoulder and hauled me back up. I had to stand on my own; there was nothing solid to lean on. The only things around us were quilts hanging from their frameworks. I steadied my knees, straightened my spine, and threw back my shoulders. It was a brave posture, one I did not feel. What had Freddy said? Fake it 'til you make it. I faked courage.

"That's not a good thing, Dewey. For you, being compared to your mother is wonderful. That's all I heard all weekend. Isn't Dewey just like her mother? Sweet, kind, sooo nice."

I'd spent the last six months trying to measure up to my mother. Was I going to get the chance to prove myself or was Myra going to cut me short?

"My mother, on the other hand, was a junkie and a whore. Although she preferred to be called a free spirit. She should have thanked me for putting her out of her misery."

"You killed your mother?" Shit, shit, shit. I was getting in deeper and deeper. I needed to get out of here now, away from Myra and her tiny, deadly gun.

Myra laughed. "Anyone can kill, Dewey. All you need to be is hungry enough, battered enough, desperate enough."

"I couldn't kill." The words came out in a squeak. I tried to clear my throat. I wanted to sound strong.

"Oh yeah? How about that stone-cold bastard who killed your mother?"

"Leave my mother out of this!" I yelled. She was closer to the truth than she knew. Many nights I had imagined what it would be like to run the unknown drunk down with my car. I hadn't acted on my impulse. Was that because I was a better person than

Myra or because I'd never had the chance?

"I can't. Your mother's the one that started all this. She had what Claire wanted, what I want, what you don't want. Quilter Paradiso. This all started with that infernal store."

"Are you saying you killed Claire because of my mother's store?"

"Let's walk. We don't have all night."

"Wait, I want you to tell me what my mother has to do with all this." I had just gotten my mother back. I wasn't going to share her with a murderer. I planted my feet, and Myra stopped, still standing in front of Claire's quilt.

"Your mother never cared about you, Dewey. She cared more about her shop than her kids."

I lunged at Myra. "That's a lie."

She hit me across the head with the gun. I saw stars and cried out, feeling my knees buckle beneath me. I struggled to stay standing, the colorful quilts competing with the sparks in my head. I grabbed onto the nearest quilt. The quilt stand swayed, but then straightened.

My head swimming, I felt a presence in the space. My mother. My mother was here with me. I cleared my head, half listening to Myra's tirade, trying to gather my strength.

"Come on, Dewey. Behave. Let's go."

"How can we get out? We're locked in."

"Not to worry. I stuck a piece of tape over one of the locks in the back. The final security check isn't until eleven. That cute little security guard likes his work. He was happy to tell me all about the schedule."

I couldn't let her take me out of the building. Myra was staring at Claire's quilt. An idea began to form. I tugged the quilt to my left. Out of the corner of my eye, I saw the joint where the quilt stands hooked together move. I pulled again and saw the wooden stand sway slightly.

"It's all very poetic," Myra said. "You commit suicide with the gun you used on Justine. I don't want to do it here. We wouldn't want to get your brain matter all over this lovely exhibit now, would we? Lark took footage of this quilt for her show about me. It would be a shame to ruin it."

With my peripheral vision, I studied the quilt stands. Each piece was dependent on the other; a kind of surface tension held the whole thing together. When I'd watched Eve's minions putting the quilt stands together, I'd been struck at how tenuous the arrangement was, how one relied on the other to stand up.

If I pulled hard enough and quickly enough, maybe I could bring down the whole display. These stands were much heavier than the stands that had fallen on Myra earlier. If I could start a domino effect, these stands with their thick wooden supports and heavy metal pipes would come crashing down on Myra's head.

The problem was my head was underneath here, too. I'd have to run as fast as I could. I bounced lightly on my toes and felt my head rock.

"I need one thing from you. Give me the notebook, Dewey."

"You lied to me." I tried to sound wounded. "You told me you didn't know anything about WGC and Claire's money lending."

Her face tightened, and she gripped the gun so hard that the tips of her fingers were white.

"I didn't. I was the only one who didn't know. Right up until Claire pulled out that little notebook to show Justine what she owed."

I held my breath, my stomach muscles shaking from the effort of keeping still. I let my hand explore behind me. I wasn't close enough to the quilt yet to get a good grip.

"You saw Justine that morning?"

"That twat," Myra sneered. "She was in and out of Claire's room, first repaying the money, then begging for it back. The last time she knocked on the door, Claire and I were having our dispute over her lending practices. Justine told me later she'd overheard."

"I saw her. She was going down the stairs when I got there."

"I told you she couldn't stay away. She knew that money was in the room, and that was all she could think about."

Or maybe she was trying to see if Claire was alive. If I hadn't been the one to find Claire's body, would it have been Justine? The last few days would have been so different.

"The thing about Justine was she didn't know when she had it good. She called me Thursday, begging for money. She'd lost all her money at the card club and was ready to go back for more. She was desperate to pay back Eve."

"And you took advantage of her vulnerability." I moved closer to the quilt behind me.

"I want that notebook," she repeated.

"I gave it to the police, Myra. That book is going to lead them right to you."

"You think so? Let's find out. Give me your cell phone," Myra demanded.

"I don't have the phone on me," I stammered. "I left it in the charger, back at the booth."

"Come on, I really want to call Officer Studly. What's he got in those pants, anyway?" She grinned lasciviously.

"Leave Buster out of this."

"Leave Buster out, leave Mom out," Myra mocked me. "Next you'll be telling me to leave Claire out. Who says you're making the rules? I'm the one with the gun."

I needed more time to figure out which pole would take down the rest. I took another baby step away from Myra. "How can you kill someone with a rotary cutter, Myra?"

"I got lucky with Claire. I mean, she gave me the idea. She was so insistent on cutting the borders herself. She was sitting down, for pity's sake. What did she think was going to happen? She pulled that rotary cutter right off the edge of the mat and into her lap. If she hadn't been using the safety cutter, she would have cut herself right then. But I took care of that."

She leaned in, and I caught a whiff of her foul scent. She was going to kill me. Would my mother be there to greet me if I died? She was surely in heaven, but I didn't know about my own life. Had I lived a good enough life to end up where she was?

I wasn't ready to die. I backed away another inch.

"It doesn't matter," I said with a bravado I barely felt. "I'm not the one who killed Claire or Justine. The police will figure out that you killed both of them." And me, I thought.

"Would your faith in the cops be so strong if you weren't banging Officer Meat? I doubt it."

"You don't need to get rid of me, Myra. Let me go. I won't tell a soul." No longer pretending, I was begging for my life.

I tried to appeal to her emotions.

"Didn't you love Claire?" I asked.

She looked up at me sharply, then focused her attention on Claire's quilt. Her features softened, and she answered me quietly. I got closer to the quilt behind me.

"I did, but it was never enough. Not enough for her to acknowledge me publicly. Not enough to keep her from starting over without me. She had been running this side business all these years and never told me. Then she was going to buy your mother's shop and leave me out of that, too."

I knew how she felt. It was not easy being the odd one out.

She shook herself, and her expression changed back to the woman ready to kill.

"She kept talking about a fresh start. I gave her a fresh start."

I flattened myself against the quilt behind me. Myra had a clear view of Claire's quilt. I needed to distract her so I could get a good grip on the quilt.

"Claire's quilt won first prize, Myra," I said, trying to inject as much sneer into my voice as I could. "But no one has given you the recognition you deserve."

Myra looked at me and then at the quilt. The metallic quilting thread glowed and reflected in her eyes. She seemed mesmerized by the quilt. This was as close to Claire as she was going to get again.

My back was right up against the crazy quilt that hung at right angles to Claire's. I felt the soft velvet, the rough edges of the embroidery, the cool metal of a charm, as my fingers scrambled for a hold.

"I made this quilt. Not her." With her open hand, Myra hit Claire's quilt. The quilt moved wildly.

"Destroy it, Myra."

She shifted the gun to her left hand and slapped at the quilt again. She grunted like a tennis player as she took the quilt by the binding and twisted.

Now was my chance. With my hand behind me, I gathered a large handful of the crazy quilt and pulled with all my might.

Nothing happened. The quilt stand rocked twice, but held fast. Myra looked back at me, her face distorted. She didn't know why the stand was moving, but she sensed I was getting away. She shifted the gun toward me.

I heard the creaking of the wooden cross stands and the clanging of the pipes as the framework struggled to stay together. The stands held steady. My escape plan wasn't working.

I looked at her face, expecting to see her exultant. Instead, her eyes flashed with terror. She was afraid. I'd thought she was powerful, but in fact, she had power only over those she killed. And I was still alive.

Keeping my eyes on her, I pulled back my right leg and cross-kicked the quilt support, using all the strength in my legs, catching the pipe fully. My hip bone resonated; the pain radiated from the ankle to the groin, setting up an answering throb in my head.

The quilt stands rumbled. It was working. The support shifted. The metal pole slipped from its crook and started down.

I ran, hands over my head. Behind me, metal rang loudly as it hit the convention center floor. The stands were toppling one after another. I ran alongside the falling supports, dodging wooden stands and jumping over rolling pipes. A pole clipped my arm painfully. I ran faster, putting all the falling stands behind me.

I made it to the doorway of the alcove and stopped and looked back. Myra was transfixed, her gun hand loose at her side, ineffectual. Poles fell like pick-up sticks all around her. I watched as a metal pole caught her on the shoulder, knocking her to the floor, toward the collapsing stands. Another pole hit her squarely on the head and she went limp. Claire's quilt settled around her, covering her.

More quilt stands fell down. I ran again. The noise was deafening, as the quilt stands in the alcove collapsed one by one, their echoes reaching out as I cleared the entrance. My breath was painful, coming in short, cutting bursts. I got into the main exhibit and leaned over my knees, chest heaving with effort. Behind me the room was in total disarray — quilts, wooden stands, and metal poles scattered like driftwood on the beach. Myra moaned.

"Stop right there!"

My little friend, the security guard, stood in front of me, large Mace can drawn like a revolver, nearly beaning me with it. I stopped, holding my hands out in front of me.

"Oh, man, am I glad to see you," I said, gasping for air.

I was so happy to see his ferret face, I grabbed him and kissed him. He jumped back and raised his Mace can at me again. I ducked, trying not to laugh at his startled expression.

"Don't shoot me. The murderer is back there, under a pile of quilt stands. Call the police."

"What's going on?" a deep voice rumbled from behind the security guard. The little guy whipped his Mace can around, pointing it directly at Buster. Buster held up his gun, and the guard backed down.

I was never happier to see him. "Myra," I said, my chest hurting with each syllable. "She killed Claire and Justine, and she's back there."

Buster barked into his cell, then pointed at the security guard. "Let's go."

They ran toward the alcove.

I sat on the floor and cradled my aching skull in my hands. Time slowed. Paramedics rushed past me. Sanchez appeared at my elbow. From my vantage point on the floor, I could see his black silk socks. Was it just two days ago I'd looked up at Sanchez from this same angle? The crease in his pants was so sharp, I could have flossed my teeth with it. The thought made me smile.

"Crimesolver Pelligrino. We've been looking for you," Sanchez said.

"I told you I didn't kill anyone. And it's Pellicano."

"That notebook gave Ms. Banks' motive, and the ME pinpointed Justine's time of death as during the time you and my detective were cavorting."

"We were having lunch," I protested.

"Oh, is that what you young folks call it these days?"

He started to walk away, but the entrance was blocked by the paramedics rushing through with a stretcher. Buster came through the doors right behind the paramedics. Sanchez followed the stretcher, telling Buster to stay with me. Nice.

He took a step toward me and held out his arms. I sank into them, relishing the warmth of his strong forearms. I began to shake, felt the answering beat of his heart, steady and strong.

"Is she dead?" I asked into his chest, relishing the warmth there. I wasn't sure I wanted to know the answer. How would I feel if I'd killed someone?

"No," he said, kissing the top of my head.

"But she's out cold and won't be coming to for a while. She caught one of those metal bars right on the noggin."

"Is that police talk — noggin?"

He laughed. I wrapped my arms tighter around Buster's back. If I could have climbed him like a tree, I would have. I didn't want to leave the safety of his arms.

"She was going to kill me and make it look like a suicide," I said into his shoulder, my voice cracking at the horror.

"Suicide?" Buster barked, his voice rough and low. "No way I'd have gone for that scenario."

He pulled back, his eyes serious, belying the light tone in his voice.

"Shoot yourself?" he continued. "Now if you'd jumped off a bridge or gone under a train, that I could believe. But shooting yourself? Remember that time Kevin shot his foot with the BB gun? You fainted at the sight of his blood."

"I didn't faint," I protested. "I sat down suddenly."

"You were out cold."

"Now you're just lying," I said, his silliness making me giddy.

He smiled, pleased that he'd made me laugh. "Look what I found. Does this belong to you?"

From behind my back he produced a QP bag. The Wild Goose Chase quilt. My eyes filled with tears. I couldn't speak, but nodded, pulling the quilt out of the bag and burying my face in it.

"Come on, I'll take you home," Buster said.

TWENTY

Kevin whispered in Kym's ear and kissed her hair. He glanced at me, and she gave him a small shrug. He gave her a little shove toward me before pushing the full dolly away from the QP booth. He gave me a quick smile. Always the baby brother, wanting everyone to be happy.

It was Sunday evening, and we were tearing down the booth. The Seventeenth Annual Northern California Quilt Extravaganza was over. Kevin was headed for the truck, the dolly loaded with the tables and shelves we'd been using in our booth. Dad had called this afternoon with tales of late spring snows, road closings, and chains. It was just as well he'd missed this weekend. I'd sworn Kevin to secrecy for now. I would tell Dad all about it when he got back. This was my story to tell.

I was taking my time undoing the computer wires, neatening the cords with tie wraps and stowing them in a plastic box at my elbow. Kym was unusually quiet, boxing up the unsold books. What had Kevin told her? I knew she was worried that I was going to look for another buyer for Quilter Paradiso.

Myra had been taken into custody last night, charged with both murders. Her injuries had put her in the hospital, but weren't fatal. She would live to stand trial for the murders of Claire and Justine. I had been in the emergency room for several hours getting my head checked out, and spent the rest of the night at the police station. Myra wasn't talking and Sanchez had plenty of questions for me. He was genuinely interested in what I had to say. A new development, one I wasn't sure I trusted.

Buster had dropped me at home at dawn. He wouldn't come in the house, and made me promise to get some rest. I'd climbed into bed, under the Wild Goose Chase quilt, but sleep never came. I stroked the quilt and thought about my mother. By the time the weak morning sun had come through my window, I knew what I had to do.

I went to the quilt show to work in the booth. For the rest of the day, I enjoyed the simple pleasure of making customers happy.

To my delight, the POS program had

worked smoothly. People flowed in and out of the booth. Kym spent several mostly successful hours on the computer. Quilter Paradiso had the best sales day of the weekend, and I was proud of what we'd done.

Now the booth was half-stripped, a shell of its former self. Kevin had already taken away the old-fashioned cooler. Piece by piece, the Dewey Mercantile booth was being dismantled.

Kym stopped, holding a book midway to a box, and cleared her throat. I looked at her. She was trying to say something.

"Dewey," she began. I waited. "I'm sorry that I gave you a hard time about the computer."

I choked back my surprise. Kym admitting she was wrong was not what I'd expected. Kevin must have insisted she apologize. I forced myself to be gracious.

"Thank you. I know if you let yourself, you might even learn to enjoy it," I said.

She looked like she was going to protest, but thought better of it and returned to packing up the books instead.

If she was going to try to make amends, I would, too. I tried to keep the conciliatory spirit going. "Thanks to you we won first place for the Best Decorated Booth," I offered. Eve had announced the results of the booth contest an hour ago when the show closed for the weekend.

She rolled her eyes and flicked her hair off her shoulder. "That was a pity vote."

"Excuse me?" I couldn't believe she wasn't happy about winning.

"We only won because they felt sorry for us."

"Kym, the judges voted Thursday morning, before Claire and Justine . . ." I stumbled over my words. "Before any of the drama took place. We won fair and square."

"Wake up, Dewey. They gave us the prize because of your mother's death. We would have won this year even if *you'd* decorated the booth."

"Hey!" There was no need to insult me.

"Sorry, but it's true."

I sighed. Kym and I would not turn into best friends overnight.

"No big deal," she said. "It just means I have to get started really early to win next year. I'm thinking a circus theme."

"Huh?" I stuttered.

"Think of it. Clowns, bareback riders. I'll be the ringleader. Oh wait, unless you want to. I could be a high-wire act."

Vangie came around the corner, dressed in sweats. Her hair was pulled into two thick braids with a Raiders cap perched on top. "I'm here to haul. What can I do?"

"Do you have a lion tamer on speed dial?" I asked.

Kym stopped her wild gesturing, her enthusiasm dying as I burst her bubble. I reminded myself that she acted a little nuts because she loved Quilter Paradiso.

"We can talk about it," I said.

She shifted her attention to Vangie. "Get over here and help me take down the QP banner," she demanded.

I gave Vangie a quick squeeze on her upper arm as she passed me, and she smiled.

Lark's head appeared over a stack of boxes. "Anyone want to be on TV?"

Kym looked up at the sound of the familiar voice. Lark stepped around the half-filled hand truck and the large plastic bins of unsold fat quarters, trying to get closer to where I was putting the cash drawer and scanner away. I looked for the cameraman, but to my relief, Lark was alone.

"I sure don't," I said. "Besides, no one wants to hear about murder on the home-decorating channel."

"Not about this weekend. I want to do a show on your shop," she said.

Kym's eyes widened in surprise. I saw her start to say something, then bite back her jealousy. She was really trying. I took a deep breath. I had to start giving Kym more of what she needed from me.

I stepped over to Kym, flinging an arm around her shoulder. She started, unable to keep the surprise off her face.

"A show on Quilter Paradiso would be brilliant. I don't want to be on camera, but I know someone who would be great," I said, pointing at my sister-in-law.

Lark looked from me to Kym. She shrugged. "You call the shots, girl. Just let me know when. Call me."

She walked away, making a phone sign, holding her thumb and pinky to her ear.

"Does this mean you're not selling Quilter Paradiso?" Kym asked warily, picking a piece of lint off my sweatshirt. I managed not to flinch this time.

I didn't answer right away, taking the Quilter Paradiso banner that my mother had sewn so long ago from Kym and folding it gently.

On the way to the show this morning, I'd stopped at the store. Since today was Sunday, the shop didn't open until eleven, so I was alone. I stood in the middle of the display floor, turning around, feeling the history — the exposed brick wall, the rows of wooden drawers left over from the hardware business, the loft that the first Dewey had stored grain in. But it was the more recent history that captured me. The bolts of colorful fabric. A hand-lettered sign pointing the way to the bathroom. A half-filled notebook in my mother's handwriting with ideas for new classes. The quilts.

Like a snake shedding its skin, there would soon be nothing left here that had my mother's stamp on it. The fabric she'd ordered would all be gone. The Blocks of the Month finished. Her favorite patterns replaced with new ones.

I'd been trying to hold on to my mother so tightly that I'd nearly lost her. I'd been willing to sell the shop, rather than be the catalyst, the one to move things forward. I couldn't keep the store stagnant and still stay in business.

Soon enough her presence would no longer be visible in the store; I would stick around at least until that happened.

I rubbed my hand along the wooden countertop. Generations of Deweys had worked here and, for a moment, I felt their warm spirit in the wood. I wouldn't be alone. I'd have help.

Myra had been wrong. My mother loved her family, and she loved quilts. I needed to do whatever I could to stay connected to both.

"So?" Kym insisted.

Vangie watched our faces closely. This was her family, too, and a divorce would be too much for her to take.

I looked into Kym's eyes and nodded. "I'm not looking for a buyer anymore."

Kym's face split in a wide grin. She grabbed my hand and let out a squeal. She didn't care why I was keeping the shop. The only thing that mattered to her was that it stay in the family.

"You'll need to take some basic computer classes," I said.

Kym's expression was agonized. Vangie stifled a chuckle. I gave her a look. With a wisdom beyond her years, she pulled Kym aside to pile more bolts on the hand truck, chattering about creating a QP line of original quilt patterns. I smiled at Vangie gratefully and was rewarded with a sweet smile from her.

"You people got everything you need?" Eve was standing in the aisle.

It was the same question Justine had asked four days ago. So much had changed since then. I couldn't speak. My eyes filled with tears. All the loss.

"Guess I'm not the only one who was up

378

all night," I said finally, looking at the bruised bags under her eyes.

"Thanks to you. That alcove was a mess." Her smile took the sting out of her words. "Not to worry, we got most of the quilts re-hung by the time we opened this morning. Two or three had too much damage."

"Ouch. I didn't mean to ruin your exhibit."

Eve held up a hand. "Hey, don't apologize. You put an end to the killing, that's what counts. Believe it or not, this was the biggest Sunday crowd we've had in years."

"So does that mean there will be an Eighteenth Annual Northern California Quilter's Extravaganza? Same time, next year?" I suggested.

Eve shrugged. "Maybe. I've worked out an installment plan to pay off the convention center, and if I finish as promised in six months, they might be willing to allow us back again next year. Don't know why, now that they've seen how much trouble quilters can really be."

"That's the truth," I agreed.

"I don't know if I want to, without Justine." Eve brushed a tear from her eye roughly. She clasped my hand with both of hers and looked into my eyes. She was wan, but I could see a spark of life returning to her.

"Thank you, Dewey, for stopping Myra. It may be silly, but I feel like Justine will rest easier now."

I nodded and squeezed her hand.

"Come to Reno and visit me sometime," she said.

"I'd like that."

"You hate Reno," Kym put in, unable to resist correcting me.

I shrugged. Maybe it was time I learned to gamble.

Kym rolled her eyes. She took the family photos from Vangie and lovingly wrapped them in batting. Eve said her goodbyes and continued toward the exit.

Freddy came by next, surprisingly with Chester and Noni in tow.

"Got time for a drink? I'm buying," he said.

"Oh, now, Freddy, this is our treat," Noni said.

I laughed. "Start without me. I'm going to spend tonight with my family."

I hugged each of them in turn, savoring Noni's caring presence, Chester's heartiness, and Freddy's sense of humor. I looked forward to seeing them next year at the show.

Kevin returned with the dolly. He smiled at me shyly. All he wanted was for Kym and I to get along. I saw the hope in his eyes. We had some long talks ahead of us, but we were family. I smiled back, letting him know we were okay.

Kevin and Kym took another load out to the van. Vangie followed them with a hand truck full of books. I stayed behind, guarding the computer equipment. My eyes burned with fatigue, and I rubbed at them viciously. When I took my hands away, Buster was standing in front of me. He was off-duty, by the look of him. He was wearing a purple shirt with black jeans. The deep plum color of his shirt complemented his eyes, making them look bluer and deeper. His sleeves were rolled up, and he had that leather thong on his left wrist. He looked great.

I sucked in a deep breath. "Hey," I said.

"Hey, yourself. You doing all right?"

I nodded, suddenly at a loss for words. What was it about Buster that made me vulnerable? He put his thumb in the cleft of my chin and raised my face so I had to meet his gaze.

I didn't know if we had a future together. I only knew that I couldn't stay closed up.

The good stuff was only there if I was open to it.

Buster's smile was gentle, softened by a sadness in his eyes. "You're amazing."

I tried to turn away from the compliment, but he held me firm. I had no choice but to watch his face. His mouth softened and he put the back of his hand on my cheek and stroked. I closed my eyes and leaned into his touch. I felt like every nerve of my body was exposed, and only his fingertips could restore me.

"I wish I could have been there for you," he said quietly.

I opened my eyes and grinned at him. "You were, in a way."

His head tilt reminded me of a dog whose supper is cold kibble instead of the steak off the grill. I laughed.

"I conjured you up, just when I needed the most strength. I pictured that old goal we had in the side yard. All those years practicing my corner kicks paid off. Those quilt stands didn't stand a chance."

Buster's smile faded and he hooked a hair behind my ear.

"You don't have to do that, you know," he said. "Not with me."

"Do what?"

"Act tough."

"I'm not," I protested.

"I've been down a dark alley with a suspect. It's a very scary place to be. You can either stand up to the evil or run away. You stood up to Myra. It takes a certain kind of person to do that. You . . ."

He caught his breath and tried to turn away. I reached up and held his face toward me. The sight of his eyes filling up with tears was the sexiest thing I'd ever seen. I felt my knees weaken and stiffened them in defense. I wasn't going to make the same mistake again. Sex with Buster was great. That I knew. It was the out-of-bed time we had to figure out.

"I wanted to protect you, Dewey."

I flicked his tears away. He grabbed my hand and kissed my palm. I felt the tingle all the way down to my toes.

"You don't need to protect me," I said.

"That's a hard pill to swallow."

"It's true, though, and you know it."

He was quiet for a moment, just holding my hand.

"I never said thank you," I said.

"For what?"

"For being with Mom when she passed."

"But I let that bastard . . ."

I held my finger to his mouth. "You'll find him."

He turned and looked at the quilt show beyond the booth. Volunteers were gently lifting the quilts from their stands, folding them onto waiting sheets. It was hard to imagine last night's chaos.

"I never did get to see the quilts," Buster said.

"You missed your chance."

"I understand there were some works of art."

"There were some real beauties," I agreed.

"Of course, I wouldn't know a good quilt from a bad one. Maybe you could teach me."

"Sure, I could show you the difference between a Baltimore Album quilt and a free-motion embroidery collage."

"Liar," he said. "Did you understand anything you just said?"

"Not a word," I admitted. "But I'm going to have to learn."

"You're going to keep the shop, Dewey?"

"Yeah, Kym needs a job, and Vangie."

"Is that the only reason?"

I could tell him. "My mother's life was tied up in the shop. I have to find out if mine is, too."

"She thought you were the best thing on earth."

"I know." And that knowledge was

enough. It would have to be enough for the rest of my life.

"I hope we can remain friends," Buster said tentatively, eyes straight ahead, staring at the quilt show. He rubbed my knuckles.

Friends? I wasn't sure that was enough. "I need some wooing, you know."

"Wooing?" His tongue tripped over the unfamiliar word. His eyes slid to mine. I struggled to keep a straight face. "What does that mean?"

"That means I'd like to go on a real date. With you picking me up at my door, and me —"

"Wearing a dress?"

"A dress?" A guy could dream. "I'm not even sure I own one."

"How about tomorrow night?"

"Too soon. If you want that dress, I'll need time to shop."

"Let's not wait too long," he said with a rasp in his voice that sent heat flowing through my body.

"Be warned — I never sleep with a guy on a first date."

"Lucky for me, we never dated."

Lucky for me, too.

"We could continue our guitar lessons," he said, eyes dancing with mischief.

I looked into his big blue eyes, wondering

what the future was. Guitar wasn't the only thing we needed to learn. "Okay, but we're going to have start over."

The disappointment registered on Buster's face for a split second, and I choked back a laugh. Was he remembering the note he'd left on the pillow, thanks for Lesson One?

"Come on," Buster said. "We've . . ." he stumbled, searching for a word. "You've progressed farther than that."

I shook my head. "I need to start at the beginning. Like, before the first lesson."

"Before Lesson One?" he said, his voice cracking.

I nodded. "Let's pretend I know nothing."

Vangie and Kym approached, the dolly now empty. I dropped Buster's hand. Kevin was right behind them. His face lit up in a big smile at the sight of his friend. He grabbed Buster. They man-hugged, bumping chests and patting backs.

"We should change the window display every month, Vangie," Kym was saying.

"We? When was the last time you climbed the ladder?" Vangie answered.

I watched as Vangie and Kym argued. Kevin and Buster had their heads together, their low voices a counterpoint to the female bickering. I couldn't contain the grin that seemed to start deep in my belly.

This was what my mother loved. Friends, family, quilts. I was right where I belonged.

ABOUT THE AUTHOR

Writing has always been a passion for **Terri Thayer** — this first volume of her quilting mystery series is the product of her decision to write the quilting mystery she could not find on the market. Terri has been sewing since her teens and quilting for twenty years. She has taught quilting, developed patterns, and made hundreds of quilts.

We hope you have enjoyed this Large Print book. Other Thorndike, Wheeler, and Chivers Press Large Print books are available at your library or directly from the publishers.

For information about current and upcoming titles, please call or write, without obligation, to:

Publisher
Thorndike Press
295 Kennedy Memorial Drive
Waterville, ME 04901
Tel. (800) 223-1244

or visit our Web site at:

http://gale.cengage.com/thorndike

OR

Chivers Large Print
published by BBC Audiobooks Ltd
St James House, The Square
Lower Bristol Road
Bath BA2 3SB
England
Tel. +44(0) 800 136919
email: bbcaudiobooks@bbc.co.uk
www.bbcaudiobooks.co.uk

All our Large Print titles are designed for easy reading, and all our books are made to last.